THE MARSHALS

Packy Trucker

Packy Publishing

Copyright © 2021 Packy Trucker

All rights reserved

The characters and events portrayed in this book are fictitious. Any similarity to real persons, living or dead, is coincidental and not intended by the author.

No part of this book may be reproduced, or stored in a retrieval system, or transmitted in any form or by any means, electronic, mechanical, photocopying, recording, or otherwise, without express written permission of the publisher.

Printed in the United States of America

CONTENTS

Title Page
Copyright
The Proposal 2
The Search for Deputies 12
Montana Territory 56
The Kidnapping of Brenda Wilson 88
Different Directions 147
Killer McBride 203
Wyoming 270
Arizona 311
The Wedding 361

Lady Marshals of the Old West

F.M. Miller

Ada Curnutt

S.M. Burche

Mamie Fossett

Phoebe Couzins

THE PROPOSAL

Fort Worth, Texas 1881

Ranger Wyatt Peterson tied his horse to the rail in front of the Fort Worth ranger office and went inside. Ranger James was on desk duty and said, "How you do, Wyatt?"

The muscular broad-shouldered six-foot-one Wyatt answered, "Doing well, but could use your help with the prisoners."

Ranger James followed Wyatt outside. "Who ya got here?"

"Just Mendoza and his so-called gang."

The rangers helped the four hand-tied prisoners off their horses and led them into the holding cells in the rear of the ranger office.

Wyatt was about to leave the building when Captain McDonald came out of his private office. "Wyatt, I have an important telegram for you from J.T. Rothschild."

"Never heard of the man. I'll look at it in the morning."

"You might want to look at it now. He's offering you five hundred dollars to come to New York. And another five hundred after you've spoken with him."

"He must be a rich man."

"He is. He has a vast fortune."

"What could he possibly want with me?" asked Wyatt.

"I've no idea, but for that kind of money I would go see him."

"I'm convinced. I'll check the train schedule for tomorrow and then I'm getting a haircut, shave and a bath. After that, this tired ranger is hitting the hay."

"You best fit a trip to the clothing store into your schedule. A man like Rothschild would be highly insulted if you were dressed like a cowboy," commented Ranger James.

"I reckon that's a good idea."

His errands done, Wyatt stopped in the Hideaway Saloon for a nightcap. Two other rangers were in there, so he sat with them. They chatted ranger talk for a while and Wyatt told them he was leaving for New York in the morning. When they asked him what for, he said he had no idea, only that some rich man was overpaying him to come.

Thirty minutes later Wyatt went to bed in the

ranger bunkhouse.

The next morning Wyatt was wearing his new western cut brown suit, boots, and a new western hat when he got on the eastbound train. He refused to buy the popular bowler hat Easterners wore. His hair was cut short, making it much easier to manage and stay cooler in the hot Texas weather. Several women smiled at the good-looking ranger. He tipped his hat and said, "Good day."

Arriving in New York City, he got off the train to see a man holding a sign reading, "Peterson." He went to the man and was led to an enclosed carriage. Wyatt got in and sat in the comfortable leather seat. Seeing crowds of people and the congestion of wagons and carriages, Wyatt was glad he was being chauffeured. He didn't understand how people could live like this. Then the carriage pulled up to an impressive white mansion with white pillars adorning the front door. A male servant had been waiting for the carriage and hustled out to open the carriage door for Wyatt. The servant led Wyatt into the library, where Mr. J.T. Rothschild was sitting in a large comfortable chair sipping on brandy while reading a newspaper. He stood immediately and met Wyatt. The two shook hands and introduced themselves.

"Mr. Peterson, let's sit at the table over there where I have some papers." As they each took a seat the servant came to the table and stood. "Mr. Peterson, may I offer you a drink?"

"I would appreciate that, thank you. Rum if you have it."

Without a word the servant went to the bar and poured a drink for Wyatt.

Rothschild waited until Wyatt had taken a sip of his rum. "Let's get down to business. We both understand it was the money that brought you here."

Wyatt grinned, "It certainly got my attention, and I am curious."

"Mister Peterson…"

"I apologize for interrupting sir, but please call me Wyatt."

"Apology accepted Wyatt, and you may call me JT. I've heard much about you. You are a very capable man, but most important to me is your honesty and the goodwill you have shown to people. You see, I have been following your exploits for the past year. I am looking for someone to fill a position for me and I believe you are that man. I am eighty years old and have no one to give my money to, and how I earned that money may be a bit questionable. It is my wish that when I die, the majority of my fortune will have been redistributed to those who need it. I have heard stories of desperate people in the West and I would like to do something for them. I need someone to travel the West, helping people that need it. Just a minute."

While JT paused to take a breath and sip his brandy, Wyatt spoke up, "Riding the West giving out money. It sounds like the ideal job, but why would you want someone like me? Anyone can do that."

"I wasn't finished. Besides dispersing money, you may be dispensing bullets. Sometimes instead of giving out money, you may be helping people with a problem. That is why I chose you. You know the law. You are one of the best with guns. And yet you have compassion."

"I can't just ride around shooting people."

"If you accept this position, you will be able to do just that. I am friends with the Attorney General, and he is aware of what I want to do and agrees with it. If you accept this position, he will make you a U.S. Marshal. As a U.S. Marshal you have the authority to appoint deputies."

JT noticed Wyatt's eyes were lighting up, "I can tell you like my offer."

Wyatt grinned, "I do. It follows why I became a Texas Ranger, but it never worked out like I had envisioned it."

"Good. The Attorney General will give you a marshal badge and two deputy badges. You will also receive a signed document by the U.S. Attorney General describing your duties. As a U.S. Marshal appointed by the US Attorney General, you will have authority everywhere in the United States. You will have authority over town sheriffs and town marshals."

"I only have one question. How much will I be paid?"

"I did forget that didn't I? It would be two hundred and fifty dollars a month. Your deputies will be paid one hundred seventy-five a month."

"Wow. That's over four times what I make as a ranger."

"It won't be easy money; you will earn it. One more thing. I am sure you won't like this, but one of your deputies must be a woman."

"A woman! They can't shoot a gun. Most can't even ride a horse! Why is a woman needed?"

"Women are more understanding, gentle, more sensitive and have more empathy for people than men do. These things will be needed to assure what I want done will get done. You will have a sealed letter for that woman. I warn you, part of her job will be to make sure that you and your male partner do not abuse your authority. I say that because besides helping the needy I want you to rid the unlawful West of scum. In extreme cases, when you know scum will legally evade our laws and remain free to put innocent lives in jeopardy, you have the power to be judge, jury and executioner. This gives you a lot of power. I know you will use it wisely. The female deputy will be required to contact me weekly. She will be your watch dog."

"I cannot imagine killing someone in cold blood."

"I knew you would feel that way; that is one reason you were chosen."

"And where will I find a woman that can ride and shoot and have the traits you mentioned?"

JT laughed, "Finding a woman with those traits and skills could prove exceedingly difficult, I'm sure. I suspect you will have to train her on the more masculine aspects of being a deputy marshal."

Wyatt looked at his drink, raised it to his mouth and downed the rest of it. "Is there any particular place you would like me to begin?"

"Not until there are three of you and you have some experience working together, then I will tell your female deputy where to go. And I'm sure the Attorney General will have some things he would like taken care of also."

"This woman will have power over me."

"Yes, to some extent she will. Any questions?"

Wyatt shook his head no.

"You have an appointment with the Attorney

General here at nine tomorrow morning. There is a room under your name at the Hotel Brunswick. They have everything you need. My carriage will take you there and pick you up tomorrow at eight-thirty. Here is a draft against my bank account for the amount you were quoted and a few blank drafts to cover expenses and gifts. I want you to open an account at a reputable bank and let me know where. Your pay will be deposited on the first of every month. The same goes for your deputies. Good hunting."

JT stood, which let Wyatt know the meeting was over, so he stood and they shook hands.

HOTEL BRUNSWICK,

Fifth Avenue, - - - - - NEW YORK.

MITCHELL & KINZLER.

See page 25 of this book for picture of this Hotel, from a painting by the celebrated artist, Wordsworth Thompson. An extensive addition is now being made on the Madison Square front, which, when completed, will add a large number of elegant rooms, and will make this Hotel one of the most complete in the city.

RESTAURANT AND CAFÉ.

Dinner, Wedding, and Outside Parties furnished in the well-known style of this house,

PRIVATE DINING-ROOMS.

ICE CREAM, CAKES, and PASTRY delivered Free of Extra Charge to all parts of the city. COLD LUNCHES PREPARED.

WINES AND LIQUORS AT WHOLESALE.

N. B.—The Coach "Tantivy" starts for Tarrytown from Hotel Brunswick, 4 P. M., daily (Sundays excepted).

While being driven to the hotel Wyatt couldn't get over the tall buildings and the mass of people. It all gave him claustrophobia. He was anxious to get back out west.

Wyatt was met at the hotel door and escorted to the desk, where he was given a key to room 405. He was told his stay was prepaid including dining and drinks. Wyatt was so impressed with the fancy hotel and its service, he felt like a king.

Wyatt enjoyed a nice meal and a drink in the hotel's bar. Exhausted from the day's events, he went to bed and was instantly asleep. The next morning, Wyatt was woken by a knock on the door at seven-thirty and told his bath was ready. Wearing the same clothes as yesterday, Wyatt sat outside on the cool morning waiting for the carriage. At eight-thirty JT's carriage arrived.

As Wyatt rode to JT's house, he wondered how close of friends JT must be with the U.S. Attorney General for him to come visiting at his house.

As the carriage pulled up at the front door, the same servant as yesterday came to the carriage and opened the door. He then led Wyatt inside. Wyatt had never been so nervous in his life. Again he was led into the library. JT and the Attorney General were standing at the bar with drinks in their hands talking. They turned towards Wyatt. JT waved Wyatt over and poured two fingers of rum into a glass and handed it to Wyatt, saying, "I'm sure you are nervous so don't say a word until you've emptied your glass."

Wyatt couldn't help smiling as he put the glass to his lips and downed it.

"Now that you are relaxed, we'll get on with it. This is United States Attorney General Joseph Whitaker. I call him Joe. Joe, meet Ranger Wyatt Peterson." The two shook hands. "Wyatt, your signed papers are on the table, but Joe would like to get to know you, so we will be having drinks and brunch."

"I understand. I haven't eaten, so brunch sounds good."

Forty-five minutes later Wyatt was on a train headed west with badges and papers. The important papers were rolled inside part of an old rain slicker. It felt good to get out of the big city. He would be going back to Fort Worth for his horse and the few personal things he owned.

The long ride to Fort Worth gave Wyatt lots of time to make his plans. He was easygoing and had no trouble making friends, but the thought of making a stranger a partner on a life and death mission was going to be difficult. Then again, doing the same with a woman would be ten times more difficult. What did he get himself into?

THE SEARCH FOR DEPUTIES

Upon returning to Fort Worth, the first thing Wyatt did was turn in his resignation. Captain McDonald was sadly disappointed to lose one of his best men but wished him well. Not wanting Captain McDonald to get involved in the deputy selection, Wyatt never mentioned he needed two deputies. It was something he would have to stumble through on his own.

Wyatt would start his new job by riding south to Waco, Austin, San Antonio, and smaller towns, and talk with their sheriffs. He would be interviewing them but they wouldn't know it. He would watch for a rancher's daughter because they are usually taught how to handle a gun early and would probably be his best chance of finding the right woman.

The next morning, he rode south out of Fort Worth. There was train service all the way to San Antonio, but he felt by riding he had a better chance to meet a prospective deputy. His first stop would be Hillsboro. It was fifty miles, or a twelve-hour ride. He hoped to make it in one day so he would not have to sleep on the ground. So, the next day he left Fort Worth at five a.m.

Arriving in Hillsboro around five p.m., the hungry Wyatt dismounted at a small no-name café where he always ate whenever in town. As he stepped up onto the boardwalk a man was leaving the café when the two recognized each other. Both surprised men went for their guns. Wyatt was faster. Knowing one bullet might not be enough to stop the threat, Wyatt usually fired twice in quick succession. This time he put three shots into the outlaw, who fell to the boardwalk dead.

Wyatt took the U.S. Marshal badge from his pocket and pinned it to his chest so people would not mistake him for an outlaw and shoot him. He ejected the three spent shell cases and thumbed in three cartridges and holstered his gun. A crowd was gathering as the town sheriff arrived with his gun out. Wyatt raised his hands. Seeing who it was, the sheriff holstered his gun.

"Hello Wyatt, who'd ya just shoot?"

"Hi Ben, Jake Halsey. I've been after him for years," answered Wyatt while checking the outlaw's pockets and finding eight dollars and change. "Like most outlaws he didn't have much money." Wyatt looked at the crowd, "Anyone know which horse belongs to this man?"

"The black mustang," yelled a man who had been eating inside the café. "We both arrived at the same time, so I saw him get off it."

"Thank you, sir," said Wyatt. Wyatt checked the saddlebags. All he found was spare ammunition and dirty clothes.

Seeing a barefoot, threadbare boy of about twelve in the crowd, Wyatt asked Ben the sheriff who he was.

"That's Jimmy Hawkins. Comes from a good family but poor as can be."

Wyatt looked at the boy, "Jimmy, come here please."

Not knowing why a U.S. Marshal would want him, the boy was hesitant.

"You are not in any trouble Jimmy, come on over. I'd just like to give you something."

Now the boy hurried over. Wyatt gave him the outlaw's money and handed him the reins to the horse.

"What would ya like me to do with the money and horse, Marshal?"

Wyatt grinned, "I want you to give them to your father."

"To keep?"

Wyatt laughed, "Yes, to keep forever, or sell for

the money. Whatever he wants."

Jimmy's eyes got big and he smiled, "Thanks Marshal!" Jimmy could be heard yelling, "Pa Pa!" as he led the horse away. Most of the crowd knew the poor family and were pleased with what the marshal had done so they clapped their hands and voiced their approval.

"Wyatt, are you thinking of running for sheriff next year and taking my job?" joked Ben.

"Nope, I've got a good one right now." Wyatt reached into a pocket and took out some money. "Usually when I find money in an outlaw's pocket, I give it to the undertaker as pay...oh well, here's five dollars for the undertaker."

"I've never realized you were so generous Wyatt."

"My new job pays well. Now I've got to get inside and put something in my stomach before it rebels and does something I won't like," grinned Wyatt.

"I'll join ya after I get the undertaker. Here he comes now. Must have heard the shots and saw dollar signs!"

"Glad to have you, Ben."

After eating, Wyatt stabled his horse, named Gotcha, got a hotel room and then went to the only saloon in the town of three hundred people. He was recognized and people were friendly. After twenty minutes and one drink he went back to the hotel and to bed.

Up the next morning at five he went to the same café for breakfast. He was always watching people, looking for possible deputies. His breakfast finished, he tipped the waitress and said, "Be sure to tell the cook that was the best breakfast I've had in months." His motto has always been to make people feel good and he would always be welcome.

Getting Gotcha from the stable, he headed south to Waco. It would be a shorter trip of thirty-five miles or about nine hours of riding.

It was around three in the afternoon when Wyatt rode into Waco. First, he got a room and locked his rifle and saddlebags in it, then stabled Gotcha. Too early to eat, he entered the first saloon he saw. With over eight thousand people living in Waco, the town had several saloons.

Before entering he could hear a ruckus going on inside. Not being in the habit of always wearing his badge, he took it from a pocket and pinned it on. Next, he removed the hammer tie down loop from his gun and went inside. To his surprise a half-breed friend of his, Jed Tucker, was backed up against a wall holding a knife. Four men were taunting him.

Wyatt moved sideways, away from the door behind him and yelled, "If anyone has a problem with my Indian friend, they have a problem with me!"

Everyone in the saloon turned to see a lawman.

One of the four antagonists yelled back, "I don't like Indians or lawmen, so I have a problem with you!"

"It's your dance, your call. Unless you are just a loudmouth."

With all his friends watching, the loudmouth knew he had to do something. Having enough alcohol in him he lacked fear and judgment and went for his gun. A second later two bullets from Wyatt's gun made holes in the loudmouth's chest and he fell to the floor.

"Anyone else have a problem they would like me to solve for them?"

No one said a word. The remaining troublemakers went to their table mumbling.

Wyatt's friend came to him with a scowl on his face. "I was right behind him! You would have killed me if you had missed! Or if a bullet would have gone through him! I didn't need any help."

"Better you get shot than me," laughed Wyatt. "And when have you known me to miss what I'm shooting at? Besides I went for his fat belly."

"I seen ya miss lots of times."

"I guess ya have at that. Grab us a table while I get us something to drink." Wyatt went to the bar, "I want a bottle and two glasses."

The bartender moved down the bar to Wyatt and said quietly, "We don't serve Indians here."

"He's only half Indian so serve his white half."

The bartender took the hint and gave Wyatt two glasses and a bottle.

Wyatt filled both glasses halfway. "It's good seeing you again Tuck. What are you doing in Waco, visiting your Waco Indian tribe's old homeland?"

"You know I go by Red Hawk. I've been looking for a man that owes me money."

"And you know I've always called you Tuck. You know if you didn't wear your hair that way and did away with the headband and feather and dressed like a white man no one would ever guess you are a half-breed."

"And desert my heritage? Never!"

"You already have deserted your heritage, your white heritage. Dressing the way you do only causes trouble and you know it."

"Maybe I like causing trouble."

"I know you do, but this time you had more than you could handle. You are lucky I came along. By the way Tuck, you have no idea how glad I am to see you. I have an offer to make you."

"Not interested."

"That's half your problem. You're stubborn besides being a troublemaker. How would you like to earn one hundred seventy-five dollars a month and have fun doing it?"

"White man been drinking spirit water," Tuck said in an Indian accent.

Wyatt laughed, "You might be right. It still sounds too good to be true to me. I'm now a U.S. Marshal and I need two deputies. We would work for two bosses, one a rich man and the other the United States Attorney General. He appointed me a marshal. The rich man wants us to help people with money or whatever they need. The attorney general wants us to capture or kill outlaws."

"Where would we work?"

"Anywhere in the U.S. we want to go, or wherever we are sent."

Tuck scratched his head, "Neither one of us has a home anyway so I guess it doesn't matter where we go. We would be getting paid to explore the country. I like it."

"You are serious?"

"I am."

Wyatt reached into a pocket, "Here's your badge."

Tuck had a pleasant smile as he stared at it. "I never in a hundred years thought I'd wear a badge." Tuck was still smiling as he pinned the badge to his buckskin shirt.

"There is one catch though."

"Here it comes. Now you are going to ruin it. What's the catch?"

"You must wear normal clothes and cut your hair short like mine."

"No headband and feather? No moccasins? What about the scalps hanging from my saddle?"

"Boots, but keep your moccasins. I have a pair too for when I want to sneak around quietly. As far as the headband, you are just trying to give me trouble, and I know you don't have any scalps which shows you aren't much of an Indian," chuckled Wyatt.

"If you are finished insulting me, I need a cash advance."

Wyatt reached into a pocket and brought out a roll of bills. "Here's fifty dollars. Now you can buy some new clothes, boots and a hat. Then get a haircut and bath. When you're done, I'll meet you at Bill's Café. I'll buy."

It was over an hour later when Tuck found Wyatt in the café drinking coffee and reading a newspaper; he took a seat across from him.

Not looking up from the paper, Wyatt said, "I'm sorry sir but that seat is reserved for my friend Tuck."

"Is that supposed to be a compliment?" asked Tuck.

"Actually, yes. But truthfully no one would recognize you. I dare you to walk into a saloon now and see if you aren't served."

A pretty waitress came to their table. "I see your friend is here now. What would you two like?" The whole time she was talking she was staring at Tuck in his new clothes with a smile. They both said they wanted the special, which consisted of a steak, green beans, mashed potatoes and bread roll. While staring at Tuck the waitress said, "By the way, my name is Celia."

"Good to meet you, Celia. I'm Tuck and that's my friend Wyatt."

Celia left with a nice smile on her face.

Wyatt was grinning when he said, "I can see I'm not going to stand a chance with the women now that you have cleaned up your act. She never once looked at me."

"You know, maybe I should have done this long ago."

When they finished eating Wyatt said, "Let's get you a hotel room, so you don't have to sleep in your teepee outside of town." Wyatt was teasing about the teepee.

"Now you're insulting me again," said Tuck with a big grin as he left a dollar tip.

Seeing the dollar tip Wyatt said, "That was an expensive smile she gave you. I'm glad she didn't smile at me." Thinking four dollars would cover the meal, Wyatt left it on the table.

After registering a room for Tuck, Wyatt said he was beat and going to bed. They would meet for breakfast at the same café at seven in the morning.

The two friends happened to meet in the hotel lobby the next morning and walked the two blocks to Bill's Café together. They hadn't even sat down when Celia was at their table with a smile and a, "Hi Tuck."

"No hi for me?" asked Wyatt.

"I apologize, I don't remember your name."

Wyatt smiled and shook his head, "It's Wyatt."

"Good morning Wyatt." Celia's eyes went to Tuck, "What will you be having this morning, Tuck?"

"Four eggs over easy, toast, potatoes and coffee."

Celia almost left when she remembered Wyatt. "What will you have Wyatt?"

"Give me the same."

Celia smiled at Tuck and left.

"This is making me sick. I never should have said anything about your appearance."

Tuck was grinning from ear to ear. "Ya got anymore advice for me?"

"Yeah, shut up."

Tuck laughed, "You sound like a poor loser."

Wyatt ignored him and looked out the window pretending to be interested in something. After a bit he said, "The telegraph office should be open at eight. I need to let our boss know I now have a deputy. Do you want to come with?"

"Nothing else to do."

Knowing it would be quite a while before they received a reply, the two sat in the office and talked.

"Tuck, we've been friends for what...eight or ten years. In all that time you never mentioned which of your parents were Waco."

"My mother was Waco. She raised me and taught me the language, which is mostly Wichita but also Pawnee. She also taught me English. My mother was killed in a fight with the Apache, our worst enemy. After that I drifted away from the tribe and became a homeless twelve-year-old scavenging to survive."

Wyatt's respect for his friend Tuck increased after hearing of his tough life. "Your mother must have instilled good values in you at a young age. Your life's experiences make you the perfect partner for the other half of our mission I haven't told you about."

"Are you saying you've held something back?"

Wyatt grinned, "Yes, I guess that's what I'm saying. The other half of our mission is helping those in need, whether it be with money or bullets."

Tuck thought for a moment, "If you had told me this yesterday, there would have been no hesitation on my part to join you. Where will we get the money?"

"A very wealthy old gentleman that wants to reform his ways and rectify his past. That is who I just sent the telegraph to."

"Gentlemen, I have a reply," said the telegraph operator.

They both stood and went to the counter. Wyatt took the message and read it, then handed it to Tuck.

When Tuck finished, he said, "It looks like we are going to Indian Territory."

"I suspect I'm going to be glad to have you for a partner," grinned Wyatt.

"You should have been anyway," laughed Tuck. "So, we're looking for four men that killed the sheriff and his deputies in Coffeeville, Kansas before robbing a bank and killing two bank workers."

"You forgot the best part. We have nothing to go on other than one of the robbers is an Indian and their horse descriptions," said Wyatt.

"But horse descriptions can be better than descriptions of the men. We will find them. I'm just wondering why they think the robbers went to Anadarko?"

"I've been wondering that also. It's too bad you cut your hair and made yourself presentable," laughed Wyatt.

"What do you mean?"

"We need to dress down and look like outlaws. The way we're dressed anyone could peg us for lawmen."

"You're right. We better buy some used clothes."

Indian Territory, as it was called, is now called Oklahoma. Indian tribes from all over the U.S. were forced to relocate there in sections designated for each tribe. The only law in Indian Territory was the Indian police. The only U.S. lawmen allowed there were the U.S. marshals. So Indian Territory became the favorite hiding place for outlaws. It was an extremely dangerous place for marshals.

The two marshals disembarked from the train at Anadarko in Indian Territory. Tuck was all smiles.

"You look like you just swallowed the canary in the mine. What are you so happy about?" questioned Wyatt.

"This is my home. This is where the Waco were forced to relocate. We're part of the Wichita now."

"Why didn't you tell me this before we left Texas?"

"Just thought I'd surprise ya."

"I don't think many outlaws ride trains, so we best get our horses and get away from here."

After getting their horses Wyatt asked, "Tuck, you're the expert here, what should we do now?"

"We go to the Indian police and tell who we are and what we are doing here and ask for their help. Mount up, it's outside of town."

The two marshals rode two miles out of town to a small collection of huts and a few teepees. Tuck led Wyatt to a hut and they both dismounted. Tuck took a large bag off the back of his horse and carried it inside. Wyatt followed. The three Indians inside wore badges on vests but otherwise they were a poor-looking lot of police officers.

Tuck greeted the three Indian officers inside with a mix of Waco and Wichita languages. After talking for a few minutes Tuck set his bag on a desk. The three Indians crowded around. Tuck opened the bag and took out two handguns with gunbelts and two Winchester 1873 rifles. There was also a box of fifty, forty-four forty cartridges for each gun.

1873 Winchester

With a big grin on his face, Tuck looked at Wyatt, "They agreed to help us."

"I'd been wondering what was in that big bag, but I figured if you wanted me to know you would have told me."

"Let's step outside." As the two stepped outside, Tuck continued, "The Indian police are poorly supported and use their own guns. What we did in there means a lot to them. It could save their lives. They will find the four men we want and will notify us. I said we would be in the hotel. Let's go get rooms."

"How will they find them?" asked Wyatt while they returned to town.

"An Indian with three white men. It will be easy. First, they will look for the horses. When they find the horses, they will make sure it's the men we want. If it is, they will notify us. The law says they cannot touch white people, so they will come to us and together we will go after them. They will only help by arresting the Indian."

"Sounds like the easiest outlaw hunt I've ever been on," said Wyatt.

"Just remember, these outlaws are wanted for murder and will not surrender; they would rather go out fighting."

"Good point."

"Doesn't look like much of a hotel with only one floor," commented Wyatt as they approached the only hotel in the small town.

"It isn't but better than sleeping on the ground in the rain."

"Let's get rooms then check out that poor excuse for a saloon," said Wyatt.

"What will we do if we see them?"

"I don't know. Let's worry about that if it happens. Besides, their Indian partner wouldn't be allowed in the saloon, so there would only be three to contend with."

"As long as the other outlaws inside left us alone, which would be unlikely," warned Tuck.

After getting their rooms the two lawmen had an uneventful afternoon in the saloon. About five o'clock they went to a dingy café to eat. Then with nothing else to do, they went back to the saloon for a couple of hours and then went to bed.

The next morning was boring for the two. It was breakfast then saloon time. Later, in the middle of their dinner an Indian policeman entered the café and went straight to Tuck. They spoke in the Wichita language for a couple of minutes.

"Let's go. We're to follow Black Feather to a small camp four miles from town, where we'll meet up with the other two officers," said Tuck.

Wyatt dropped some money on the table, and they were out the door walking fast to the stable while the Indian officer rode alongside them.

Riding fast, they were at the small camp in forty minutes. The camp consisted of a couple of grass huts and a teepee. The two Indian police officers were waiting in a small grove of trees a couple hundred yards from the camp.

Wichita Indian Grass Huts

"How can we do this without hurting innocents?" asked Wyatt.

Wyatt and Tuck thought for a while. "The only thing I can think of," said Wyatt, "is to take them when they go to town."

"Sounds good, but how do we get them to decide to leave for town?" asked Tuck.

"I don't know."

"They weren't in town last night, so I bet they're

bored and they go tonight," suggested Tuck.

"So, we sit here and wait for them to leave. We can do that, but let's move farther away so they don't see us."

Tuck spoke with the Indians for a minute. "They think it's a good plan. Black Feather will stay with us tonight."

The group moved further away down the trail to town. The other two officers left. The horses were unsaddled and picketed in a grassy area.

"Let's pick our ambush spots so we're ready for them." Tuck chose a spot behind some rocks while Wyatt picked a spot on the other side of the road between two trees. Black Feather would be with Tuck. After picking their fighting places, Wyatt, Tuck and Black Feather got comfortable for the long, boring wait.

Evening approached and nothing happened. Then it was dark and still no outlaws. Black Feather said he was tired of waiting and going home.

"What are we going to do now? I can't believe they didn't go to town. They must be paying a squaw to keep them happy," said Tuck.

"I'm sure they are. We will get them in the morning when they come out to relieve themselves. In the meantime, I'll heat water for coffee. Looks like it's hardtack and jerky for supper."

"I'm glad we brought blankets with," said Tuck.

After their meager meal the two men found a heavy stick to use to subdue the outlaws.

The next morning before sunup the two marshals saddled their horses and led them to the small stand of trees where they watched the camp the first time.

"We don't know which hut they are in," complained Tuck.

"You take one, I'll take the other."

"What if a woman or child comes out?"

"Point your gun at them and put your finger in front of your lips and motion them to keep going. Put your badge on."

With their badges displayed, both men stood outside the open doorways with a big heavy stick waiting.

It was now light out. Wyatt was nervous and getting tired of standing when a white man walked sleepily out the open doorway. Wyatt swung his stick almost as hard as he could, hitting the man in the back of his head with a loud thunk. The man fell to the ground unconscious. Wyatt dragged him away from the door, put irons on his hands and was tying the feet when he heard shuffling. He picked up his stick and hurried to the doorway arriving just in time. It was another white man, so Wyatt thumped him over the head hard. The man let out a loud, "Ohhh" and looked at Wyatt. Wyatt hit him again harder. This time he fell. Wyatt dragged him over to the other man, put irons on his hands and tied his feet. Then he finished tying the first one's feet.

A woman came out of the hut Tuck was watching. He told her quietly to be quiet and keep going. She ran off scared.

Wyatt was waiting by the opening when he saw a hand holding a gun coming out of the opening. Wyatt waited until the man was almost all the way out when he brought the stick down hard on the man's wrist, breaking it. The gun fell to the ground. The man swore loudly. Wyatt quickly grabbed the damaged wrist and pulled the man screaming out of the hut. Tuck ran over with his gun in hand.

"Tuck, watch the door for the outlaw Indian while I tie this one up."

What they didn't know was the outlaw Indian was in the hut Tuck had just left, with his woman. He came out with a gun in his hand. Seeing two white men he didn't recognize, he shot at them. The bullet whizzed past Tuck's ear. Tuck turned towards the Indian and fired, missing him. The Indian ran to the horses, untied one from the string and rode off bareback.

A baby was crying and people were talking rapidly, but so far everyone was staying inside the huts hiding.

"Tuck, see if you can find out which horses are theirs."

Tuck yelled something in Wichita and an old man came out. They spoke for a minute. Slowly the rest of the Indians came out talking amongst themselves. Two women started cooking fires.

"He's getting their horses."

Wyatt went inside the hut. He found three saddlebags next to bedrolls and carried them outside. He then went into the other hut and found the Indian's saddlebags. Once outside he went through the bags and found a bundle of money in each. He put all the money together in one saddlebag. Then he found a buffalo bladder with water in it and poured it over an outlaw's head. He sputtered and came awake moaning his head hurt.

"I'm going to untie you and you are going to saddle all your horses."

"My head hurts too bad to do anything," moaned the outlaw.

Wyatt held the heavy stick over the man's head, "It will hurt worse if you don't get started. Be warned, I will not hesitate to shoot you. It will be much easier for me to take only two of you back to Coffeyville instead of three."

The outlaw moved slowly toward the tack and

started saddling a horse. Wyatt poured water over the other two outlaws, waking them. They also awoke moaning and complaining their heads hurt.

Once the horses were saddled, they were told to mount up. They complained they were hungry and needed to eat. The one with the broken wrist said he needed a doctor.

"You will eat when my deputy and I eat," said Wyatt.

On the way back to town they stopped at the Indian police hut and told them the Indian outlaw had escaped. They said they would find him and deliver him or his body to Coffeyville, Kansas.

When they got to Anadarko, the northbound train to Wichita was about to leave. Being a U.S. marshal, Wyatt was able to delay the train long enough so they could load the horses. The marshals and the outlaws all went without breakfast. With all the stops for passengers, water and coal, it would be a seven-hour train ride to Wichita. It was a small local railroad company and they didn't have a club car with food.

Arriving in Wichita seven hours later, the horses were unloaded. It would be a two-day layover before the small Southern Kansas Railroad had a train going to Independence, so using directions the conductor gave Wyatt, they rode to the Sedgwick County sheriff's office. Wyatt led the prisoners inside while Tuck followed the last one.

The small female deputy that was on desk duty stood, "Good morning marshals, what did you bring us?"

"The Coffeyville bank robbers," replied Wyatt. "We would appreciate it if we could keep them in your jail for two days while we wait on a train to Independence. Independence is as close as we can get to Coffeyville by train. The U.S. Government will pay boarding costs. I'm United States Marshal Wyatt Peterson and this is my deputy Tuck Tucker."

"Good to meet you two. I'm Deputy Cory Jackson."

"I've heard of you," grinned Wyatt, "I'd like to talk to you later."

Before Deputy Jackson could respond, Sheriff Drake exited his office, "I heard that. I suspect you want to steal my deputy. Everyone wants my little deputy. The Texas Rangers want her as a full-time ranger, the local police department and I don't know how many towns and cities have tried to get her. Go find your own deputy."

Wyatt grinned, "That's exactly why I wanted to talk with her."

"Marshal, just forget it; I'm not letting her go!" said the sheriff in a stern voice.

Hearing the sheriff talk about her, Deputy Jackson couldn't keep the smile off of her face. "Sorry Marshal Peterson, but I am happy where I am."

"Why would anyone want a tiny female deputy?" asked Tuck.

Deputy Jackson was shooting icicles at Tuck when the sheriff said, "I'd be very careful what you say about her. I made her mad one day, and I found my surprised self on the floor looking up. Don't make a bad assumption due to her size."

Wyatt chuckled, "I guess my deputy never heard of the Ice Lady. Let's get these yahoos locked up."

After the prisoners were locked up and the money was locked in the sheriff's safe, Wyatt saw his chance, "Deputy Jackson, I'd like to take you to supper."

"Please call me Cory. I would like that, but you won't have any luck making a marshal out of me. Did you know I'm also a Texas Ranger?"

"Up until two weeks ago I was a Texas Ranger myself, so I know all about you. In fact, we've been at the same parties, but you never once looked my way."

Cory gave Wyatt a flirtatious smile, "That was my loss."

"We'll be back for you at six."

"Make it five, that's when I get off. We have a stable around back where you can put all your horses. It'll be a bit tight but they'll fit."

While they were stabling their horses Tuck said, "Are you looking for a deputy or a wife?"

"Why not both? She would be a good catch."

"She's small but she is good-looking," agreed Tuck.

"We should have asked her where there is a hotel."

"You were too busy flirting with her. We've been sitting too much so let's walk around and see if we find one," said Tuck.

"I need to stretch my legs too."

"Why is Cory called the Ice Lady?" asked Tuck while they walked.

"They say she has no fear. Cold as ice in a shootout. And she is lightning fast with a gun, even won a shooting match here in Wichita."

After walking for forty-five minutes, they came across the Occidental Hotel and got rooms. They had baths, shaved, and changed into clean clothes. At four-thirty they were ready and started walking back to the sheriff's office.

"Good evening Cory," said Wyatt, followed by Tuck saying, "Good evening."

Cory smiled nicely, "Look at you two, all decked out for an evening with little Cory. The Detroit Dining Parlor is three blocks down the street."

Cory put her right arm around Wyatt's arm and her left arm around Tuck's arm. "This is my lucky night," chuckled Cory as she looked up to the tall Wyatt then Tuck.

"It's our lucky night also," said Wyatt with a smile.

After finishing their meal, the three sat back with a beer and talked. The first thing out of Tuck's mouth was, "Why do they call you the Ice Lady?" even though Wyatt had told him he wanted to hear it from Cory herself.

Cory shrugged her shoulders, "When I'm in a gunfight I don't fear death because my best friend claims she met with me in the future. It was called the Great Depression and the Dust Bowl. She said I was sixty-seven. So, I guess I don't have to worry about getting killed."

"Even if what she says is true, don't you think you can change the future? What if I put a gun to your head right now and pull the trigger?"

Cory smiled, "You won't because you want to make me an offer."

Wyatt laughed, "You're right. I need a female deputy. My boss requires it."

"Why?" asked Cory.

"To make sure Tuck and I don't lose our empathy for our fellow humans or abuse the power or money we have. And he thinks she will have more compassion for the downtrodden than a man."

"After the men I've killed with my knife and my gun I don't think your boss would approve of me at all," laughed Cory.

"It pays one hundred seventy-five dollars a month!"

Cory grinned, "That's hard to pass up, but I have someone I'm taking care of and I don't want to ride all over this land and be away from home. I do appreciate the offer and the dinner. It's time I get to my ranch."

"You have a ranch?"

"Yes, the man I take care of put me in his will."

"It sounds like you have your life in order, except for possibly a man."

"That's not my fault! Deputy Grant is taking his sweet time about deciding to court me."

"Maybe you need someone to make him jealous," grinned Tuck.

"If you two were to stay around longer that would be fun."

"I wish we could." Wyatt looked at Tuck, "You know, Wichita is located in the center of the country; I think it would be a great place to open up our bank accounts for our pay."

"That's a good idea. Then we could visit Cory all

the time," grinned Tuck.

"Cory, meeting you has been a delight. We will probably see more of you," said Wyatt while getting up and going to Cory's chair and pulling it back for her, "but for now we need to get some shuteye."

"Thank you, Wyatt."

"Cory, the same goes for me. If Grant fails you, get a hold of me," grinned Tuck.

"Choosing between the two of you is a decision no woman should ever have to make," said a smiling Cory as she stood.

Wyatt and Tuck laughed. "If I see this Grant fellow in the next two days, I'll straighten out his head!" said Tuck rather forcefully.

Two days later they were picking up their prisoners and saying goodbye to Cory. Grant was there so both Wyatt and Tuck thought this would be a good time to help Cory by instilling some jealousy into him.

"Cory, it's been a great two days. Dining and drinking with you has been a lot of fun. I'll be back," grinned Wyatt.

Grant had a look of shock on his face. "Cory what's he talking about?"

Before Cory could answer Grant, Tuck chimed in, "You're quite the party girl, Cory. You've been a lot of fun. Especially when you've had too much to drink. We'll be seeing you again."

Grant was now flabbergasted, "Cory, did you go out with these two?"

Knowing that Wyatt and Tuck were helping her with Grant, Cory played along. "Of course, these are two good-looking men. I couldn't decide which one I liked the best, so we went out together. I was overwhelmed with the attention of two perfect gentlemen, though I don't remember much after it got late."

Grant was upset and looked like he wanted to cry. He moved in front of Cory, standing close to her, "But I love you. How could you do this to me? I thought we were a couple."

"You refuse to show your love by courting me, so I have to move on with my life and have a little fun."

"I will start courting you tonight with dinner. Will you accept my courtship?"

Cory threw her arms around Grant in a tight hug and gave him a long kiss on his lips. After a minute she pulled away. "How's that for an answer?"

Wyatt and Tuck were laughing their heads off.

Grant finally realized he had been hoodwinked and said, "I've been tricked."

"Big boy, you made a commitment and I'm holding you to it! Thanks for the help Wyatt and Tuck."

"The both of us did take her out for dinner and drinks. She's a wonderful woman. You are a lucky man, Grant. Cory, if he doesn't follow through on his commitment let us know and we'll be back," said a smiling Wyatt.

"We sure will, Cory," added Tuck.

"That would be hell for me," laughed Cory, "how could I ever decide between the two of you?"

As the two marshals left the office Wyatt said, "She's quite a woman, isn't she?"

"I certainly wouldn't have to think about courting her," grinned Tuck.

It would be a three-hour train ride to Independence, Kansas. It was a small train consisting of only one passenger car, four stock cars and one freight car. The passenger car had eight other people in it. They were about an hour out from Wichita when one of the prisoners said he needed to use the toilet. Tuck took him to the rear of the car where the toilet was and opened the door for the prisoner and he went in. The prisoner was taking too long so Tuck yelled, "Come out now or I'm coming in!"

The door suddenly burst open, banging into Tuck and knocking him backwards, slamming him into the wall. The prisoner was on Tuck smashing fists into his face, stunning him. The prisoner exited the rear of the car and jumped off the train just as a deep gorge appeared. Tuck had followed the prisoner outside and watched the prisoner fall into the deep gorge. Tuck went back to Wyatt and the other two prisoners. "That's one less prisoner Coffeyville will have to deal with."

At Independence, the saddled horses were unloaded from the stock car. It would be an eighteen-mile ride to Coffeyville, which should take about four and a half hours. Tuck had the two prisoners and the riderless horse tethered behind him. Wyatt rode in the rear, keeping a close eye on the remaining prisoners. If they were to try something, this was their last opportunity.

The trip to Coffeyville was uneventful. It seemed the two prisoners were resigned to their fate. The prisoners were locked up in the town jail, the one with the broken wrist asking for a doctor. Wyatt and Tuck then delivered the money to the Condon Bank president. "I don't know how much was taken but I suspect most of your money is here," said Wyatt.

"Thank you marshals. I thought that money was gone for good. You've done a great job."

When they got outside Wyatt said, "I think we deserve a day off. If you take care of the horses,

I'll send a telegram to JT. I'll meet you at the hotel."

"We just had a couple of days off, but another wouldn't hurt," chuckled Tuck.

Wyatt and Tuck were sitting on the hotel's front porch drinking coffee, quietly talking and watching the activity of the town of nine hundred people.

"What'd JT have to say?" asked Tuck.

"Complimented us on a job well done but was disappointed I hadn't found a female deputy."

"Finding a female deputy is the toughest part of this job," said Tuck.

"It surely is."

"JT didn't give us an assignment?"

"Nope. He said to keep looking for a deputy and give away some of his money," laughed Wyatt. "Oh, I did give him the name of the Wichita bank and our account numbers."

"Good. I think we have a good spot sitting here watching for the needy."

"Yes, we do," said Wyatt as he leaned back and put his feet up on the porch railing.

While the two were relaxing in the shade of the porch, a young barefoot boy holding a wooden box by a handle came around. "Would you like your boots shined marshals?"

Tuck right away said, "If my boots saw any polish, they'd probably jump off my feet and run down the street looking for a pair of women's high heels."

"Ignore him," said Wyatt, "and yes, we'd both would like our boots polished. How much do you charge?"

The boy smiled, "Five cents for both boots."

"That's a good deal."

The boy was still smiling happily while he got out the polish and a few rags and went to work on Wyatt's boots.

While the boy worked, Wyatt studied him. He was barefoot, wearing raggedy corduroy pants and a torn shirt. He had a clean face and long hair. The boy and his clothes were clean, just old, showing he was cared for. Wyatt had a plan. "Tuck when our boots are polished, I'm going to start taking care of JT's business."

Tuck gave Wyatt a questioning look.

"You'll see."

When the boy had finished Tuck's boots, Wyatt gave the boy a silver dollar. The boy's smile vanished, "Sir, I don't have change for this."

"I don't want money back, that's your pay."

A smile burst on the boy's face. "Wow, thank you mister! I never seen a silver dollar before. I can't wait to show my mother!"

"Where is your mother?" asked Wyatt.

"She's going through town selling the eggs our chickens laid."

"Sound like a hard-working family," said Tuck.

"Yes, it does. What's your name boy?"

"Tyler, sir."

"Tyler, if you would come with me I would like to buy you some things," smiled Wyatt.

"I don't know sir, my mother warned me about strangers."

"But we are United States Marshals; you have nothing to fear from us," said Wyatt gently.

Tyler looked at their badges, "I guess it would be alright."

"How old are you, Tyler?" asked Wyatt.

"Eleven sir."

"Let's get you some new clothes and surprise your mother. But first you need a haircut. I bet you know where the barber shop is. Take me to it."

After a haircut and new clothes, Tyler was unrecognizable from the shoeshine boy. They were walking along the boardwalk when a distressed woman ran up to Wyatt. "Marshal, I can't find my boy! Could you please…" the woman looked at Tyler. "Tyler what's happened to you? I didn't recognize you!" She hugged Tyler tightly. "I was so worried. We were supposed to meet outside the town hall thirty minutes ago."

"Sorry Ma. I was busy and forgot."

"Where'd you get the nice clothes? And shoes too?"

"The marshal got them for me."

The woman took a long look at Wyatt's badge, then his face. "I've never heard of such a thing. Are you rich?"

"No ma'am, but someone I know is and he gives me money for things like this."

"My manners! I've forgotten my manners. Please forgive me. I'm Mrs. Stone. This is my son Tyler."

"I'm Marshal Wyatt Peterson. Tyler and I have already met," laughed Wyatt.

"Of course you have! I hate to rush off, but I must find my daughter."

"I'll go with you."

Mrs. Stone saw her daughter sitting on the steps to the town hall and ran to her. Squeezing her in a tight hug, she said to Wyatt, "This is my daughter Silvia." Silvia looked to be about fourteen. Wyatt tipped his hat. "I'm Marshal Peterson. Nice meeting you, Silvia."

Mrs. Stone and Wyatt both noticed Silvia staring

at her brother's new clothes.

"Mrs. Stone, I think Silvia needs some new clothes also."

"Please call me Sharon. That would be so kind of you."

After new clothes were bought for Silvia and Sharon, Wyatt offered lunch. They went back to the hotel for Tuck and the five of them went for lunch.

While the five were eating, Wyatt said to Sharon, "Tell us about yourself."

"The three of us live on a small plot of land outside of town. My husband died last year of tetanus. We've been trying to survive by selling things from our garden."

"Gardening is a lot of work," said Tuck. "I would suspect all of your work is keeping the kids from school."

A look of sadness struck Sharon's face. "I've been homeschooling them. We are doing our best to get by. Wyatt, you have been a blessing. Every night I pray for help. We thank you so much."

"It's been my pleasure. You are a handsome hardworking woman; I suspect a man will come along soon to court you. In the meantime, take this money." Wyatt handed Sharon five hundred dollars. "I'd like to give you the address of the man that made this possible. I'm sure he would greatly appreciate hearing from you."

"Please do, I would like to thank him."

With the lunch finished, everyone shook hands. When Wyatt went to shake Sharon's hand, she hugged him instead.

Wyatt and Tuck went back to the hotel where they sat and watched people going about their business.

"You know Tuck, we need an address so people can get a hold of us."

"The last thing I need is a house," replied Tuck.

"No, not a house, just an address. Maybe we should see if Cory would take care of our mail."

"Might as well; we're banking in Wichita, so we might as well use it for an address also."

"Next time we're in Wichita we'll ask her," said Wyatt.

The chatter ended when they saw an extremely attractive woman of about twenty-five stopping a wagon at a dress shop across the street. They watched as she got down and picked up the rifle that had been propped against the bench seat. She had long brown hair hanging from underneath a hat and was wearing corduroy pants and a shirt. While she was reaching for the rifle, a grungy man that appeared to have had too much to drink grabbed her rear end. She spun around and smacked him on the side of his head with the shoulder stock of her rifle. He went down hard. His head was bleeding when he looked up at her. Losing his temper, he went for the gun on his hip. The woman must have had a round in the chamber because she only had to cock the hammer and pull the trigger, shooting the downed man in the center of his chest. He put both hands on his chest, attempting to stop the bleeding.

The town sheriff must have been close because it wasn't a minute later he was at the woman's side. Looking at the dead man he noticed the gun was still in its holster. When the sheriff took the rifle away from the woman and was arresting her for murder, Wyatt and Tuck were up and moving quickly towards the sheriff.

"Sheriff you can't arrest this woman. We saw it all; it was self-defense. The man was going for his gun. This woman was so handy with her rifle he never got his gun out of its holster, but he was going for it. My deputy and I both saw it."

"His hand is nowhere near his gun. Both hands are on his chest. I think you are just trying to make favor with the young woman in hopes of female compensation."

Wyatt was steaming mad and about to lose his temper. Tuck noticed and quickly moved in front of Wyatt.

"Marshal, Sheriff Watkins has had it in for me ever since I turned him down when he came to court me. I think he wants me helpless in his jail for his benefit," explained the woman.

Wyatt pushed Tuck out of the way. "Sheriff, if you try to arrest her, I will take your badge and you will be out of a job."

"You can't do that. I'm a duly elected sheriff."

"You need to bone up on the law. A United States marshal does have that power. Just try me."

A large crowd had formed and were quietly watching to see the outcome. The sheriff was not well-liked.

Sheriff Watkins roughly grabbed the woman by the arm, pulling her with him.

Wyatt took the sheriff's gun out of its holster and hit him over the head with it, knocking him to the ground where he laid holding his bloody head.

"Tuck, yank that badge off him."

Tuck reached down and ripped the badge from the ex-sheriff's shirt.

"You can't do this!"

"I just did."

"Ma'am, I am Marshal Wyatt Peterson. This is my deputy Jed Tucker. Could you take me to the mayor?"

"I'm Cindy Harper. Sure, I can take you. It's just a few blocks."

As the three were leaving Watkins yelled, "What about my gun? You can't take my gun."

"You can have it tomorrow. Come to your old office," replied Wyatt.

Cindy Harper took Wyatt and Tuck to the hardware store the mayor owned.

"Mr. Mayor, I'm U.S. Marshal Wyatt Peterson and this is my deputy, Jed Tucker. Sheriff Watkins was unbecoming of his position, so I relieved him of his office. He tried to arrest Miss Harper for murder after I told him my deputy and I both saw it was self-defense."

"Glad to meet you. I'm Mayor Thompkins. You have the authority to relieve a law officer of his position?"

"Yes, I can do that."

"Actually, I'm glad you did because Watkins hasn't lived up to what everyone expected. He was doing a poor job."

"If you have a deputy sheriff, I suggest making him temporary sheriff until you can hold another election."

"I'll do that."

"Right now, I have some business to attend to, but my deputy and I will be around for another day if you should need anything."

"Thank you marshals."

After they were outside the mayor's store Wyatt asked, "Miss Harper, I'm impressed by how you handle yourself. I have an offer to make. May I do it over supper?"

Miss Harper smiled, "I would gladly go to supper with you two handsome marshals, but please call me Cindy."

"We're new in town so please, you pick the place."

She led them to Pete's Diner a few blocks away.

After placing their order Cindy looked Wyatt in the eyes with smile and said coquettishly, "If the offer isn't marriage I'm not interested."

Wyatt was taken aback by this bold, forward woman. She appeared to be serious. Caught off guard as he was, instead of replying he only stared.

Tuck came to Wyatt's rescue. "We are looking for a woman to help us with distributing a rich man's wealth among the needy. This woman will also be a deputy marshal; that's the reason skill with a firearm is necessary."

Coming out of his shock, Wyatt said, "We feel you may be the person we have been looking for."

"Tell me more. What will my responsibilities be?"

"You will help us decide who should be helped and how much help they should get. But be warned, the help might not always be monetary. It might require force to right a wrong or get someone out of a jam."

"Fine so far, but for some reason I feel you are holding something back."

"He is. Tell her Wyatt," laughed Tuck.

Wyatt frowned at Tuck. "There is one more thing. You will be required to keep records and report to the patron, Mr. J.T. Rothschild, weekly."

Cindy grinned, "I can tell there's more. Keep going."

Tuck laughed, "Wyatt, she can read you like a book."

Wyatt grimaced, "You will have some control over Tuck and me. It will be your job to see that Tuck and I don't abuse the power of the badge or misuse the money."

Cindy grinned mischievously, "So that's the worm in the pie that bothers you, being controlled by a woman! It sounds like the perfect job!"

Tuck laughed again, "Wyatt, I think she's too much for you!"

"You haven't even asked what it pays; aren't you interested?"

"Not in the least. The job sounds perfect. Working with and controlling two handsome men, what could be better?"

"It pays one hundred seventy-five a month," said a grim-faced Wyatt.

Tuck laughed some more, "You're a strong woman Cindy, and perfect for this job and will make it fun…for me anyway."

MONTANA TERRITORY

"I have to telegraph Rothschild and let him know I have a female deputy and have him send money to the Condon Bank. Let's meet at the hotel. I have a sealed letter from Rothschild for you, Cindy. It's with my things; I'll give it to you when I get back," said Wyatt.

"Maybe he will have something for us to do," said Tuck.

Twenty minutes later Wyatt found Tuck and Cindy sitting on the hotel front porch. "I've got to get that letter; I'll be right back." Wyatt went upstairs and dug through the bundle of papers wrapped in a piece of old rain slicker. Finding the sealed envelope from Rothschild, he went back downstairs.

Wyatt handed the envelope to Cindy with a badge.

"Thank you," she said with a big smile.

"Rothschild is sending us to Miles City, Montana.

It's the site of numerous killings due to a range war. After the sheriff was killed, two marshals were sent in and were both killed in their first month."

"Sounds like a tough one, like maybe the AG should be sending in the army instead of us," said Tuck.

"The army is a good idea. Maybe we'll request it when we get there."

Cindy had been reading the letter from Rothschild while the two men talked. A smile came to her face and she said, "This job keeps getting better and better."

"What's it say?" Wyatt wanted to know.

"It says, for my eyes only."

"You're an impossible woman!" complained Wyatt.

Tuck was laughing, "I agree with Cindy, this job keeps getting better and better."

"I have to get back to my father's ranch and tell him I'm now a deputy marshal. He will be shocked and won't like losing his best worker," said Cindy while putting on her badge.

"We will meet at Pete's Diner for breakfast at six. Be ready to depart for Independence from Pete's. At Independence we take a train to Kansas City. Cindy, do you have a pistol?" asked Wyatt.

"No. I'm good with my rifle. It's all I want. You two keep your baby guns; I'll keep my rifle which has twice as many bullets as your pistols."

Wyatt looked at Tuck. Tuck shrugged his shoulders.

At breakfast, the next morning Wyatt asked, "Cindy, how did it go with your father?"

"He was not happy with me at all, but I think he was proud I was a United States Deputy Marshal."

The three marshals arrived in Independence, Kansas at eleven that morning and were on the train to Kansas City by one o'clock in the afternoon. At Kansas City they had a six-hour layover for the train to Sioux City. At Sioux City they took the Sioux City/St. Paul Railroad train to Minneapolis. At Minneapolis they took the Northern Pacific Railroad train west through Bismarck to Miles City.

Miles City had a population of about eight hundred. It had two hotels, three saloons, two cafés, a general store, lumber yard, two hardware stores, two banks, a brewery, and a few other stores.

While on the train they made their plans.

"We'll separate before disembarking. I'll just be a cowboy looking for work. I'll try to get hired by the outfit that is causing all the trouble. You two can play husband and wife and look for a ranch to buy. There should be several of them for sale during this range war," instructed Wyatt.

"Wait," said Cindy, "what if I don't want to be married to Tuck?"

"Why not?" asked Wyatt.

"Maybe I'd rather be married to you."

Wyatt blushed, "This is a pretend marriage."

"I know but I'd rather pretend with you."

Tuck's grin was about to split his face in two. "Wyatt, I can be a better bad guy than you any day of the week," claimed Tuck.

Wyatt thought a moment. "You are right about being a better bad guy. You always were a troublemaker. Okay it's settled. You're the bad guy Tuck."

Cindy was happy with the change and it showed on her face.

They arrived three days after leaving Independence, Kansas.

The railway clerk suggested the Miles Hotel; he said the other one was the Lodging House and with its billiard tables tended to have lots of fights, so Wyatt and Cindy went to the Miles Hotel first to get a room. Tuck would go to a saloon first then to the Miles Hotel and register.

After tying their horses at the hotel's hitchrail, as they were walking up the steps Cindy put an arm through Wyatt's left arm and smiled, "We need to look like we're married."

Wyatt couldn't help grinning.

They registered under the name of Mr. and Mrs. Peterson. Cindy still had her arm through Wyatt's while going up the stairs.

After entering their room Wyatt asked, "How are we going to do this?"

"Do what?" asked Cindy with a knowing grin.

"There's only one bed."

"I see that. If you are afraid to sleep with me, you can always sleep on the floor."

"But, but..."

"But what Wyatt?"

"Let's go get a drink."

"Sounds good, I think you need one," grinned Cindy.

The Cow Bell saloon was across the street so that was where they went. Cindy slipped her arm in Wyatt's again. She was enjoying herself.

When the two entered the Cow Bell, all the men's eyes were on the brown-haired beauty wearing pants and carrying a Winchester rifle. Only working girls were usually in saloons.

The two took an empty table in the front of the room. Wyatt noticed all the men looking at Cindy. A waitress came to their table, "What will you two be having?"

"A bottle of your best whiskey," answered Wyatt.

In a minute, the waitress was back with a bottle and two glasses. She looked at Cindy quizzically and shrugged her shoulders.

"I hope bringing you in here won't be a lot of trouble," said Wyatt.

"Back in Coffeyville, I was the only woman that went into the saloons besides the soiled doves. The men liked it. They always hoped I had had a bad day so I would drink too much and be easy prey. I never drank more than two drinks. The men were always disappointed to see me go."

"No one ever bothered you?"

"Once in a while I had to hit someone with my rifle. You've seen how I use it as a club. That's why

I like carrying a rifle."

"I just hope you never use it on me," chuckled Wyatt.

"Behave yourself and I won't."

"What day is this?" asked Wyatt.

"Friday."

"That means this place will be packed later with cowboys. Not a place for a woman."

"I have been taking care of myself just fine for five years."

"It's almost six, let's go for supper," suggested Wyatt.

Cindy had an impish look, "I'm sharing a room with a man and being taken out for supper, what a perfect job."

"You might not be so happy when the fireworks start."

They had finished eating when Cindy asked, "What do we do now?"

"There isn't much to do. Drink, gamble, eat and sleep. But I think we should hangout a bit and see what we can learn."

"We should find a confidant to catch us up on what has happened and keep us informed."

"Great idea Cindy. The question is, who?"

"It would be someone that has made an investment in the town and has lots to lose with this lawlessness."

"That would be a business owner that isn't afraid of reprisals," said Wyatt.

"A banker would have the most to lose."

"You are right, Cindy, a banker would. We'll go to the bank in the morning and see what's for sale and see how he feels about what is happening. Let's check out that Yellowstone Saloon we passed on our way here."

As they entered the Yellowstone Saloon all eyes were on the woman wearing pants and carrying a rifle. Some devious minds immediately started working on how to rid the woman of her man. It was early enough there were still a few empty tables. Wyatt led Cindy to one by the wall. He pulled out a chair for her then went to the bar. No sooner was Wyatt gone than a drunken, dirty man left the table next to Cindy's, and moved to the round table Cindy sat at. He put a chair right next to her and sat down. Wyatt noticed. He knew Cindy could handle him. After getting the drinks and paying for them, Wyatt stayed at the bar. He wanted to see what Cindy would do.

When the man leaned against Cindy and put his right arm around her, she became a wild, screeching bobcat. As she twisted to the left towards him, she gave him a roundhouse to his nose. It made a popping sound. He fell backwards off his chair onto the floor, holding his nose.

Cindy's screech had alerted the entire saloon, so everyone saw what she did to the drunk. Everyone roared with laughter, including Wyatt.

The three men from the drunk's table rose yelling, "That was our brother you just smacked. We're going to have some fun with you and make you pay!"

As they moved towards her, Cindy grabbed her rifle and rose to meet them. Spectators blocked Wyatt's path to Cindy. Cindy became a whirlwind with her rifle, spinning one way, then the other. When the person she was swinging at was close, her right hand slid from the two-handed barrel grip, to the fore stock. If her attacker was farther away, her right hand would slide back towards the end of the barrel next to her left hand, giving her a longer swing. The man whose nose she had bloodied joined the melee. In less than a minute the battle was over. Cindy was standing, rifle in hand, untouched. The four brothers were lying on the wood floor moaning and bloody.

Wyatt was finally able to get through to Cindy. Amazement was showing on his face as he looked at the bloody scene. "I couldn't have done as well." He proudly put his arm around her and led her out. His other hand carried the bottle. "Let's go to our room and talk."

Cindy smiled up at him, "I'd like that."

The two were sitting at a table in their room.

"Wyatt, the way I behave towards you, you probably think I'm a loose wanton woman. I am not. I have only been with a man once and that was when I was eighteen and dumb. He gave me too much to drink and took advantage of me. At twenty-five I am still single because, until you, I have never met a man I wanted."

"You might be surprised, but I have never thought of you as a wanton woman."

"If you climb into bed with me tonight, you'll change your mind," laughed Cindy.

"Maybe I'd better sleep on the floor then," grinned Wyatt.

"It would be safer for you," laughed Cindy. "If you will be a gentleman and turn around, I'm going to prepare for bed."

Wyatt stayed seated at the table but turned his chair around. A couple of minutes later Cindy said, "Okay, you can turn around now."

Wyatt turned around to see Cindy in a thin clingy nightgown. She took her toothbrush and toothpowder to the cabinet with the basin and pitcher of water. As she brushed her teeth, unknown to Wyatt she watched him through the mirror. She saw how he stared at her. She poured water into a glass and rinsed her mouth, spitting the water into the basin. When she turned around Wyatt was busy getting out his toothbrush and toothpowder.

While Wyatt brushed his teeth, Cindy got into bed and under the covers. Finished brushing, Wyatt rolled out his bedroll on the floor. Cindy watched. She would give him one night. She knew he would never make a second night sleeping on the floor. She rolled over and went to sleep with a smile on her face.

They were having breakfast the next morning at Carol's Café, which was next door to the hotel, when Tuck walked in. Seeing only two other people in the café he thought it would be safe to sit with Wyatt and Cindy. With a smug look on his face he asked, "How'd you two sleep last night?"

Cindy spoke up before Wyatt, "I slept really good, thank you. Wyatt though, has been complaining all morning about being sore from sleeping on that awful wood floor."

Tuck looked surprised, "I bet he learned his lesson."

Cindy smiled smugly, "I think so. I doubt he will sleep on the floor tonight."

"Tuck, did you come here just to spite me or do have any information?"

"Our troublemaker is Andy Rowland. He owns

the Rolling R Ranch. He feels because he was here before anyone else, he owns the whole territory. He's doing all he can to push the small ranchers out. When lawmen get in his way, he tries to buy them off. If that doesn't work, he has them killed. He runs off ranchers with threats. If that doesn't work, he makes them go broke by stealing their stock."

"So, we now need to get proof of his shenanigans. That will be mine and Cindy's job. We'll buy a ranch today and stock it."

"I've had breakfast, I'll check with you later," said Tuck as he left.

"Let's get to the bank," said Wyatt.

Wyatt and Cindy told a teller they wanted to speak with the bank president. They watched as he went and knocked on the president's office door then went inside. A moment later the teller returned.

"President Jeffries will see you."

After entering the president's office Wyatt and Jefferies shook hands. Jeffries nodded at Cindy. The three took seats.

"What may I do for you today?"

"I'm Mr. Peterson. My wife and I are looking for a ranch to purchase."

"I have three ranches available. The smallest is four hundred acres. Has a small house. Price is ten thousand dollars. The next one is six hundred and fifty acres with a four-bedroom house for seventeen thousand dollars. The third is two thousand acres with a large six-bedroom home and bunkhouse for numerous cowboys. It's stocked with twenty-two hundred head of cattle. The price is twenty-two thousand dollars and it's available immediately."

"Twenty-two thousand is a low price for that much land with a large house. Why?" asked Wyatt.

Jeffries looked down at the papers on his desk, then at Cindy and back to Wyatt. "There is an element around here that is running people off their property. I…I can't say anymore other than I need the money to cover accounts. And the people who owned it lost their entire investment. They just wanted out of this area."

Wyatt looked at Cindy, "I think we can trust him, what do you think?"

"I think so."

Mr. Jeffries, I'm a United States Marshal. Cindy is one of my deputies. I have another deputy working undercover. We could use your help. I am not really interested in buying a ranch. I only want to use one to trap the cattle thieves. Would you be willing to help us?"

Mr. Jeffries thought for a moment. "This country is an ideal place to raise cattle. With an end to the killing and taking of land this area will rebound and grow rapidly. Yes, I will help."

"You and I will put the word that I have purchased the twenty-two-thousand-acre ranch and we will set our trap. What was the name of this ranch?"

"Big Sky Ranch. And I forgot to mention, it's furnished."

"That's great. Thank you, Mr. Jeffries, we will move in today."

The two men stood and shook. "Good luck to you Marshal Peterson." Mr. Jeffries went to a cabinet, grabbed a set of keys and handed them to Wyatt.

"Before we go to the ranch let's hire a printer to print Help Wanted posters to post around town," said Wyatt.

"Good idea."

The local newspaper office would print and post the posters. Cowboy pay would be double the normal thirty dollars a month. It mentioned cowboys, cook, and maid needed.

Before leaving town for the Big Sky Ranch, they purchased as many supplies as they could carry on their horses. Wyatt said once they had some help, he would send someone in a wagon to buy supplies.

Both Wyatt and Cindy were stunned with the

size of the ranch house and the bunkhouse. The bunkhouse had a kitchen and dining room and had enough bunks for twenty cowboys. After looking at the bunkhouse they went inside the house. The furniture was nicely made with leather cushions.

"I could live here," said Cindy.

"I could too if it wasn't so cold in the winter."

"We should make our marriage official and make this our home," smiled Cindy seductively.

"You're putting the wagon ahead of the horse."

"I know," sighed Cindy.

"Besides, winters up here are too cold for me."

As they toured the house, they came to the master bedroom.

"Look at the size of that bed," said Cindy with a grin. "Will you be sleeping on the floor tonight or in a different room?"

Wyatt looked at Cindy and saw her mischievous grin. "We'll see."

Hearing someone clomping around downstairs, Wyatt pulled his gun and rushed down the stairs only to find it was Tuck.

"I hear this ranch is hiring. I'd like a job," said Tuck with a big smile.

"You're hired!" laughed Wyatt.

"Looks like you two have been checking out the bedrooms," grinned Tuck.

"Careful or you'll be fired on your first day," quipped Wyatt.

"Your posters are working. There are a lot of cowboys out of work right now. You should have a crew this afternoon," said Tuck.

"Good. I imagine Rowland will start right away tonight trying to run off this new rancher. We'll have to set a schedule for guards starting tonight. What we want to do is capture some of his men for witnesses. Let's ride out and find a good place to set a trap for the Rolling R rustlers," said Wyatt.

"What about me?" Cindy wanted to know.

"You've worked a ranch, so you are in charge of the hiring. I wouldn't be fussy though, we need lots of riders right away," answered Wyatt.

Wyatt and Tuck rode a mile to where the herd was grazing. For a minute they studied the area. Finally, Wyatt said, "There's two hills with a swale between them. There will be a full moon tonight, so I imagine rustlers will come through the swale between the hills to keep from being seen from the house. We will put guards on each hilltop."

"Do you think they'll come tonight?" asked Tuck.

"I do. They will figure we will think we won't get

hit on our first night and so won't be prepared or be organized. You will be on one hill with men, and I'll be on the other. When they move between the hills, we will come down behind them, trapping them."

"We should also have men in front of them so we will have a circle around them," suggested Tuck.

"Good idea." Wyatt thought for a moment, then started drawing in the dirt. "The circles are the two hilltops. The arrow between them represents the rustlers moving through the swale between the hills. The little circles are cattle. The Xs represent us. The dotted lines from the Xs represent shooting direction. This is so we don't shoot each other."

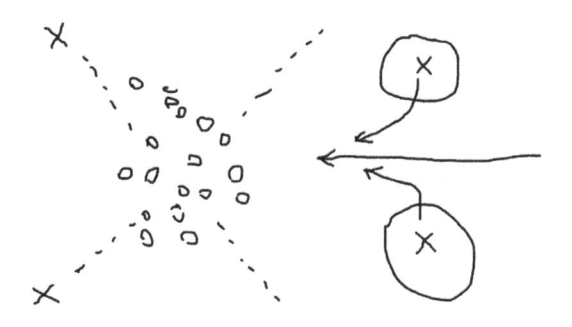

"But I don't want any shooting," continued Wyatt. "Everyone will yell, 'No shooting. We want to talk.' We want to take them prisoner. We will identify ourselves as US Marshals and promise them release if they testify against their boss.

Which I'm sure will be Rowland."

"Sounds good," said Tuck.

"If we must shoot, we have to be sure everyone knows which way to aim so we don't shoot each other. There should be one person with a torch in the groups on the east side. But they are not to light it until we yell, 'No shooting.' This way the rustlers will see how many of us there are, and that they are surrounded."

When they arrived back at the house, Cindy said she had hired twenty-two cowboys.

"Cindy, would you and Tuck please take a wagon into town and purchase supplies? Now we must feed all these cowboys."

"Are you doing the cooking Wyatt?" laughed Cindy.

"For twenty-five people? You were supposed to hire a cook! Better find one when you get to town or you will be doing the cooking."

Cindy stuck her tongue out at Wyatt which made him burst out laughing.

"Let's go Cookie," laughed Tuck. Cookie being what cooks were generally called.

Cindy and Tuck were back two hours later.

"Cindy, I hope you found a cook. I think our new cowboys are about to mutiny," said Wyatt.

"I did. Meet Curly McIntire."

"Irish are usually the best cooks," smiled Wyatt as he shook the elderly Curly's hand.

"We are at that lad."

After everyone had eaten, Wyatt, Tuck and Cindy put on their badges and spoke to the cowboys in the bunkhouse dining room. The cowboys were greatly surprised to find out they had been hired by US Marshals. The cowboys were told rustlers were expected tonight. Two would remain here at the headquarters as guards. All the rest would be assigned places for the ambush and capture of the rustlers.

"No one shoot unless fired upon. We don't want anyone hurt. We just want to capture the rustlers," said Wyatt loudly.

Two of the cowboys were only seventeen years old. They were told to stay and watch the buildings. The rest were divided into four groups. The marshals would lead three groups; the fourth group would be led by an older, experienced cowboy. At evening the four groups rode out to their assigned areas.

It was a cool enjoyable evening as the men waited. It was close to midnight when the two groups on the hilltops saw movement and heard voices talking quietly. As the would-be rustlers rode between the hills Wyatt counted ten riders. Wyatt waited until the rustlers had passed, then his group and Tuck's rode quietly down the small hills and formed a line, blocking escape.

Wyatt yelled as loud as he could, "We are US Marshals. You are surrounded. Put up your hands and no one will get hurt."

The torches were lit. When the ten rustlers saw they were surrounded by so many they raised their hands.

"If you cooperate you will be released. I repeat. We don't want you. We only want your leader. If you cooperate you will be released." Seeing everyone had their hands up, Wyatt said to Tuck, "Let's get their guns." They went around and took everyone's gunbelts and hung them from their saddle horns.

"Cindy take all the men back to bunkhouse while we take these would be rustlers into town," ordered Wyatt.

The ten rustlers were locked in the city jail and their guns hung from pegs on the wall.

"Who is your boss?" asked Wyatt. A young cowboy answered, "Rowland."

"Are you willing to testify against him for your freedom?" asked Wyatt.

"Yes, I don't want to go to jail," he replied.

"How about the rest of you?"

One or two said yes, the others were quiet.

"Someone said, "We ride for the brand."

"That's fine, you can ride for the brand right into prison. Or the judge might hang the bunch of you for the sheriff and marshal murders."

"Let's put the ones willing to testify in a separate cell," suggested Tuck.

"Good idea."

All but two decided to testify, so they were left where they were while the two holdouts were moved to a different cell.

"You two will change your mind when you hear what I'm going to do next," said Wyatt.

"What are you going to do Wyatt?" asked Tuck.

"I will be leaving in the morning to see Colonel Miles at Fort Keogh. It's only two miles west of here. You stay and watch the jail."

"Will do."

"You're going to use the army against Rowland?" asked one of the two holdouts.

"I sure am."

"Rowland and his men won't stand a chance," said the same man.

"That's the idea."

"I change my mind, I'll testify."

"I will too," yelled the last holdout.

"You will be glad you did. Anyone that causes any trouble while they are locked up will be prosecuted along with Rowland."

When Wyatt got to the ranch house everything was quiet. The front door was locked so he had to knock. Cindy was at the door right away and opened it.

"You must not have gone to bed."

"I haven't. I've been waiting for you."

Like a wife waiting up for her husband, thought Wyatt. "That's nice of you."

Wyatt locked the door behind him and the two went upstairs. Stopping outside the door to the master bedroom Cindy asked with a seductive smile, "Will you be sleeping on the floor tonight or in a different bedroom?"

"I only have two choices?"

"Would you like a third?" she asked teasingly.

"More choices make decisions more complicated, but they might also make life more, ah…fulfilling."

"I could give you another choice, but you wouldn't get any sleep," the teasing smile was still on Cindy's face.

"Sleep, who needs sleep."

Cindy turned and entered the bedroom followed by Wyatt. Cindy went to her unpacked saddlebags and took out her toothbrush and powder. "I'm going to brush my teeth at the kitchen sink."

"I'm going to do the same."

Using the pump at the kitchen sink the two brushed their teeth then went back upstairs.

"Please turn your back for a moment while I get into my nightgown."

"Do you trust me not to sneak a look?" asked Wyatt with a big grin.

"I'd be disappointed if you didn't."

Wearing her nightgown Cindy got into bed. Wyatt turned down the wick on the lamp to a low glow. It would probably burn the rest of the night.

At breakfast the next morning Wyatt told Cindy he was going to Fort Keogh to speak with Colonel Nelson Miles. While he was gone Cindy would appoint a ranch foreman to run things.

On the way to Fort Keogh, Wyatt stopped at the city jail where he found Tuck sleeping on the cot in the office.

"It looks like you caught up on your sleep," said Wyatt.

"I did, but you look like you were up all night," said Tuck with a snide grin.

Wyatt responded with, "I'll have the café send over eleven breakfasts. I'm going to see the colonel now. I'll come back here afterwards."

"Good luck."

Fort Keogh was an open fort, there was no wall surrounding the buildings. Seeing a sign saying Commandant on a building, Wyatt went to it and entered.

"What can I do for you sir?" said a corporal sitting at a desk.

"I'm United States Marshal Wyatt Peterson. I'd like to see the Colonel."

The corporal stood and knocked on the door behind his desk. "Enter," someone inside said.

"A US Marshal here to see you sir."

"Send him in."

Wyatt could hear everything.

The corporal returned, "You may go in marshal."

"Good morning Colonel, I'm United States Marshal Wyatt Peterson. I'm here under the orders of United States Attorney General Joseph Whitaker to investigate the killing of two US marshals and the sheriff. I need your help."

"You are under orders from AG Whitaker himself, I'm impressed. I have never known him to get involved in things personally. I am aware of what has been going on here, but civilian matters are out of my hands. Besides, I am having enough trouble keeping the Blackfeet on their reservation. It has to be a really serious circumstance for the army to get involved in a civil matter."

"The lives of myself and two of my deputies as well as other people are dependent on getting help from the army. I have witnesses willing to testify against Andy Rowland in the murders of the three lawmen and other people. But it is three against forty, so I need your help. Here is a letter from Whitaker."

Wyatt handed the letter to Colonel Miles. For three minutes he read it, then studied it in silence. One part stood out from the rest, "It doesn't matter if you are a lawman or part of the military, if Marshal Peterson asks for your help, you must give it to him."

The colonel looked up, "You have our help, what would you like the army to do?"

"I would like you to ride with my deputies and me to the Rolling R Ranch so I can arrest Andy Rowland for murder and theft. As I mentioned earlier, he has forty men working for him."

The colonel thought for a moment then yelled, "Corporal Higgins."

The corporal was immediately in the room. "Yes, Colonel."

"Tell Captain Wakefield I want to see him."

"Yes sir." The corporal was out the door like Indians were chasing him.

Two minutes later a captain knocked and entered. "Captain Wakefield reporting as ordered."

"Captain, this is US Marshal Peterson. You will assemble A Company and assist Marshal Peterson in arresting Andy Rowland. Follow Marshal Peterson's orders as if they were mine."

"I understand, sir."

"Dismissed."

The captain did an about face and left. He could be heard giving the corporal orders. "Have the bugler sound assembly for A Company."

"Thank you, Colonel," said Wyatt.

"You're welcome. If you see Whitaker be sure to say hello for me."

The colonel stood and shook hands with Wyatt.

Wyatt left the building to the sounds of a bugle sounding assembly. Wyatt was impressed with the power the US Attorney General had given him. Thirty minutes later he was riding ahead of two columns of cavalry soldiers alongside Captain Wakefield.

Thirty minutes later the cavalry company rode down the main street of Miles City, where Tuck joined them. Big Sky Ranch was on the way to the Rolling R so they stopped there so Cindy could also join them. After saddling her horse, she rode alongside Wyatt at the head of the long column. "You keep impressive company, Wyatt," grinned Cindy.

Wyatt just grinned at her.

An hour later the marshals and Company A rode down the lane to the Rolling R buildings. When they were two hundred yards from the buildings the right column of soldiers circled the buildings around the right. The left column of soldiers circled the buildings to the left. Rowlands' cowhands were watching and wondering what was about to happen.

The three marshals, Captain Wakefield and a sergeant rode to the center of the buildings. "You cowhands, it's your lucky day because we don't want you. Mount your horses and ride out," yelled Wyatt as loud as he could. The cowboys hurriedly saddled their horses and rode out.

Rowland had seen the cavalry circling his ranch and he had seen the three marshals wearing their badges. He knew he was in trouble and there was no escape. That is when a cornered animal is most dangerous, and Rowland was no different. When he died, he would take the three marshals with him. His three best men were inside the ranch house with him and they felt the same as their boss. They were outlaws and killers and would rather die fighting than by a rope.

"Captain Wakefield, you have done your part, but now it's time for us marshals to earn our money. I would appreciate it if you would stand by until we are finished. If anyone tries to escape have your men stop them by any means necessary."

"As you say, Marshal Peterson. Sergeant, pass that order to the men."

"Yes sir." The sergeant rode back to the men. He told them to pass the order down the line of circled soldiers, "No one is to escape."

The three marshals dismounted and tied their horses to the corral fence.

"Rowland," yelled Wyatt, "come out with your hands up or we're coming in."

"Come on in and get me."

"Cindy, you're staying here. Shoot anyone that comes out with a gun in his hand."

"I'm a deputy same as Tuck. I don't want to be treated any differently because I'm a woman."

Wyatt stared at her for a moment. "Okay, I want you behind me watching my back. I'm not worried about anyone running out the back door and getting away, so we will go in together. Undoubtedly someone will have a gun aimed at the door, so we won't go in that way right off. Tuck, you go to the left of the door, Cindy and I will go to the right. On my signal we three will stick our heads up and shoot through the windows."

"It's a good thing it's a warm day, all the windows are open," stated Tuck.

"That certainly will help. There won't be a reflection when we look in," said Wyatt.

The three moved quickly to the porch. Moving bent over below window height, they took their places. When they were squatted below the windows, Wyatt looked at Tuck and nodded his head. They both popped up and stuck their handguns through the windows. A man was standing in the middle of the main room with his gun aimed at the door. When he saw the heads pop up, he started swiveling his gun to the left to shoot Wyatt, but he wasn't fast enough. A bullet from both Wyatt and Tuck slammed into his chest, killing him. Knowing a rifle would not work in this situation, Cindy had stayed below the window.

"Let's go!" yelled Wyatt and the three rushed through the front door. As they entered the main room someone shot at them from a hallway. The three marshals returned fire. It was too much for the shooter, so he ran down the hallway and into a room.

"He's yours, Tuck," yelled Wyatt as he bounded for the stairs with Cindy right behind him.

As they topped the stairs Rowland and Wyatt saw each other at the same time. They both fired and missed each other. Someone came from the side and grabbed Cindy's rifle, trying to pull it away from her. Wyatt backed up by the edge of the staircase while shooting at Rowland.

Being used to always having a tight grip on her

rifle, Cindy had strong fingers. The man she was fighting with was about her size. The two were struggling fiercely. Seeing a window behind the man, Cindy put everything she had into a push. The man was going backwards when his boots tripped over the loose carpet. He fell backwards out the window, taking Cindy's rifle with him.

Wyatt and Rowland had been shooting at each other and missing. Wyatt's gun clicked on an empty chamber. When he lowered his gun to reload, Rowland stepped out from the doorway he had been standing behind.

"Drop the gun, marshal, or I shoot the girl!" yelled Rowland.

Wyatt looked at Cindy, then dropped his gun.

Two gunshots were heard downstairs.

"Marshal, I'm going to kill you first, then the girl."

While Rowland was cocking the hammer, Cindy jumped in front of Wyatt, taking the bullet meant for him. She crumpled to the floor. At the same time Tuck got to the top of the stairs and shot Rowland.

Wyatt yelled "No!" and dropped to his knees. He rolled Cindy over. She was shot just below the heart. She opened her eyes and looked at Wyatt. She gave a small smile and said, "Last night was wonderful."

Tears were streaming down Wyatt's face. "Cindy,

I'm so sorry."

Cindy coughed up blood. "It's okay Wyatt. Don't hold yourself responsible and promise me you will find another woman and live a happy life."

"I can't promise that." Wyatt was crying like a child.

Cindy coughed up more blood, "Please promise me before I'm gone."

"Promise her Wyatt," said Tuck sternly.

"I promise Cindy. I'll do my best."

"Now kiss me."

Wyatt bent down and kissed Cindy's bloody lips. Cindy was returning the kiss, then stopped. Wyatt pulled his head up. She was gone. He pulled her to his chest in a tight hug and cried.

Coffeyville, Kansas

Cindy's mother saw the two men standing a hundred yards away. They were watching the Police Funeral for Cindy that AG Whitaker had organized. There was a flag-draped coffin and the playing of bagpipes. She went to them. As she got closer, she saw the tears flowing down Wyatt's face.

"Wyatt, I apologize for Cindy's father's behavior when you brought her home."

"No need apologizing, I'd have acted the same. I

should be the one in that coffin, not Cindy."

"Still, he should have allowed you at her funeral." Cindy's mother turned and went back to her husband.

"What do we do now?" asked Tuck.

"All the trains go to Wichita so let's stop there, set up mailing addresses and take a few days off," answered Wyatt while wiping his tears away.

THE KIDNAPPING OF BRENDA WILSON

Wichita, Kansas

Deputy Cory Jackson was walking through town, leading her horse Socks, named as such due to the bottom portion of his brown legs being white. She saw Wyatt and Tuck sitting outside of Paul's Pub on the raised walkway, drinking. They had brought out two chairs and a small table.

"You two look comfortable. I suspect you will start a new fad, outdoor drinking," smiled Cory.

"The air inside is terrible," said Tuck while making a face.

Cory tied her horse to the hitch rail and was wondering where to sit when Tuck noticed her quandary and said, "Just a minute while I get you a chair."

Tuck brought a chair out and with an extra glass.

After seating Cory, he poured two fingers into the glass for her.

"You are such a gentleman, Tuck, thank you. What's the matter with the quiet one?" Cory nodded at Wyatt.

Tuck sighed, "It's a bad news story for another time."

"The woman of my life took a bullet for me," said Wyatt with wet eyes.

With a shocked look on her face, Cory picked up her chair and put it alongside Wyatt. "Tuck, pass me my drink please."

"Wyatt, tell me what happened."

"The most wonderful woman I've ever known saved my life by stepping in front of me and taking a bullet meant for me. She died in my arms."

A couple of tears rolled down Cory's face as she put an arm around Wyatt, "That's so sad. I'm so sorry to hear that."

Wanting to change the subject, Tuck asked, "Cory what are you doing wandering around town?"

"Things are slow, so Sheriff told me to move around, letting people think we're protecting them. Patrolling the town is actually the police department's job, but this is what we do when nothing's going on."

Not wanting to listen to the two talk, Wyatt got up and went inside.

When Cory knew Wyatt was out of earshot, she said, "Tell me what happened."

"While in Coffeyville we met this woman that was good with a rifle. Her name was Cindy Harper. She carried that rifle everywhere. In fights she used it as a club, spinning and hitting with it. In one saloon she whipped four brothers that wanted to have their way with her. I could not have done as well. She wasn't only tough, but sweet as honey and a lot of fun." Cory noticed Tuck's eyes were tearing up. Then a tear ran down his face. He wiped it away. "She knew from the beginning she wanted Wyatt. I think it was love at first sight for her. It didn't take long for Wyatt to fall head over his boots for her. When she gave her life for him by jumping in front of a bullet, it was more than Wyatt could handle."

"She sounds like quite a woman. I'd liked to have met her."

"I don't know what's going to happen to our agreement with the attorney general or Rothschild. Wyatt is about worthless. All he wants to do is drink. He feels sorry for himself and feels sorry for Cindy. When we took the coffin to Cindy's father, I thought he was going to shoot Wyatt and me while brandishing his shotgun. Besides, finding women that fit our requirements is nearly impossible. We were lucky finding Cindy. Are you sure we couldn't steal you away?"

"Nope, I'm happy where I am." Cory finished her drink. "I've got to get back to pretending I'm working. Maybe I'll see you both tomorrow."

"Why do you lead your horse around?" Tuck wanted to know.

"In case I have to get somewhere fast. I like to walk for the exercise."

"Bye Cory."

For the next couple of days Cory found herself looking at women, hoping she would find someone that would meet the deputy marshal requirements.

It was another slow day for the sheriff's office and Cory was doing her town patrol. She was on the west side of town walking past a saloon she had never noticed when she heard lots of shouting and laughter coming from it. She tied Socks to the hitch rail and went inside. To her surprise a woman was in a fistfight with a man and appeared to be winning and the men in the bar were laughing and enjoying what the woman was doing to the beat-up man. The woman appeared to be a trained boxer. When the man collapsed on the floor everyone cheered. The woman yelled, "Drinks are on me!" which brought another cheer.

When the female boxer saw Cory staring at her, she went to Cory. "Hello Deputy Jackson. Get yourself a drink and join me."

Cory looked at the woman and smiled, "I will. How do you know me?"

"Everyone knows about 'The Ice Lady;' your picture has been in all the papers. I just never realized you were so tiny. What are you, about four foot eleven?"

"About that, I'll get that drink and be right back. I have something to talk to you about."

Cory was returning with a glass of whiskey when she saw the woman seated at a table. Cory sat down across from her and grinned, "I sure hope I never have to arrest you. Poor little me wouldn't stand a chance."

"I would never hit another woman. By the way, I'm Morgan Foster, please call me Morgan."

"It's good meeting you Morgan. I must ask, how did you learn to fight like that?"

"Most people don't realize but the name Foster is from Ireland and means 'forest guardian.' Anyway,

my Irish father was a boxer, and he taught his children to box. Every weekend we would practice. I was the youngest and the only girl. Because my brothers picked on me, I strove to be better than them and practiced weeknights with my father. He tried not to show it, but I think he liked me the best, so he gave me lots of help."

"And the Irish like their ale!" laughed Cory.

"That we do! But some frown on women being in a pub."

"I'm so glad I got to meet you Morgan. I have two US Marshal friends who are in need of a female deputy marshal. I think you would be perfect for them. It pays one hundred seventy-five dollars a month. I'll let Marshal Wyatt explain why they need a woman. They tried to hire me, but I told them I didn't want to travel."

"One hundred seventy-five dollars is an incredibly lot of money. I would be interested."

"Before I recommend you, I need to find out how well you can shoot. I'd like to take you to the police department's shooting range. Can you shoot guns?"

Morgan smiled, "You want to have a shooting contest?"

"When would you be available?"

"Right now. I'll get my gun and meet you back here in an hour or less."

"Great. I love shooting contests. We just need to think of a prize."

Cory is an extremely popular person in Wichita,

so after Morgan left, different men joined Cory in friendly conversation. Cory enjoyed it. The hour went by fast.

When the batwings opened, letting light into the saloon, naturally all eyes turned to see who was entering. Seeing a pretty woman wearing a gun and cowboy hat, a murmur arose. When Morgan came to Cory's table the man that had been visiting Cory stood, held a chair for Morgan and left.

"Morgan, you changed your clothes, you look sharp. We'd better leave before you get into another fight with a drunk that wants to take you home," laughed Cory as she stood.

The two women rode side by side to the Wichita Police Department shooting range. Finding a box of empty cans for targets, Cory stood them up about thirty feet away.

"Before we start, what's the prize?" asked Cory.

"When I win you will have to date one of my brothers. I don't know which one, but they would love going out with you."

"You sound confident of winning. When I win you have to go out with a friend of mine who desperately needs help right now."

"You sound confident also," chuckled Morgan.

"How many cartridges in your gun?" asked Cory.

"Only five of course."

"Good. Now put in a sixth one. There are six cans. Let me see what you can do. I forgot to tell you, I want you to draw and fire."

Morgan loosened the gun in its holster. She spread her feet apart, took a deep breath, exhaled and drew her gun. Of the six cans, she knocked down four. She had a smile and looked proud of what she had done. "Your turn, Deputy. Let's see what you can do."

"First thing I have to do is move the cans twenty feet farther out. They're just too close to be fair for you."

As Morgan watched Cory move the cans farther away her smile fell like a hot branding iron.

"This will be a little fairer," said Cory with a straight face.

Cory pushed a sixth round into her gun and holstered it. She moved her left foot out in front of her right, relaxed for a second then drew. Cory's speed was astonishing, but even more stunning was the speed of the shots. All six cans had flown into the air.

Cory was not a person to brag or mock another, so without a comment, she loaded five cartridges into her gun and holstered it.

An amazed Morgan said, "I have never seen anyone shoot like that. I didn't think it was possible."

"That is why some gunfighters lose; they don't

think anyone could be better than them. You are dead," grinned Cory.

"I guess I am. You've taught me a valuable lesson."

"Something else, never holster an empty or partially empty gun."

Morgan looked at her holstered gun and felt foolish. She pulled it out and reloaded it.

"How do you shoot so fast?"

"First, I never take my finger off the trigger, it's always holding it to the rear. My first shot is from the hip. This takes a lot of practice. After the first shot I have my gun at eye level with a two-handed grip. My left thumb does the cocking and letting go. This also takes a lot of practice. Here, take my gun and try it." Cory pushed a sixth round into the empty chamber, then handed it to Morgan.

Morgan handed Cory her gun and holstered Cory's.

"Would you like me to bring the cans in closer?" asked Cory as she moved to collect and set up the cans.

"Put them where they were last."

"Try my stance this time, left foot forward, feet shoulder-width apart."

Morgan did as she was told, took a breath and

exhaled half of it. She drew and fired. Of course, cocking with her left thumb was new to her and slow, but she knocked down five of the six cans from fifty feet.

Cory clapped, "Excellent shooting."

"I just need to practice with my left thumb."

"Yes, practice with an empty gun."

"Your gun is so smooth. I've never felt anything like it. It's why my shooting improved."

"A good friend of mine in Colorado tuned it for me."

"What's his name in case I'm ever out there?"

"Thomasina, but most call her Tommy."

"A female gunsmith! No thanks!"

"I'm surprised that came from you, a woman. It's due to prejudiced people like you that sometimes she dresses as a man. Just because we are women doesn't mean we can't shoot as well or better than the men. It's the same with gunsmithing. I'm disappointed in you." Cory turned and was walking away when Morgan said, "Wait. I'm sorry. You are right. Now tell me how ugly this guy is that you have to get dates for him?"

"All I can say is you will be shocked when you see him. He won't be in town for long. Would you be able to see him tonight?"

"Tonight…yeah, I suppose so. Might as well get

it over with. But what about that job you were talking about, the deputy marshal position. I'm twenty-four years old and can't find work. If I want to eat, my only option is to marry someone."

Cory chuckled, "Beats starving. I had that problem once. I became an outlaw and hated it. I wanted to die. Once I put a gun to my head but was too big of a coward to pull the trigger."

"So what did you do?"

"I got into a gunfight against a sheriff and his deputies with an empty gun."

"You're still alive so I guess that didn't work."

"It worked. I survived the gunshot due to help from my best friend. You might have heard of her; they call her Lady Fury."

"I have heard of her."

"So then what did you do?"

"I changed my name, then I saved two Wichita policemen's lives and was able to get this job."

"I remember hearing of that. What's my date's name?"

"Marshal Wyatt Peterson."

"Ah, he's the one looking for a deputy. I'll just pretend Wyatt Peterson is the most handsome man I ever met and maybe he'll hire me."

"I'll put a good word in for you. Where can I meet

you after I set this up?"

At my father's blacksmith shop on McCormick Street. I live above the shop."

"Your father is Darby? I know him! Great guy. Him and I go back three years. Can't wait to see him again. Now I must go find Wyatt. I'll see you later."

"Bye, and thanks for all your help."

Cory mounted Socks and rode off quickly, hoping to find Wyatt and Tuck at Paul's Pub. Five minutes later she saw them sitting in the same place as the other day, drinking. As she dismounted Tuck yelled, "I'll get another chair and a glass."

In a minute he was back with both.

"Thanks Tuck, you are the sweetest."

"Just keep thinking that way because I want to be first in line if Grant ever dumps you," chuckled Tuck.

"He better not. Wyatt, I have a date for you."

"What? Not interested."

"You would be if you saw her. She makes me look like a cow turd."

Tuck laughed, "Impossible."

Wyatt grinned. "Why would you find me a date?"

"To get you out of your doldrums and it seems

to be working a little bit because you just smiled. Besides, I just vetted her and she's a great pick for a female deputy."

"What makes you think she's a good deputy candidate?"

"I saw her whip a man in a fistfight. After that I took her to the police shooting range. She's good."

"Good looking, good with her fists, and good with a gun. What more could we ask for Wyatt?"

"I'm not interested. No more female deputies."

"Wyatt, if we fold, a lot of people won't get the financial help they need. Get over your pity for yourself and for Cindy. Life goes on."

"When's my date?"

"Tonight. After you buy some new clothes and take a bath. Wear a suit coat and tie. No suit pants. You'll look good that way."

"Tonight!"

"I told her you wouldn't be in town long."

"That's true. The attorney general has a job in Texas for us, and we should get going. Where do I meet my date?"

"At the Occidental's restaurant."

"Okay, I'd better get going," said Wyatt as he stood and looked at Cory. "Come here you little imp."

Cory stood and went to Wyatt. "What?"

"Telling me how to dress, you remind me of my mother," said Wyatt as he picked Cory up and slung her over his shoulder. Cory screamed, "Put me down!"

"The Arkansas River is only two blocks from here. You don't weigh more than a half-loaded saddlebag, so I think I can throw you that far. If you ever set me up with a date again that's what I'm going to do."

Cory's little fists were beating on Wyatt's lower back as she yelled again, "Put me down!"

"Do we have a deal?"

"Yes! Put me down!"

Wyatt brought her back over his shoulder but didn't quite put her on the ground. They were practically nose to nose looking at each other. Wyatt winked at her. Cory bit Wyatt on his nose. When Wyatt dropped her to hold his nose, Cory ran off laughing.

"That little imp bit me on my nose Tuck!"

"Let me see, not even a bite mark, what a baby."

Still laughing, Cory mounted Socks and galloped off for Darby's Blacksmith Shop.

Tuck was still laughing, "She's quite a gal."

"She is," said a smiling Wyatt. "Tuck, will you be going on my date with me?"

"It's your date, not mine."

"You can sit off to the side, she won't know you. I might need your opinion if I should hire her."

"Alright, I'd like to see who it is that could make Cory look bad anyway."

Morgan just happened to be looking out the upstairs window when Cory arrived at the blacksmith shop. When she got downstairs her tall father was giving Cory a big hug. She looked tiny in his big muscular arms, her feet a foot off the ground. "You're squeezing too hard!" yelled Cory. Darby laughed and released her.

Morgan was laughing, "He does that to me too!"

"A few minutes ago, your date threw me over his shoulder!"

"You're a popular girl Cory," smiled Morgan.

Darby chuckled, "She's the best, I didn't know you two were friends."

"We just met," said Morgan. "I'm surprised you two know each other."

"She saved my life a couple years ago," said Darby with a smile. "I told you about it."

"I had no idea it was Cory. I thought it was a man that saved you from those road agents."

"Nope. It was this little woman that put those two six feet under and saved my behind."

Morgan had a look of gratitude on her face as she said, "Now I have more to thank you for, but tell me about my date."

"He'll be waiting in the restaurant at the Occidental Hotel at six."

"What should I wear?"

"A nice dress, nothing special."

"Good because I don't have many dresses and none of them are special."

"I've got to go. Darby, it was good seeing you again but no more hugs."

Darby smiled, "Then don't stay away so long."

"Cory wait," Morgan moved close to Cory and said quietly, "I would greatly appreciate it if you were there."

"You don't need me. You can take care of yourself."

"You're my new friend and I would feel so much better if you were there."

"Okay, I'll be there. I keep a dress at the office for emergencies; my house is eight miles from here."

After Cory had left, Morgan was surprised to find herself getting excited about her date. Just because he isn't good-looking doesn't mean he won't be nice.

Wyatt was dressed neatly and sitting by himself in the restaurant.

Cory was wearing a dress and sitting with Tuck when a waiter came to their table. "Good evening sir. Would you and your daughter like to order?"

Not wanting to look like a pervert with a young girl he let the waiter think they were father and daughter. "I'll take the special and a glass of water. What would you like Cory?"

Cory answered with a big grin, "Just a beef sandwich and water, Pa."

After the waiter had gone Cory said, "Now you see why I like wearing pants and a gun."

As they were talking Morgan entered. She and Wyatt locked eyes for a moment and smiled at each other. Not recognizing Cory in a dress, and not knowing Tuck, Morgan took a seat at an empty table. "May I help you ma'am?" asked the waiter.

"I'm waiting for someone."

The waiter left.

Cory saw it all, chuckled and said quietly to Tuck, "That's Morgan."

"That's her? She's beautiful!"

"I told you that. Guess I'd better go introduce those two or they'll be waiting for someone all night," chuckled Cory.

Cory rose and walked over to Morgan and sat down.

"Hi Cory, I didn't recognize you in the dim light and wearing a dress. You look so young."

Cory ignored the remark and said, "Your date is here."

Morgan looked around, "I don't see him."

Cory grinned and pointed at Wyatt, "That's him."

"Him! He's the most handsome man I've ever seen!"

"Yep, that's Wyatt. Come on and I'll introduce you."

Morgan didn't get up.

"Let's go."

"I'm nervous."

Giving up on Morgan, Cory stood and went to Wyatt. "Hi Wyatt. Waiting for your date?"

"Yeah, she's late."

"No, she isn't. That's her over there. Come and I'll introduce you."

"She's my date?"

"I told you she was beautiful. Come on."

Cory led Wyatt to Morgan and introduced the two. "Now you two behave yourselves." Cory rejoined Tuck and resumed eating her beef sandwich.

Cory kicked Tuck in the leg, "Stop staring, it's impolite; besides, I might get jealous."

When Tuck and Cory finished eating, Cory said, "I have to leave. I have an eight-mile ride to my place. Thanks for the dinner and company."

"You're welcome for the dinner, I'm afraid I was poor company though."

Cory left for the sheriff's office where she would change back into pants for the ride home. Tuck followed Cory out then walked to his hotel room.

The evening had started out well, thought Morgan. She and Wyatt seemed to get along well. So, what happened? She realized it was after Wyatt told her she was hired that his demeanor changed. She noticed how sometimes he would stare off into space like he was in another world. He was now abrupt with her. When they had finished eating a short time after Wyatt and Cory had left, he told her to be here at one in the afternoon. They shook hands. Wyatt went upstairs while Morgan walked home.

It was one in the afternoon. Wyatt, Tuck and Morgan were having lunch in the hotel's restaurant.

"Are we going to Texas in the morning?" asked Tuck.

"Yep, I got the order about an hour ago. We're going to Houston. A wealthy attorney's daughter has been kidnapped. He must have connections in Washington to get us involved in a kidnapping. There are no trains that go south from Wichita due to it being Indian Territory, so we must go to Emporia to get a train that goes south to Houston. Train leaves at eight am, so be at the depot a half hour early to get your horses loaded. See you in the morning, I'm going to take a nap."

After Wyatt left, Morgan said to Tuck, "Have you noticed how Wyatt avoids me? He never looks at me when he talks, just you."

"Yes, I have."

"Do you know why he's doing this?"

"I think so."

"Please tell me."

"I think I need a nap too. See you at the depot in the morning."

Morgan watched as Tuck left. When he was gone, she got up and rode home.

Because the seats only sat two people, Morgan and Tuck were sitting together behind Wyatt.

It was their second day on the train when a family of four took two seats across the aisle from the marshals. The husband was a handsome man about twenty-eight. His pants were old and tattered. His wife was thin but pretty. Her dress was homemade and had seen better days. Their boy looked to be eight or nine and his sister a year or so younger. The children were dressed well and wearing shoes. It was evident the parents thought more of their children than themselves.

Morgan noticed how Wyatt stared at the family with a smile on his face. The husband and Wyatt appeared to be the same age. She suspected Wyatt saw in the family what he was lacking.

Wyatt turned around and said, "I'll be right back." A couple minutes later Wyatt was back with some hard candy. He stopped by the husband and wife, "May I give your children some candy?"

The mother looked up at the big man wearing a badge and smiled. "Yes, you may. That is very thoughtful of you, they never get candy."

The children had been listening attentively. Hearing his mother's reply the boy yelled, "Yippie!"

Wyatt handed the children the candy and sat down. Immediately the two children were crowded on Wyatt's bench seat with him. He had to scoot over against the wall to make room. Of course, Morgan and Tuck couldn't help seeing everything and were smiling.

With two pieces of hard candy stuffed in his mouth the boy asked Wyatt, "Are you three really sheriffs?"

"No, we're United States Marshals."

"Wow. Why do you wear two guns? No one else

does."

"So I don't run out of ammunition when I'm in a gunfight."

Tuck had been wondering why Wyatt had taken to wearing two guns. He suspected it was due to what happened in Montana, now he knew for sure. Morgan knew nothing of Montana or Cindy, and simply thought he had always worn two.

The children were well-behaved and spent a lot of time sitting with Wyatt, who seemed to really enjoy them. The mother had brought a bag with sandwiches, but when the sandwiches ran out, they seemed to go without eating. The children were good about it, they never complained of being hungry. Finally, Wyatt said, "Come on kids let's get some lunch." The kids squealed with glee and headed for the dinner car holding Wyatt's hands. When Wyatt returned, he had a sack he gave to the mother. "We ordered too much and couldn't eat everything."

She looked inside the sack and saw four sandwiches. She then looked up at Wyatt with teary eyes, "You are so kind. Thank you, Mister Wyatt." She knew Wyatt's name from hearing the kids saying it.

Wyatt smiled, "I think it's about time we get to know each other. I'm Marshall Peterson. Sitting behind me is Deputy Morgan Foster and Deputy…well, we just call him Tuck."

"I'm Geraldine Hancock and my husband Rick. Of course, you know the kids, Scott and Nora."

Morgan and Tuck came over and everyone shook hands.

Geraldine was smiling when she said, "A while ago I told Rick I've never felt so safe."

That evening Wyatt took the two children to supper. While they were sitting at a table eating, Wyatt asked, "Young Scott, where is your family going?"

"We're going to New Orleans. Ma's father died. They argued about going. Pa said we don't have any money. I think they borrowed money for the train from someone."

Wyatt ordered four sandwiches wrapped to go. When the sandwiches arrived, Wyatt led the two children back to their parents. He handed Geraldine the sandwiches and she asked him, "You are so kind, but how can you afford this?"

"We are special marshals working out of Washington D.C. and are extremely well paid."

Geraldine grabbed Wyatt's hand, "You are a special man, thank you."

"Yes, thank you, Wyatt," said Rick.

Morgan watched it all, realizing Wyatt wasn't the heartless grumpy soul she had thought he was.

The marshals were about three hours from

Houston when Wyatt called Scott over to him. Morgan saw Wyatt take out his wallet. She looked at Tuck. He was sound asleep with his head against the wall. Morgan leaned forward to see better and saw Wyatt stuff a five-hundred-dollar bill into a pocket in Scott's pants along with a business card. He had earlier written on the back, "If you ever need help."

Wyatt whispered in Scott's ear, "This is a secret so don't tell anyone. I want you to give it to your pa after I get off in Houston. Do we have a deal?"

"Yes sir," said the wide-eyed Scott.

"Do you promise?"

"I promise not to say anything."

"Good."

The five hundred dollars was J.T. Rothschild's money, but the money spent on candy and food was Wyatt's personal money.

Three hours later the marshals said goodbye to their new friends.

After the train was rolling again Scott yelled, "Pa! I have something for you!" and pulled the money and business card from his pants pocket and gave both to his father.

Rick was stunned speechless and became wet-eyed. All he could do was hand the money and card to Geraldine. Looking at the money and the card, she couldn't help crying.

As the marshals were walking to the railroad corral to get their horses, Morgan got close to Wyatt and slipped her arm around his and was about to say something when he roughly pushed her away.

"I don't know what you are so angry about, but I know it's not the normal you. I saw what you did for that family."

"It was no big deal. It's easy to give someone else's money away."

"It was more than just giving away money."

It was evening as the three claimed their horses and rode towards the center of Houston. The marshals got separate rooms at the Capital Hotel and stabled their horses in the hotel's barn. On the first floor of the hotel was a restaurant, lounge and the lobby. The upper four floors were the guest's rooms.

The marshals were having supper in the hotel's restaurant. "Here's what we're doing tomorrow," said Wyatt, "I'm going to talk with the county sheriff and see what I can learn about Larry Crenshaw. Tuck, I want you to do the same at the main police station."

"What am I doing?" asked Morgan.

Wyatt looked at her, dissatisfaction showing on his face, "You are going to interview Crenshaw."

"But I'm a woman. He won't like that."

"That's why I'm sending you. There is a reason for it. Everything is all set up. He is expecting Deputy Morgan Foster. Try to get a picture of his daughter."

Morgan nodded.

"I'm going upstairs and to bed. I expect you both out of here and doing your job by eight o'clock tomorrow. We'll meet here at one tomorrow afternoon." With that said, Wyatt got up and left the room.

"Whew!" said Morgan. "Is he always like this?"

"No. He's changed. Let's go across to the hotel's lounge and have a drink and I'll explain what happened to him."

As they walked into the lounge Tuck asked Morgan, "Do you drink?"

"Yes. Being in Houston, I'm sure they have rum here. Get me a rum please."

Morgan saw an empty table with two padded chairs and sat down. A minute later Tuck joined her. They each took a drink then Tuck said, "You're a beautiful woman."

Morgan blushed, "Thank you. You are a handsome man. Are you part Indian?"

"Yes, I'm part Waco."

"Ah, that's where the ruggedness comes from that adds so much to your looks," said Morgan with a nice smile. "So, tell me what changed Wyatt?"

"Before you there was another woman in your place. She only survived one mission. She was a very likeable woman. It didn't take long for her to worm her way into both Wyatt's and my hearts. We were up in Montana taking down a man that thought he owned the whole territory. His name was Andy Rowland. He killed a sheriff and two marshals amongst others. When we were arresting him, Wyatt ran out of ammunition, so Rowland had the drop on him and was about to shoot him when Cindy moved in front of the bullet. I then shot and killed Rowland. Cindy died in Wyatt's arms."

"Were they lovers?"

"They had just become lovers the night before."

"That's so sad. It appears he doesn't want that to happen again."

"You're right, he doesn't. I don't think Wyatt will ever get over what happened. He didn't want a woman in our group in the beginning and now he's even more against it."

"Now that I understand, I won't think of him as a perpetual grouch anymore," laughed Morgan.

"If he ever lets you in, you will see he is a great, caring guy."

"I'm bushed. I'll see you in the morning, Tuck,

and thanks for the drink."

"You are welcome. I'll walk upstairs with you."

Tuck was up early, and he was ready to go, but wanting to share breakfast with Morgan, he waited and listened, hoping to hear when she left. When he heard her door close, he stepped out his room.

"Good morning Morgan. I was just going for breakfast; would you like to join me?"

"I'd be glad to." With a smile on her face, Morgan walked over to Tuck and put her arm through his. As they were walking down the hall Tuck asked, "Why are you wearing a dress?"

"It's going to be another hot day and I thought this thin dress would be cooler than pants. And looking like a helpless woman might be an advantage. Besides, before I go to Crenshaw's office, I thought I'd go to his house while he's at work and not home. I might be able to learn more as a woman rather than a marshal."

"Good idea."

The dining room was crowded so they had to wait for a table. Once they were seated Tuck asked the waitress if a US Marshal had been in and was told he had eaten an hour ago.

When it was time to pay, Tuck paid for them both.

"I can pay my own way," complained Morgan.

"You haven't been paid yet and I'm making more money than I can spend."

"That's very sweet of you."

Tuck grinned boyishly.

A cab was waiting next to the hotel. Morgan told the driver the address and ten minutes later she was at a large stately house. She told the driver to wait; she would be back in fifteen minutes.

Her knock on the door was answered by a young man.

"Hello, I'm Morgan, I'm a friend of Brenda's and I just got in town. Is she home?"

"I'm her brother Benjamin. She's upstairs taking a bath and should be down in fifteen minutes or so. Please step inside."

Knowing Benjamin was lying, Morgan was curious to see what he was up to. Besides, she wanted in the house anyway.

"Follow me and we'll wait for her in the library."

Morgan's eyes were taking everything in. She saw a picture of a young woman on a shelf and would somehow get it. While she was looking at the picture Benjamin turned around quickly and grabbed the neck of her dress and pulled it towards him, ripping the thin material down the middle, exposing her chest.

Morgan hit Benjamin in the face. Her fist glanced off his nose and landed in his left eye. He was surprised and caught off-guard. He backed up with a hand on his eye.

"A spirited woman, I like that. Nice looking too."

"I hope you are enjoying the view because you are going to pay for it." Morgan was ready to fight so she wasn't worried about her open dress, besides she hoped it would entice him into attacking her again. She wanted to damage his face badly so everyone would know he'd been beaten by a woman.

Sure enough, he came towards her and swung a fist, which she easily ducked. Then Morgan used his head as a speed bag. When he collapsed on the floor both his eyes were swelling closed, his nose and mouth were bleeding, and his left cheek had a nasty bruise.

Morgan grabbed two pictures from a shelf, pulled her dress together and hurried out the door to the waiting cab.

The driver noticed her torn dress, "Are you hurt miss?"

"I'm fine. What's your name in case I need you for a witness for my torn dress?"

"Jeff Dukes."

"Thanks Jeff. Take me back to the hotel." Morgan sat inside the cab looking at her scraped knuckles while she opened and closed her sore fingers.

Holding her dress closed with one hand and carrying the two pictures in the other, she hurried to her room. Now she had to decide if she should wear a dress or pants to Crenshaw's office. She decided on the tough marshal look, so she would wear pants and her badge. His office was in the center of town within walking distance. She took her ripped dress with her.

The office was large and well-appointed for an attorney's office. A young pretty woman sat behind a large desk. Morgan couldn't help wondering if Benjamin had ever gotten his hands on her as she walked up to the desk.

"Deputy Marshal Morgan Foster for Mr. Crenshaw."

"We've been expecting ah…you," she said as she stood and went down a short hall.

Morgan knew they were expecting a man. She wondered how this would affect her interview with Crenshaw. Possibly anger him enough he might let something slip. Or maybe he would refuse to even talk to her.

"Mr. Crenshaw will see you now," said the secretary on her return.

Morgan found the office door open. She knocked and entered.

Crenshaw studied her silently for a good minute.

He noticed her bruised and scraped fingers. Morgan stood waiting politely.

Crenshaw stepped around his desk and held out his hand, "I was expecting a man. Apparently, the marshal's office has confidence you can do the job."

Morgan took his outstretched hand. Crenshaw purposely squeezed tightly, knowing it would hurt her fingers. Morgan kept a straight face as if nothing was wrong even though it hurt like hell. Crenshaw was impressed by Morgan. He had expected her to cry out in pain, but she didn't even flinch. She might be a tough adversary.

"Have a seat Miss Foster."

Morgan sat. "Mr. Crenshaw, do you have any idea who kidnapped your daughter and why?"

"A lazy flea-bitten cowboy name of Bill Rafferty. He's twenty-five. Too old for my eighteen-year-old daughter."

Morgan wanted to make a comment about the age difference but knew she should not. "How do you know the name of the man?"

"He took her out once or twice. Then when he told her he wanted to court her she turned him down. I guess he decided he would just take her."

"Do you have any idea where he took her?"

Crenshaw sat quietly for a moment before saying, "He took her to New York City."

"New York? That seems a strange place to take her. How do you know this?"

"I have sources."

"I need to know who your sources are."

"I can't divulge them."

"Anything else you can tell me?"

"That's about it."

"Well, I have something else. Before coming here, I went to your house. Your son Benjamin assaulted me with the intentions of raping me. He almost ripped this dress completely off me. I want ten dollars for a new dress."

"Ten dollars! That dress isn't worth five dollars!"

"No, it isn't. But it's a lot cheaper than having to defend him in court for assault and attempted rape."

Crenshaw swore while taking a ten-dollar bill from his wallet. He threw it at Morgan. She picked it up off the floor. "Thank you, Mr. Crenshaw. I might be back for more information."

As Morgan was leaving, he asked, "How did you scrape your knuckles?"

"I gave your son a boxing lesson."

"But you don't look hurt."

"I'm fine. He was not man enough to best a woman. Good day Mr. Crenshaw." Morgan left with a big grin on her face.

At one in the afternoon the three marshals were gathered in the Capital Hotel's restaurant for lunch and briefing. Morgan was a couple of minutes late arriving.

As they ate, Wyatt noticed Morgan's scraped and bruised fingers.

Morgan suggested they go to the lounge for their briefing. Wyatt paid the bill and they walked across the lobby into the lounge.

Finding a table for three, Morgan and Tuck sat while Wyatt remained standing, "What would you two like?"

"Morgan's a rum drinker," grinned Tuck.

Wyatt had a questioning look as he said, "Oh. Sounds like you two have been getting to know each other."

Tuck sheepishly said, "I'll take a whiskey."

"I do like rum," said Morgan with a winsome smile.

Wyatt left, then returned with the drinks.

"I'll start," said Wyatt. "First, I spoke to the Harris County sheriff. I don't know if this has anything to do with our case or not, but he said the two Crenshaw boys are nothing but trouble. They would be in jail if not for their father. Crenshaw either pays someone off or threatens them until they drop the charges. If that doesn't work, he gets them off in court. Let me catch my breath for a minute." Wyatt took a couple swigs of his whiskey. "Another thing that baffles me is the man that kidnapped Brenda was a sheriff in Cotulla for three years." Wyatt took another swig.

Wyatt continued, "After leaving the sheriff's office I went to the telegraph office. When I asked to see any telegrams Crenshaw might have sent or received, the operator on duty refused. He said it was against company policy. I had to threaten him with arrest for hindering an investigation, but I got some good info. He has the gunfighter Bob Longley out in Colorado looking for them with orders to kill both Brenda and Bill Rafferty. The telegram didn't say that exactly but that's the way I took it. Crenshaw talked about an accident."

"Crenshaw told me they were in New York City," interrupted Morgan.

"Why would he want to kill his daughter?" asked Tuck.

"Oh, I forgot to mention, the sheriff said Brenda's name isn't Crenshaw but Wilson. She's his stepdaughter. He married her mother."

"But why would he want to kill his stepdaughter?" questioned Morgan.

Wyatt shrugged his shoulders and took a drink.

"What'd you find out from the police, Tuck?"

"Mostly the same as you. The two brothers are troublemakers. The police captain I spoke with said Rafferty had been courting Brenda for four months and was a good man. He would never kidnap someone. He thinks they eloped together."

"Ahh now things are coming together," said Wyatt. "But that still doesn't answer the question why Crenshaw wants to kill the two."

Morgan was flustered. She looked at Tuck then Wyatt. "What about me? Don't you want to know what I found out?"

Wyatt looked at Morgan, "Okay, what did you find out?"

Morgan took the two pictures from her bag. "I've got these. I think the man is Rafferty. I got them from Crenshaw's home."

"You went to his house?" asked a surprised Wyatt. "I thought you would only go to his office. Is that where you got the bruised knuckles?"

Morgan ignored the question. "When I went to Crenshaw's office, he told me Rafferty kidnapped his daughter after she refused his request to court her."

"Hmm…I doubt it. Rafferty sounds like a good man. I suspect they eloped. You two have the afternoon off. Let's meet here at seven. I'm going to check with the three depots in town. Hopefully, I can find out where those two went. The pictures will be a big help, Morgan."

Morgan smiled.

"What will you two do with your time off, Morgan?"

"I will be shopping for a dress. Would you like to join me Tuck?"

"Gladly."

"Morgan, before you go, a word of advice. Never use your gun hand to punch someone in the head. If you must hit them in the head use the heel of your hand. It works well against a nose or a chin."

"That's good advice Wyatt, I'll remember that," said Morgan.

"Is that a dress you have in your hand?" asked Wyatt as Morgan was leaving the table.

"Yes."

"May I see it?"

Morgan handed Wyatt her dress. He unraveled it and held it up. He saw where the front was ripped open. "Pretty flimsy dress."

Morgan grinned, "It's hot down here. I thought it would be cooler."

Wyatt laughed, "From the way it looks, I imagine you were very cool in it," as he handed it back to her.

Morgan's face turned red as she blushed.

As they walked through the downtown district Morgan slipped an arm through Tuck's and said, "Let's just explore this big city. If we see a dress shop fine, it not, that's okay."

"After seeing the ripped dress it's pretty obvious one of Crenshaw's sons tried to rip it off you. Lucky guy."

"You think so? If you saw him, you might change your mind."

Tuck laughed, "I must remember to behave with you."

Morgan laughed, "That would be in your best interest."

After walking for an hour, they came to a small park and sat on a bench and talked. A half hour later they were walking and discovered a clothing store and went inside. Morgan found a dress she liked, and Tuck bought two new a pairs of blue Levi jeans. He liked jeans but they were hard to find, especially in his size. When Morgan saw the jeans Tuck had bought, she got a pair for herself. They were made for a man so she would have to roll up the cuffs.

Walking back to the hotel, the two deputies stopped in a nice-looking restaurant for supper. When they were finished, the tired deputies went back to the hotel for hot baths and a nap.

It was almost seven when Tuck awoke and hurriedly dressed. He crossed the hall and knocked on Morgan's door. When she opened it, Tuck was stunned. Morgan was wearing her new dress and it was cut low in the front, unlike most Victorian dresses. Her brown hair with gentle curls was hanging on her shoulders.

Noticing Tuck's open mouth and wandering eyes Morgan asked with a smile, "Do you like it?"

Without looking Morgan in the face, Tuck nodded dumbly.

"If we hurry, we will be on time. Let's go cowboy." Morgan put her hands on Tuck's chest and gave him a light push out of her way.

Seeing Wyatt at a table with a drink, Morgan made her way over and took a seat. Tuck went straight to the bar and returned with a glass of rum and one of whiskey.

"Thank you, Tuck."

"You're welcome."

Noticing Wyatt staring at her dress, Morgan asked, "Do you like my new dress Wyatt? Crenshaw was kind enough to buy it for me."

Noticing the sparkle in Morgan's eyes and her smile, Tuck sadly realized she wore the dress for Wyatt and not him.

Instead of answering, Wyatt asked, "Where is your gun?"

"In my room."

"You are a deputy marshal. You should always have a gun with you," said Wyatt sternly.

"But you said we were off duty," said Morgan, the disappointment noticeable in her voice and showing on her face.

"You were off duty, but still on the job. Marshals must always be prepared."

Morgan took a couple of swallows of her rum. Off duty but still on the job, does that make any sense?

"Using the pictures you got Morgan, the clerk at the Union Station recognized Brenda and Raffety traveling under the name of Mr. and Mrs. Compton. They were going to Denver."

Morgan noticed while Wyatt spoke his eyes kept traveling to her cleavage. She smiled to herself; she knew she had control of him.

Wyatt tried not to look but it was as if his eyes had a will of their own. He was captivated by Morgan's beauty. When he was able to force his eyes to look into her face, he noticed the twinkle in her large brown eyes and the hint of a smile. He realized she was enjoying his unabashed helplessness. The power of a beautiful woman.

When Wyatt regained his composure he said, "I

have tickets for us and our horses. Train leaves at nine so be at the Union Station at least a half hour early to load your horse. I'm going to bed, see you all tomorrow." Wyatt stood, turned and left.

Morgan stood, "It's been a long day, I'm going to bed too. How about you Tuck?"

"I'm staying for a bit."

Morgan hurried after Wyatt. She caught up with him in the lobby and put an arm through his left arm and pulled him tightly to her.

"What are you doing?" he said loudly while trying to pull his arm out.

Morgan was holding tightly, "I know you're heartbroken and don't want anything like that to happen again, but you must move on with your life. Let me try to help you. Tuck told me Cindy's last words."

Wyatt stopped trying to pull away and turned to Morgan. She saw tears in his eyes. "No one has ever captivated me like she did. She was wild and free-spirited."

Morgan pulled Wyatt into a hug. She could hear him crying softly. She patted his back like a mother with her upset child.

Finally, Wyatt pulled away and wiped his tears and said, "I'm afraid of you."

Morgan grinned, "You should be afraid of me. I

should knock you senseless for saying I was off duty but still on the job."

Wyatt grinned, "It didn't make any sense did it?"

"Walk me to my room, Wyatt."

When they got to her door Morgan quickly gave Wyatt a quick kiss on his cheek.

"You have me all mixed up," said Wyatt.

"That's the way us women like it. Take your time Wyatt, I'm a patient woman."

Tuck sat in the lounge for another half-hour, sipping his whiskey and sadly thinking about Morgan. She's a fine woman. Where Cindy was brash and forward and easy to like, Morgan is reserved and quiet. Two completely different women, but both extremely beautiful and sweet. If a man had to choose between the two…well, it just would not be fair. Time to turn in.

Brenda and Bill Rafferty had arrived in Walsenburg by train late at night. Bill was the first to awaken. He slipped out of bed, quietly washed up at the water basin and dressed. He was looking out the window at the street below.

"Good morning Mr. Rafferty," said Brenda with a happy smile.

"Good morning to you, Mrs. Rafferty," grinned Bill. "Let's get something to eat, I'm famished."

"You sure you don't want to come back to bed first?" asked Brenda with a seductive smile.

Bill couldn't get undressed quickly enough.

An hour later after having breakfast the young couple entered Jim's General Store. They went right to the counter.

"Hello, I'm Bill Rafferty and this is my wife Brenda. We would appreciate it if you would put together everything we will need for a week in the mountains. I also want a pan for placer mining and a couple of small cloth bags in case I get lucky. Oh, we will need a tent and two wooden chairs."

"I can do that for you. I have to be honest; nobody pans for gold around here anymore."

"That's good. I don't have the gold bug. I really don't care if I find anything or not. I don't want to be where everyone else is panning and it's crowded and dangerous. We're from Texas, I've always had the desire to pan for gold. It will be just a quiet vacation."

"When would you like this ready?"

"However long it takes you. We will be back in an hour. I have to go buy horses."

"You best get yourself a pack mule and pack saddle. The livery should have a used one. The livery is on the southside of town. Just follow this street south."

"Good idea and thank you for the directions." Bill and Brenda walked out and headed for the livery.

An hour later Bill and Brenda returned to the general store. After riding to the store wearing a dress, Brenda wanted pants and was looking at the men's pants. Seeing a pair of blue pants with a tag saying Levi she fell in love with them right off. She found a pair she thought would fit and took them to the counter.

Jim the owner commented, "I just got those in yesterday. People seem to like 'em. They are very hard to get."

After getting the pack saddle on the mule and saddlebags loaded, the pair went back to their hotel room to get their things. Not having any room in the saddlebags, they had to hang bags from the saddle horn.

As they rode away from the hotel Bill said, "We need to stop back at the general store. I forgot to get cartridges for my rifle and handgun."

"That was dumb," said Brenda. Bill was surprised at the retort, but he let it go.

Bill and Brenda found the ideal spot between Rough Mountain and Mt. Mestas on North Abeyta Creek. It was all grass around the creek with spotty pine trees back a little way. It was just beautiful.

Bill pitched the large tent far enough away from

the creek to be safe from a flash flood, which is common in the mountains. After pitching the tent, he built a fire to cook lunch on.

"The fire is ready honey."

"What do you mean, the fire is ready?"

"It's ready for you to cook lunch."

"I'm not cooking over a fire! I have never cooked a meal. The servants have always done it."

"That's okay honey, I'll do the cooking."

They were having a late breakfast. Bill first cooked the bacon then used the grease in the pan for cooking eggs. In the meantime, biscuits were baking in the Dutch oven. It all smelled good.

When the food was ready Bill did the serving.

"This is so good. You're a good cook, Bill."

"Thanks Brenda."

After lunch it started raining so the rest of the day was spent inside the tent. At first it was fun for young lovers but then things got boring and Brenda complained about being cooped up in a tent with nothing to do.

Adam Lipinski was a lazy no-good outlaw who had never worked a day in his life. Most called him Lippy. He wanted easy money, so he robbed and killed for it. He had been hired by the attorney Larry Crenshaw to kill Brenda and make it look like an accident resulting in her death. But first he needed to kill Bill Rafferty. He was laying in the prone position with his rifle a hundred yards up the mountain. He had the rifle sighted in on Rafferty when the rain started, and Rafferty went inside the tent. Even with his slicker on, Lippy was cold and wet sitting on the log. He was waiting for the rain to stop so Rafferty would come out of the tent.

Being bored waiting, Lippy had dozed off. Hours later he woke to sunshine. Looking down on the campsite he saw Rafferty panning for gold. This would be the perfect time to shoot him and he aligned his sights on Rafferty's head.

Rafferty was panning when out of the sand in the pan he spotted a large nugget. Excited, he turned and yelled, "Brenda..." That was all he got out of his mouth when the pan he was holding was torn from his hand. Having been a lawman he'd seen lots of action and responded quickly by rolling and grabbing his nearby rifle. Seeing the smoke on the side of mountain he fired three quick shots into it. That was enough to scare Lippy. Rafferty saw him stand and run off.

Rafferty looked at the hole in his pan, tossed it and started looking for the nugget. Finding it, he yelled for Brenda.

"I have to go into town for another pan. You

should come with."

"Yes, I'm coming. It's too boring here."

"I was almost killed, and you call it boring," laughed Rafferty. "I'll get the horses saddled."

Five hours later they tied their horses in front of the same general store. The street was a mixture of mud and horse manure from the earlier rain, so Rafferty was a gentleman and carried Brenda to the walkway in front of the store. They were about to go inside when a man yelled, "Rafferty you killer. You're a dead man! You killed my little brother in Cotulla!" and went for his gun.

Not having time to say anything, Rafferty gave Brenda a huge shove with his left hand. She went flying off the boardwalk into the smelly mud face-down and slid.

Both men fired their guns at the same time. The other man missed but Rafferty didn't. Rafferty went to the dying man. "Was your brother Sam Westfall?"

"Yeah," the wounded man barely got out.

"He was wanted for murder and robbery. He deserved to die. If you'd have left it alone, you'd still be alive."

"You're right...big mistake." When Rafferty saw the eyes glaze over, he knew the man was dead.

Having been close by and hearing gunshots, the town marshal came running. "What happened?"

"I saw it all marshal. It was self-defense," said a man in the crowd. Others said the same.

Rafferty said to the town marshal, "I was a sheriff in Texas and killed his younger brother, he was looking for revenge."

"You're good to go, I'll take care of the body."

"Thank you marshal."

In the meantime, Brenda was getting up when she slipped and fell in the mud again. Upon getting up a second time a passing horse bumped her, knocking her down again. Mad as a hornet, Brenda screamed. Rafferty rushed to her. "There's not enough time to go back to the campsite so we'll get a room for the night."

"I want my own room and I want you to get all my things. I don't want to see you again. In the morning I'm going home!"

Rafferty was stunned. Now he realized his friends that tried to warn him about Brenda were right. She's a spoiled brat who has always had everything. How could he have been so blind? Let her go back. She was not going to mess up his life. He would pan for gold for a week then, using his savings to buy a ranch as he had planned. He took Brenda to the same hotel where they had stayed before and left her there. Knowing it would be dark when he arrived back at his campsite, he left anyway after buying a new pan. He was glad he never said anything to Brenda about the nugget because if she'd thought he would become rich she might have hidden her true colors.

The next day while Rafferty was panning for gold, Brenda was on a train for home and the marshals had just arrived in Walsenburg and were in a restaurant about to have breakfast.

The pretty waitress arrived at their table and seeing Tuck she became spellbound. Wyatt and Morgan both noticed. They also noticed Tuck was as bad as the waitress. Finally, Wyatt spoke up, "We'd like to order," breaking the trance between the two.

After ordering Morgan asked Tuck in a teasing way, "Tuck what just happened?"

Tuck was embarrassed, "I'm not sure."

"She is beautiful. She appears to be Indian or part Indian," added Morgan. "You should ask her when she returns."

When the waitress brought their food Tuck spoke Waco, which is a branch of the Caddoan language, to the waitress. A large grin came to her face as she and Tuck rattled on together, sometimes laughing. It didn't appear they were going to stop talking so Wyatt said, "Tuck!" loudly to get his attention, "Your food is getting cold." The waitress was embarrassed, "Excuse me, I must go."

Looking like the happiest man in the world Tuck said, "She's Pawnee. We speak mostly the same language. We had a little trouble on a few words, but we worked it out."

Having finished eating the three were getting ready to leave. While Wyatt was paying the clerk at a counter near the entrance, Tuck threw a ten-dollar bill onto the table. Morgan noticed and asked laughingly, "Are you trying to buy her?"

Noticing they were leaving the waitress rushed over and grabbed Tuck's arm. They spoke in Indian. They both grinned and nodded their heads.

When they were outside Morgan asked, "What was that all about?"

"She just wanted to make sure I would come back."

"I never knew there was such a thing as love at first sight until now," grinned Morgan.

"Morgan, stop teasing me," groaned Tuck.

"It looked like a match made in heaven to me," laughed Wyatt. "Tuck's going to be useless today Morgan."

"I think you're right. Tuck, what's her name?"

"Lomasi. It means pretty flower."

"So fitting," smiled Morgan.

"Tuck, get us three rooms while Morgan and I take different sides of the street showing

Brenda's picture to people."

"I don't know if Tuck can handle that in his current state of mind," teased Morgan.

Tuck mounted his horse and rode off in a huff to the laughter of Wyatt and Morgan.

After finding out from the owner of the general store that Brenda and Rafferty went west to the mountains, the marshals left town on the only road going west. After a few miles the road disappeared as people went different directions. At this point Tuck took over leading the way using his tracking skills. They followed the tracks to the foothills where some tracks split off. Most of the tracks went right; only a few went left. It was decided Tuck would follow the ones to the left while Wyatt and Morgan went right.

A short while after the tracks had split, Wyatt and Morgan came across a camp. They stopped. Wyatt yelled, "Hello the camp."

From down at the creek, behind some trees, came a reply, "Come on in if you're friendly."

"We are US Marshals," yelled Wyatt.

When the man came from behind the trees holding a pan Wyatt knew he had been panning for gold.

Morgan recognized Rafferty from the picture and whispered, "It's Rafferty."

Meanwhile on the side of the mountain, Tuck came across a man with a rifle. The rifle was aimed at the camp. Tuck took off his boots and slipped into his knee-high moccasins so he could quietly sneak up on the man. When he was close enough, he jumped and came down on the sniper's right arm, breaking it.

The man screamed loudly. Tuck pulled the man's pistol from its holster and grabbed the rifle. He tossed both aside. The man rolled over holding his right arm. "You broke my arm! Who are you?"

"Deputy Marshal Tucker. Why were you going to shoot those people?"

"I was only going to shoot the one that's camped there."

"You're under arrest for attempted murder."

Tuck found two short sticks which he used to splint the man's arm. Taking a shirt from the man's saddlebags, he ripped it into strips and wrapped up the arm.

"Get on your horse. We're riding down to the camp."

Wyatt, Morgan and Rafferty had heard the scream.

"Tuck must have found someone up there. He'll be down with him shortly," said Wyatt.

"It sounded like Tuck disemboweled someone," laughed Morgan.

"It must be the same person that tried to kill me yesterday," said Rafferty.

A few minutes later Tuck rode up with his prisoner. Wyatt looked at him and said, "Get down." After the man complied, Wyatt asked, "What's your name and why are you trying to kill this man Rafferty?"

"Jack Jones."

"You didn't answer my question Mr. Jones, why did you try to kill Rafferty?"

Jones stood silently.

"Make it easier on yourself. You know I can get it out of you. I could start cutting off fingers or pushing splinters under your fingernails. I could put your hand into a fire. Or I could just start twisting your broken arm. Need I go on?" questioned Wyatt.

"Wyatt let me take care of the questioning. Being half Indian I'm sure I can get it out of him much quicker than you," mentioned Tuck.

"You are right Tuck, take over."

"I'll talk," said Jones nervously. "Larry Crenshaw in Houston promised me a thousand dollars if I killed his daughter and made it look like an accident. He gave me five hundred dollars with the other five after she was dead. He also gave me five hundred for expenses."

"So why kill Rafferty?" asked Wyatt.

"He was in the way. I had to get rid of him first."

"Do you know why Crenshaw wants Brenda dead?" asked Wyatt.

"Crenshaw is not really Brenda's father. Her real father died leaving her a great sum of money. Crenshaw figures if she's dead he can get the money."

"I bet she doesn't even know her father died."

"She doesn't. Crenshaw hid the letter from her."

"Gee Rafferty, it sounds like you might be married to a rich woman," said Morgan.

"Doesn't matter. I made a mistake marrying her. I doubt we will be married much longer. She's on her way back to Houston. I don't know what will happen to her when she gets there."

"We'd better get to town and send a telegram to the Houston police. Maybe they can warn her at the depot," said Wyatt.

"You should let him know we have a witness that Crenshaw wants her dead," said Tuck.

"Good idea. I will." Wyatt looked at Jones, "If you go back to Houston, Crenshaw will most likely have you killed. Which wouldn't bother me because I can't stand people that would kill an innocent person for money, but you might be needed as a witness against Crenshaw." Wyatt took out a piece of paper and pencil and did some writing. "Here's my address. Let me know where you are and if you are ever needed to testify against Crenshaw, I'll pay you a thousand dollars. How's that?"

"Sounds good. I'll do that."

"Tuck, give Jones his guns back, he's free to go. Once I get these telegrams sent our job is done. Let's go celebrate."

The telegrams sent and their work done for now, the marshals were relaxing in a saloon. They had taken their badges off for the night. Wyatt had been watching a young, saloon girl for some time.

Morgan noticed and was watching Wyatt. She knew she shouldn't say anything, she didn't know if it was jealousy or something else, but she couldn't help asking, "She's young and pretty, are you going to take her upstairs, Wyatt?" The question shocked both Wyatt and Tuck.

Anger was evident on Wyatt's face when he looked at her in silence for a moment. "Yes, she is young, that's one of the reasons I'm looking at her. If I want to take a soiled dove upstairs it's my business, not yours. Tuck, you tell her."

"Wyatt isn't interested in taking her upstairs, he's interested in why she's here and helping her. I have been watching her also, I'm just not as obvious as Wyatt is. I noticed how sad she is and how the owner was berating her for not approaching men and selling herself. I think it's time Wyatt."

"I agree," said Wyatt as he motioned to the girl to come over. She tried to put a smile on her face but failed miserably. "Please take a seat miss."

The young girl was confused as she looked at the three. Knowing the saloon owner was watching, Wyatt motioned her to come closer and said, "We're US Marshals, we just want to talk." Wyatt made a big deal of giving the girl a couple of silver dollars so the owner would see.

The girl sat in the remaining chair.

"I'm Wyatt, my friends are Morgan and Tuck. What's your name?"

"Tricia."

"How old are you Tricia? Your true age."

Tricia looked back at her boss. Seeing he was busy with someone she answered, "Fifteen."

"Why are you doing this?" Wyatt asked.

"It's the only work I can find. I'm trying to support my twelve-year-old brother."

The owner bartender had been watching the marshals and Tricia. He was upset with Tricia to begin with and seeing her talking to those people about who knows what upset him further. He stomped over to their table.

"Is one of you going to take her upstairs or not?" he asked gruffly.

Wyatt didn't like the man right off, and stood. Standing over six foot and muscular, Wyatt was an imposing figure, and the scowl on his face made him even more so. It was enough to scare the owner and he backed up.

"Tricia doesn't work for you anymore. I'm a United States Marshal," said Wyatt while pinning on his badge. "I should arrest you for hiring a child."

"She said she was eighteen."

"And you believed her. Get out of my sight before I throw you in jail!"

The owner scampered behind his bar.

"But Wyatt I need this job. How will I support myself and my brother?"

"You don't need to work anymore. Change into something decent and come with us."

"Really?" asked the happy Tricia.

Wyatt laughed, "You're much prettier when you smile. Yes, really. Go change."

The young girl was so happy she ran up the stairs. In just a couple of minutes she was back, wearing a plain dress with a number of patches and a big smile.

"Are we going to get my brother now?"

"Yes, we are. You lead the way."

She led them back around the saloon, down a couple of streets to a rickety shack with a leaky roof that had been abandoned. A shirtless young boy was working hard outside cutting and splitting firewood with a saw and axe. He was surprised to see his sister coming home this early.

"Hi sis, who's with you?" Then he saw the badges.

"These are my new friends. Wyatt is a US Marshal, and the woman is Morgan, and the other man is Tuck. This is my brother Sammy."

"Good to meet ya all," said a smiling Sammy.

"It's only three o'clock so how about we take you two to a clothing store and get you some new clothes. Then you both can have a bath at our hotel. And after the bath we'll get something to eat. How's that sound?" said Wyatt with a smile.

"Sounds great! I'm hungry!" said Sammy excitedly.

"And I know just the restaurant to go to," grinned Tuck.

"I thought we should go somewhere else this time," teased Morgan.

"If you weren't a woman."

Morgan smiled mischievously, "What are you saying big boy, you want to box with me? I'm game."

"Guess I forgot who you are, I take it all back!"

Morgan smiled and gave Tuck a light loving punch to his belly.

Tricia had been watching the banter between the two and thought, "These are really good people."

As the group walked back to the main part of town, Tricia walked next to Wyatt and asked, "Why are you doing this for us?"

"Because you need help and because us three marshals are being paid by a rich man to help people that need it."

"That's nice of him. Be sure to thank him for me."

"I will. He'll be pleased to find out he helped two children."

DIFFERENT DIRECTIONS

After returning to the main street, Morgan told Wyatt, "I'm going to Trinidad to see someone. I'll leave my horse here and take the train. It's less than an hour ride. I've already checked. The next train leaves at five."

Wyatt was surprised, "You know someone in Trinidad?"

"There's someone I need to look up," said Morgan, avoiding the question.

"Will you need any help? Tuck could go with you."

"I'll be fine."

"When will you be back?"

"It will probably be two days. I'll meet you back in Wichita."

It was with a concerned look on his face when Wyatt said, "Okay, we'll see you in Wichita."

"Please let the liveryman know I'll pay him when

I return."

"Will do."

Morgan went to her hotel room, got her things and checked out.

After baths and new clothes, the two children were excited to eat in a restaurant.

When Tuck and Lomasi saw each other they both smiled. While Lomasi took the order, she couldn't keep her eyes off of Tuck.

While eating, Tricia asked, "What's to become of Sammy and me?"

"I know two good people that lost their only child recently. I'm thinking they might adopt you both. If they don't, there is a good orphanage in Wichita."

"Even though you two have been so good to Sammy and me, all these changes are so frightening," said Tricia.

"What happened to your parents?" asked Tuck.

"My mother died in childbirth with Sammy. My father was a cowboy for a large ranch. He had an argument with another cowboy and was killed. The bank took the house. Sammy and I were used to being alone due to Pa working, so we found that abandoned shack and moved in."

"Don't worry, Tuck and I will look after you." Wyatt wished Morgan were here. The girl and boy needed the comfort and caring of a woman, not two old lawmen. "We'll be leaving by train for Wichita in the morning."

Tuck put another ten-dollar tip on the table and went to a quiet corner of the room where he motioned for Lomasi to join him. They spoke rapidly for a few minutes then Tuck joined Wyatt and the children. "Lomasi will be traveling with us tomorrow."

Wyatt wasn't surprised, "I figured as much, Tuck."

Arriving in Trinidad, Morgan got directions to Taylor's Guns. With her saddlebags over a shoulder and her rifle in hand, Morgan walked the three blocks. Seeing the sign 'Taylor Guns' on a nicely maintained two story wooden building, Morgan opened the door. A small bell alerted a girl behind the counter. She looked up and smiled.

"Good afternoon ma'am, I'm JoEllen, what can I do for you?"

Morgan was mildly excited as she smiled, "I would like to see Tommy."

JoEllen yelled, "Tommy, someone here to see you."

A tall pretty woman wearing pants stepped out from a back room, "I'm Tommy, what can I do for you?" Tommy's real name was Thomasina, but everyone called her Tommy.

"Cory Jackson in Wichita told me if I was ever in the area to have you modify my gun."

Thomasina became excited, "You know little Cory! JoEllen, let's lock up and take the lady to supper!"

Morgan chuckled happily, "I'm Morgan Foster. This sounds like fun."

"I'm so excited I forgot my manners. This is my sister JoEllen. Everyone calls her Jo. We have so much to talk about." Thomasina was putting on her gun. "I haven't worn this for a while. I'm a deputy sheriff, but it's sort of an honorary unpaid position."

"Have you ever arrested anyone?"

"Sakes yes. A number of times."

"I'm a deputy US Marshal."

"Really! I'm impressed. That says a lot for a woman. I'm proud of my badge. Let's wear our badges."

Morgan grinned, "Okay," and put hers on.

Thomasina led Morgan across the street to the small café. Because the two women talked so much it took them forty-five minutes to eat their cold food.

Having finished eating, Morgan said, "I should

get going, I need to get a room."

"Nonsense. You're staying with us. Jo can sleep with me and you can have her room. Jo, could you take care of that for me while Morgan and I go to the Trinidad Tavern?"

"Sure, Tommy. Remember, you have lots to do tomorrow so don't stay out too late." JoEllen crossed the street and went into the shop.

Thomasina laughed happily, "She sounds more like a mother than a fifteen-year-old sister, doesn't she?"

"She sounds like she cares for you a lot," observed Morgan.

"We are close. We are not really sisters; I sort of adopted her. Follow me, I want to make sure she locked the door behind her. We've had some trouble in the past." Thomasina found the door locked.

"Where are we going?" asked Morgan.

"The Trinidad Tavern. Ted Hamilton owns it. He's a friend of mine."

As usual whenever anyone entered a saloon all eyes turn to the door to see who it is. Ted was bartending and he yelled a greeting to Thomasina. Thomasina led Morgan to the bar.

"Ted, this is Morgan. She's a new friend of mine. She'll be returning to Wichita in a day or so."

"Nice meeting you Morgan. It's a shame you don't stay," Ted smiled and winked at her.

"Ted, do you have any rum?" asked Morgan.

"I do. It's not popular here but I keep a bit on hand for two of my customers." Ted poured a glass. "What are you having Tommy?"

"I've never had rum, so I think I'll try it."

"Good choice, Tommy," grinned Morgan.

The two women went to a table to be more comfortable.

"It's bad enough we have one woman deputy in town, now it looks like we have two," a man sitting at a table with two others said loudly enough for all to hear.

"Here we go again," said Thomasina with a serious look on her face.

Morgan smiled at Thomasina, "I can handle this." She stood and walked over to the loudmouth's table.

Morgan smiled at the man nicely. "What's your problem? You don't think a woman can handle the job?"

Everyone in the tavern was waiting to see how this new woman would handle the situation.

"I don't want any shooting in my place," yelled Ted Hamilton, the owner.

"Don't worry Ted, there won't be any shooting. I

don't want to kill this man, just teach him a lesson." Morgan looked the loudmouth in the eyes, "I'm United States Deputy Marshal Morgan Foster. I have earned this badge. What's your name sir?"

"Mark Bundy."

Morgan unbuckled her gunbelt, "Mr. Bundy, I challenge you. I'll give my gun to my friend Tommy and be right back."

Thomasina couldn't believe what Morgan was doing as she took off her gunbelt and badge. "You are going to take on Bundy in a fistfight?"

"Sure, nothing to it."

Bundy was taking off his gunbelt when someone yelled, "Don't you two get in a hurry. Who wants to place bets?"

Everyone liked this idea and started lining up to place their bets. Someone else cleared the tables and chairs out of the center of the room.

"Ted, I need a pencil and paper," said the betting organizer.

When Sheriff Rice walked in the door he was flummoxed. "What's going on?" he yelled.

"Over here, sheriff," yelled Thomasina.

Seeing Tommy with a strange woman, he hurried over. "What's going on?"

"My new friend Morgan just challenged Bundy to

a fistfight."

Sheriff Rice's mouth fell open. "You, a woman, challenged Bundy to a fight?"

Morgan grinned, "He didn't think women should be deputies. I thought I'd teach him a lesson."

Sheriff Rice had a doubtful look as he said, "Tommy here has taught me a lot about what a woman can do, but I can't believe a woman would stand a chance against a man in a fistfight."

"Then go put your money on Bundy," grinned Morgan.

"Somehow I don't think so. You're just too confident."

"Come on sheriff, let's go put some money on Morgan," said Thomasina as she grabbed the sheriff's arm.

"Tommy, put twenty down for me," said Morgan.

"Are all the bets in?" yelled the betting organizer.

"Get on with it," someone yelled.

"Yeah, let's go!" someone else yelled.

Morgan and Bundy moved to the open area and stared at each other.

"This will be sweet and short," claimed Bundy as he suddenly charged Morgan with all the speed he could muster.

Morgan sidestepped and Bundy crashed into a stack of chairs with one falling on his head, causing everyone to roar with laughter, angering Bundy.

He got up. This time he moved in slowly, swinging his fists. Morgan ducked and swayed. Bundy's swings only pushed air while making him gasp for breath. Most of the crowd had bet on Bundy so in the beginning they were cheering for him, but as the fight progressed with Morgan getting the best of Bundy, they started cheering for her.

Morgan stepped up to Bundy and let loose with a right jab, using the heel of her hand to Bundy's nose followed by a left to his right eye. Next, she let loose a right to Bundy's sternum, knocking the breath from his lungs. This was followed by a left to his stomach which caused him to double up. Using an uppercut, she brought the heel of her right hand to Bundy's forehead with enough force to slam it up and backwards, almost breaking his neck. Bundy crashed to the floor, banging the back of his head, knocking him out.

One man yelled, "Best dollar I ever lost!"

"I wouldn't believe it if I hadn't seen it, and I still don't believe it!"

The place was going crazy.

An overexcited Thomasina ran over to Morgan and started pounding on her back.

"Easiest ten dollars I ever made," said Sheriff Rice with a grin.

"Easiest twenty dollars I ever made," grinned Thomasina.

Morgan went to Ted, "Ted, I'd like a pitcher of water and a towel please." Ted gave her the water and towel. Morgan took both to Bundy and squatted down by him. She wet the towel with water and started gently sponging Bundy's face like he was an injured best friend. As people saw what she was doing the place quieted.

Bundy's eyes slowly opened. "Am I dead? Are you an angel?"

In a soft voice Morgan said, "I'm just someone that feels bad for what I did to you. Just lay there for a while."

"I don't care what anyone says, I think you're an angel. Help me up."

Morgan helped Bundy up. Then with an arm around his waist she walked him to his table and helped him sit down. The men in the bar were stunned. They had never seen compassion like this before.

"Drinks on me!" yelled Morgan, causing another uproar with lots of nice comments. "How are you feeling Mr. Bundy?"

"Like a horse ran over me."

"Here, you can have my winnings. From now on

treat women like you would like to be treated, okay?"

Bundy tried to smile but it hurt. "You really are an angel."

"Now behave yourself," said Morgan as she patted him lightly on his head. She then joined Sheriff Rice and Thomasina at their table.

Thomasina was full of excitement, "I can't wait to tell Jo, Sky and Rex about this! I almost forgot, here's your badge back."

Seeing the badge, the surprised sheriff said to Morgan, "You are some woman. If you ever want to be a deputy sheriff you're welcome here! By the way, I'm Sheriff Rice."

"Glad to meet you Sheriff Rice, I'm US Deputy Marshal Morgan Foster."

"The lucky man that wins your heart," grinned the sheriff.

"I don't think so sheriff. Her husband will always be afraid he might say the wrong thing," laughed Thomasina.

"He sure won't complain about my cooking," laughed Morgan.

The three sat and drank for another half hour when Morgan said she was tired. She said goodbye to Sheriff Rice and shook his hand.

Morgan and Thomasina walked to the gunshop.

It was a tired Morgan that went to sleep in JoEllen's bed.

The next morning Morgan woke to the smell of bacon cooking. She body-washed herself with water in the basin and put on clean clothes. She was surprised to find JoEllen fixing breakfast.

"Good morning Jo."

"Good morning Morgan. I heard about your fight. I wish I could do that."

"It took years of training."

"Hi Morgan," said Thomasina as she came upstairs from her shop. "We never got around to talking about why you came here. Did you want me to do some work for you?"

"Yes. Cory showed me her gun and I'd like that done to mine."

Thomasina thought for a moment, "How long will you be staying?"

"I need to get back to Wichita as soon as I can. My partners have already left."

Thomasina smiled. "I think I can help you. I'll be right back." She turned and went back downstairs. A moment later she was back. "Here's one of my guns. It's empty but you check it and make sure."

Morgan checked the gun; it was empty.

"Put these empty shells in it. Now try it."

Morgan tried it. A smile formed on her face. "I like it."

"Just give me your gun and that one is yours."

"Tommy, I can't do that. This is your gun. It even has your name on it."

"I have another identical to that one. Besides, I don't need two and you would be stuck here for another day if I do your gun."

Morgan pulled her cash out of a pocket and counted it. "I never should have given my winnings away. I barely have enough money for the train. I must get an advance on my pay from Wyatt. He's the marshal in charge."

Thomasina noticed the worried look on Morgan's face and pulled a chair over next to her. "What is bothering you?"

"I don't have enough to pay you and I feel I should have two guns on me when going after someone. The woman who had this job before me was killed when Wyatt's gun was empty. Now he carries two."

"You are the most trustful person I know, keep your old gun and mail me twenty-five dollars for mine. How's that?"

Morgan looked Thomasina in the eyes, "That's very trusting of you."

"Go catch your train and your partners. I can't wait to write Cory in Wichita about last night."

Morgan stood and hugged Thomasina, "Thank you so much. If you ever need help, I'll be here for you." Seeing a piece of paper and pencil, Morgan wrote down her name and address.

"I have lots of help around here, but I'll remember that. Write me sometime and let me know how things are going."

"I will."

Wyatt, Tuck and the children were about to board the train. Wyatt noticed Tuck was in a foul mood. Not seeing Lomasi, Wyatt asked Tuck, "Where's Lomasi? I thought she might be going with us."

With a scowl on his face, Tuck stared at Wyatt. Finally, he said, "She went back to the reservation with her husband."

"Whoa, I didn't think she was married."

"I didn't either," said Tuck angrily. "When I looked for her at the restaurant they told me a big Indian she was married to had taken her back to the reservation."

The four boarded the train and were headed to Wichita.

Morgan arrived in Walsenburg an hour after

Wyatt, Tuck and the children had left. Finding out the next train going east wouldn't be here until ten tomorrow morning, she was about to leave the depot and get a room for the rest of the day and night when she saw Lomasi. Lomasi had a worried look on her face.

"Lomasi, what's the matter? I thought you were leaving with Tuck."

"Morgan, I'm so glad to see you. I came here to take a train to Wichita. Kuruk came to the restaurant and forced me back to the reservation. My mother wants me to marry him. I have refused him many times. I want to get away from Indian ways. I see no future there. Therefore, I have studied the English language. I'm afraid of Kuruk, which means bear. He is well-named because he is as big and mean as a bear. If he finds me, he will beat me and take me back and force me to marry him."

"You speak perfect English with no accent. The next train leaves tomorrow. I'll get us tickets and a room." Morgan realized she didn't have enough money for both of them. "I don't have enough money; do you have any?"

"Yes, let's get the tickets and get out of here. I'm sure Kuruk will be coming here looking for me."

Lomasi was too scared to have her own room, so the two women shared one.

"Lomasi, we have to get you into different

clothes. That buckskin skirt makes you stick out like a herd of buffalo. If you will give me some money, I'll get you different clothes. I'm sure Kuruk will be at the depot in the morning looking for you."

"I saved this money while working at the restaurant," said Lomasi as she handed Morgan ten dollars.

"I promise to spend it wisely. Don't go anywhere, stay in the room. I'll bring something to eat when I return."

Two hours later Morgan returned with a plain-looking grey dress that should not attract any attention and a black pair of boots. She also had a sack of sandwiches.

Lomasi tried on the dress. It came down to just below the top of the new boots.

"I'm so glad everything fits. I was worried about that. And here is a brown wig to cover your beautiful long black hair. Let's tie your hair up and see how you look as a brunette."

Seeing herself in the small mirror, Lomasi smiled. "I like it."

"You're beautiful. Tuck is a lucky man. I also bought some makeup. We'll put it on you tomorrow and you won't be recognizable."

"Thank you, Morgan, you are so kind."

"You're welcome. Here's the sandwiches. Tonight

we can try out your disguise when we go out to eat."

"That sounds like fun."

Wyatt, Tuck and the two children arrived in Wichita. It would be two days before a train would leave for Independence, so Wyatt got a room in their hotel for the siblings to share. Tuck would take them to Coffeeville, hoping the Harpers, Cindy's parents, would adopt them.

Wyatt had only been back for two hours when Deputy Cory came asking for his help.

"Wyatt, I hear you are a fair tracker. I need help. I'm being sent to Viola, that's twenty-five miles from here, to look for a missing woman. I think she's a well-to-do rancher's wife."

Wyatt thought for a moment. He was looking forward to some time off, but he liked the diminutive deputy and didn't want to turn her down. Besides, it sounded like a woman might need help. "If you're trying to get me alone, there's better ways," he teased.

Cory smiled, "It's the best I could come up with."

"A missing woman, I'd be glad to help. I haven't stabled my horse yet so he's out front. He's due for some exercise too. First, I need to leave a note for Morgan and talk to Tuck. Tuck is going to take a couple of kids to Coffeyville."

Five hours later Wyatt and Cory entered the small town of Viola, population two hundred. Seeing the sheriff's office as they rode in, they stopped and introduced themselves.

This was Cory's case, so Wyatt stood back and let her handle it. "Sheriff, what do you know about Tom Baxter and his wife Celia?"

The sheriff thought for a moment, "Well, Baxter thinks highly of himself and thinks everyone else is a rung below him and he's a know-it-all. No one knows much about his wife Celia. She's only been in town a few times and she was always with Baxter's foreman. She's a shy little thing, just a bit taller than you deputy. She's about sixteen years old, much younger than Baxter. Some would say too young for him. That's all I know."

"How come you haven't looked into this case?" asked Wyatt.

"I'm just a town sheriff, so it's out of my jurisdiction. I'm surprised to see the marshal service involved in a little case like this."

"It's not a little case, a woman is missing," said Wyatt sternly.

As Wyatt and Cory rode up to the Baxter's ranch house, a man with a low-slung gun walked towards them from a barn. A moment later another man with the looks of a hired gun stepped out from the house onto the porch, followed by a fortyish portly man. Wyatt slipped off the hammer loop holding his gun. He noticed Cory doing the same. "This girl knows what's going on," he thought to himself.

"Well, a US Marshal and the Ice Lady, I didn't think my Celia would draw so much interest. How can I help?"

Cory surprised Baxter by answering, "When did you find Celia missing?"

Baxter turned to Cory, "Yesterday morning I got up expecting my breakfast to be ready and she was gone. Took my best horse too!"

"Is she your wife?" Cory wanted to know.

Baxter hesitated, "She's my woman."

"Was she kidnapped or did she leave on her own?" asked Cory.

"She would never leave me. She's well taken care of and has money, so she must have been kidnapped."

"Any idea which way they might have gone?" questioned Cory.

"She went through the woods in that direction," Baxter pointed southwest.

"One more thing, Mr. Baxter, did she take any supplies or gear?" asked Cory.

Baxter shrugged, "Her saddlebags are gone."

"Thanks Mr. Baxter. We will be on your property following her trail," said Cory as she reigned Socks towards the southwest as Baxter had pointed.

"Crow, follow them. Keep in touch with me. Use the telegraph," ordered Baxter.

"Will do, boss."

Once they were out of earshot, Wyatt complimented Cory. "You did a good job. Asked all the right questions. You didn't leave anything for me."

Cory smiled at the praise. "Thank you, Wyatt, your praise means a lot to me."

"I didn't like Baxter. He's overbearing and sees himself as better than others. I bet he beat her."

"I didn't like him either," said Cory.

They both put the hammer loops back on their gun's hammer.

"Why would a rancher need two hired guns?" asked Wyatt.

"I had been wondering the same thing. They certainly weren't cowboys."

"When that gunhawk on the porch heard 'Ice Lady' he sure perked up. I suspect he'd like to make a name for himself by killing you."

"I noticed it too."

"You make a good partner Cory; sure wish you would join Tuck and me."

"What about Morgan?"

"She hasn't shown me anything."

"Give her a chance, I'm sure she will work out just fine."

"These must be Celia's tracks." Wyatt stopped and dismounted. He studied the tracks closely looking for some kind of identifying mark. He re-mounted. "Let's go. The way the dirt is kicked up she was riding fast, and the right rear shoe is loose. She's going to have to get that taken care of."

"Now it's my turn to compliment you. I would never have known those things. Sure glad you came along."

Wyatt smiled at Cory. "What's the next town going southwest?"

"I think it's Milton, ten miles from here, which is in Sumner County. Out of my jurisdiction."

"No, it's not," said Wyatt while reaching back into a saddlebag.

"It sure is."

"Hold up a minute."

Cory stopped alongside Wyatt.

"Hold out your hand."

Cory frowned but stuck her hand out. Wyatt dropped a badge into her hand. Cory looked at her hand and saw a US Deputy Marshal badge. Her smile went from ear to ear. "Wyatt, I have to tell you, I'm a badge nut, you might not get it back." Cory took off her deputy sheriff badge and pinned on the deputy marshal badge.

"From what I've heard you've worked hard to get where you are."

"You have no idea. I used to be an outlaw. Maybe sometime I can tell you my story."

"Sweet Cory, an outlaw. You will never convince me."

"I hope you don't expect this badge back," said Cory with a devilish look.

"I'll get it back if I have to turn you upside down and shake you."

Cory gigged her horse and took off following Celia's tracks.

Wyatt grinned and galloped after her.

As the two rode into the tiny town of Milton, Wyatt heard the clanging of metal on metal. The noise could only be coming from a blacksmith shop. A couple hundred yards later they saw it, stopped, and dismounted.

"I'll take it, Cory."

Seeing the two marshals, the blacksmith stopped

pounding a red-hot piece of steel. "What can I do for you marshals?"

"Did you fix a loose shoe for a woman yesterday?" asked Wyatt.

"I did. She had to wait because I had three people ahead of her. She wasn't happy about the wait. She sat in the chair over there watching me for four hours."

"What time did she leave?"

"Four-thirty I suppose."

"Did you notice which way she went?"

"West."

"Thanks for your help." As they walked back to their horses, Wyatt said, "That late in the day I would have thought she'd have gotten a room."

"Maybe she doesn't have any money," said Cory.

"Must not. Apparently, instead of getting something to eat, she waited with the blacksmith. We just might be able to catch up with her tonight if we ride late enough."

It was eleven at night and the two marshals were still riding. Wyatt and Cory were both hungry. Wyatt took a bag of jerky from a saddlebag and passed it to Cory. After taking three she passed the bag back. They chewed on jerky as they rode. Finally, at midnight Wyatt said, "Let's stop. We should have caught her. She's pushing that horse too hard."

"If it wasn't for chewing on the jerky, I would have fallen asleep," said Cory.

"Me too. This looks like a good place. Let's get off the road a way."

After their horses were picketed, Wyatt and Cory laid out their bedrolls. Cory put her gun next to the saddle she was using for a pillow and put her sheath knife inside her bedroll. Wyatt had been watching her.

"You sleep with a knife?"

"You bet. Once it kept two men from joining me in my bedroll."

"What did you do to them?"

"Gutted 'em."

"You're serious?"

"I'm serious as a rattlesnake."

"You keep surprising me."

Cory pulled off her boots and slid into her bedroll. "Night Wyatt."

"Good night Cory and thanks for the warning," laughed Wyatt.

Sunlight woke Wyatt the next morning. He was shocked to see Cory in his bedroll with him, an arm over his chest. Having to pee badly, Wyatt was trying to slide quietly from his bedroll but stopped and laid still when Cory's eyes popped open looking at him.

A worried-sounding Wyatt said quickly, "This is my bedroll. You don't have your knife, do you?"

Cory's right hand emerged holding a shiny eight-inch-long knife. Cory had a serious look on her face, scaring Wyatt. "Cory, be careful with that. Please don't use it, I'm getting out."

Cory started laughing. "Did I scare you?"

"You have no idea how close I came to wetting my pants. What are you doing in my bedroll?"

"Wolves were howling. I was cold and scared."

"I don't mind sharing my bedroll with you, but please leave the knife," said Wyatt as he moved off behind some trees to take care of business.

Cory was still chuckling as she went behind some trees in the other direction.

"That takes care of the makeup," said Morgan as she put the final touches on Lomasi's face.

"I know a place to eat. They would not hire me because I'm Indian. They serve drinks too."

"I bet they won't know you have Indian blood tonight," grinned Morgan.

After eating, the two women had enough to drink to make them giggly. As the two walked back to the hotel Lomasi said, "I'm so lucky I met you three."

"Tuck is lucky he met you," giggled Morgan. "Thank you for paying for everything. I will pay back every cent when we get to Wichita."

"Morgan, you don't owe me anything. I'm the one that owes you."

"That's silly."

At nine o'clock the next morning, Morgan had her horse in the railway's corral. She and Lomasi were sitting in the depot waiting for the train. So they would look like two traveling companions, Morgan was also wearing a dress. She had the gun from Thomasina inside a pocket hidden in the folds of the dress. They both wore large Victorian hats. Lomasi had hers pulled down in front.

Lomasi's foot bumped Morgan's, "That's him."

Morgan looked and saw a bare-chested, muscular Indian wearing buckskin pants and knee-high moccasins. On his hip a knife hung from a belt. Kuruc had a stern, mean look on his face as he looked around. When he glanced at Lomasi, Lomasi shuddered. When his eyes continued to roam, she relaxed, but only a little, as she was scared to death. Morgan was doing her best not to look at Kuruc and draw attention to herself.

When the train came into the depot with a hiss of steam and the clanking of its bell, both the women rose and moved towards the loading platform. When Morgan saw Kuruc moving towards them she placed her right hand inside her pocket and grabbed her gun. She was about to pull it and shoot Kuruc, when he moved past them.

Morgan picked up her carpetbag and followed Lomasi onto the train. They took a seat on the far side. Ten minutes later it was steaming north to Denver where they would switch trains. Lomasi looked at Morgan and screeched, "We did it!"

"Yes, we did."

It was a long two day wait for Tuck. Finally, they boarded a train for Independence, Kansas. A couple of hours later they got off. They walked to the livery where Tuck rented a carriage for the eighteen-mile ride to Coffeyville, Kansas.

Arriving in Coffeyville, Tuck watered the two horses. Finding a café, he and the two kids ate.

It was a two-mile ride to the Harper's small ranch. The Harpers heard the horses and stepped outside to see who arrived. Mr. Harper recognized Tuck, waved his hand in disgust and went back inside.

"Good afternoon Mrs. Harper. We came across these two orphans living by themselves in a leaky-roofed shack in Colorado. They need a home. They are well-behaved and hardworking.

They…"

"Let me see them," interrupted Mrs. Harper as she walked towards the carriage with a small smile.

"Hi. I'm Mrs. Harper, what's your names?"

"I'm Tricia Wilcox and this is my brother Sammy."

Mrs. Harper noted the desperate lonely smiles. She'd seen enough, her mind was made up. She turned and went back to Tuck. "I'm forty-three, a little old to be raising children but I want these two and we are taking them if I have to beat Harold over the head with a broom. I'll be right back."

Thirty seconds later Tuck could hear yelling and mumbling inside the house. A couple of minutes later Mrs. Harper was back. "We'll take them, and we will give them a good home."

Tuck smiled in relief, "Wyatt thought you might."

"They will help fill the void in our hearts."

"I'm sure they will. I've been with these kids for four days and I don't think you could find better. Let me go talk to them first."

Tuck went to the carriage. "These are good people here. They lost their daughter recently. You have lost your parents. I'm sure you four are a match made in heaven and will share a lot of love for each other. I will be checking on you from time to time so if for any reason you want out, I will see to it. There is no doubt in my mind that you will be happy here. Tricia, they know nothing about what you were doing to support you and your brother. They don't need to know either."

Tricia climbed down out of the carriage and gave Tuck a tight hug. "Thank Wyatt for me."

"I will."

Tuck watched the children as they carried the bags containing their new clothes. Suddenly he realized he'd forgotten something and ran to Mrs. Harper.

"I forgot to give you this." Tuck handed her two folded up five-hundred-dollar bills. "This is to cover any expenses or whatever."

Mrs. Harper tucked the money into a pocket on her sweater and grinned, "I bet that was to be bribe money if we had said no."

Tuck shrugged his shoulders and held out open palms.

"It will help Harold get over any qualms he might have," chuckled Mrs. Harper.

"I've got to go. The best to you and your new family, Mrs. Harper."

When Tuck got to Independence and was told the next train to Wichita wouldn't be here for three days, he became upset. What was he to do for three days? If he had his horse with, he could ride the one hundred ten miles in two days.

When Morgan and Lomasi arrived in Wichita they were both disappointed to find Tuck and Wyatt gone. Morgan got Lomasi a room in the Occidental Hotel on the same floor as the marshals. Morgan asked the desk clerk if he knew where Wyatt and Tuck were. He said Tuck was in Coffeyville while Wyatt was helping Cory in southern Kansas.

Morgan then went to the telegraph office and sent a message to Rothschild requesting money. A return message said to check her bank account in thirty minutes. She went straight to the bank and waited. Thirty minutes later a teller told her five hundred dollars had been deposited in her account. She withdrew two hundred. Morgan then went to a gun shop and purchased an 1876 Winchester Carbine and three boxes of 44 – 40 cartridges. She would practice using the shorter barreled rifle as a club, the way Cindy had. Back at her hotel she paid Lomasi the money she owed her and bought an envelope and stationery from the hotel clerk. She wrote a letter to Thomasina in Trinidad and enclosed the money she owed her. The hotel would see it got mailed.

While Morgan was doing her errands, Lomasi was looking for work. The Detroit Dining Parlor was the fourth place Lomasi went to. They told her she would start the next morning at seven.

That evening Morgan and Lomasi went out together for supper. Morgan was surprised by the quickness with which Lomasi had found work. What a hardworking, industrious woman.

Back at the hotel that night, Morgan started practicing holding and swinging the rifle at imaginary attackers.

When Morgan got up the next morning, she found a telegram had been pushed under her door. She was being sent to Las Vegas, New Mexico to help a town marshal. His deputy had been shot by a group of roughnecks. The marshal thought they might be an outlaw gang.

The next morning Morgan went for breakfast at the Detroit Dining Parlor and was waited on by a happy Lomasi. Morgan told her Tuck should be back in a few days, Wyatt was in southern Kansas with a sheriff's deputy friend, and she was being sent to Las Vegas, New Mexico.

"We're all going in different directions. I never thought we'd be split up like this," she told Lomasi. "I don't know what I'm supposed to do, and don't like being by myself; I'm scared."

"When I see Tuck, I'll tell him where you are. I'm sure he'll get there as fast as he can to help you."

"Thank you, Lomasi."

Wyatt and Cory had been following the road southwest when they saw a farmer plowing a field. They rode over to him.

"Good morning," said Wyatt. "Could you tell me what the next town is going southwest and how far it is?"

"The next town is Harper, about fifteen miles."

"Thank you."

They had been riding another thirty minutes when Wyatt spotted horse tracks leaving the road. "Wait, let's see where these tracks go."

The tracks led them to a small clump of trees. Wyatt dismounted and studied the area. "I would guess this is where Celia spent the night. Over there is where she picketed her horse in the grass. See the horse dung. See the small boot prints?"

"I see them. Must be from a woman. She never built a fire though," said Cory.

"Nope. Either she ate jerky or she doesn't have any food."

"It's been two days. I hope she has something to eat," said Cory, sounding a bit worried.

Wyatt and Cory had ridden about five miles when they saw a small stream of smoke rising in a group of trees a couple hundred yards from the road.

"Let's check it out," said Wyatt. "There are tracks from about four horses going and coming."

A minute later at a deserted campsite, Cory said, "They didn't even put out their fire."

Wyatt had dismounted and was studying the campsite closely. He didn't look happy, "Cory, it looks like Celia met up with these men. A group of men camping along a road are most likely outlaws."

"Why would she join them?"

"Let's hurry. They're not far in front of us. I suspect they plan on pulling something off in Harper."

Wyatt and Cory were about two miles from Harper when they heard gunshots and gigged their horses into a gallop. Upon entering the town, they found a dead deputy sheriff laying in the middle of the street being looked after by the town sheriff.

Hearing riders approaching, the sheriff stood. Wyatt and Cory stopped next to him.

"What happened?" asked Wyatt.

"They robbed the bank and killed my deputy."

Cory looked worried, "Celia could hang for this."

"Let's go," said Wyatt as he spurred his horse.

Thirty minutes later the outlaws stopped. The leader got out a spyglass and checked their back trail. "Two following us. It looks like a man and woman."

"Are ya sure they're after us?" asked one of the robbers.

"I'm sure. They're both wearing badges. We'll wait here for 'em."

"This is no place for an ambush," said the same robber as before.

"No, it isn't. This land is flat and almost treeless. There isn't a good place for an ambush for a couple hundred miles. But I don't want them tailing us and picking us off one by one or attacking us while we sleep. There is only two and one's a woman. Shouldn't be a problem. We'll make a stand right here," said the leader. "Jack, tie the horses to that lone tree where the horses will be out of the line of fire. Let's line up. Celia, you're in the middle. Maybe having a girl in the middle will affect their aim."

Wyatt and Cory stopped a half mile from the outlaws.

"It looks like they want to take us on," said Wyatt. "Wish I had a shotgun."

"It looks like Celia is standing in the middle," said Cory.

Wyatt looked at Cory, "Are you as good as they say?"

Cory grinned, "I'm better. You take the one on the

far left and I'll get the other three."

"Are you trying to make fun of me?" grinned Wyatt.

"Just trying to spur you to your competitive best. I know I won't be killed. I'm going to live until I'm sixty-seven."

"I've heard that rumor. I don't think I believe it."

"Wyatt, what about Celia?"

Wyatt reached into a saddlebag and pulled out his spyglass. He aimed it at Celia. "I don't think she's a threat. There are tears running down her cheeks."

"Maybe she's being forced."

"I think so. Let's get this over with." Wyatt looked around for a place to tie their horses. Not seeing anything, he said, "I'm going to pound a stake into the ground. We'll tie 'em to it."

With the horses staked, Wyatt walked towards the outlaws on the far left side of the road. Cory was on the far right.

"Let's stop here. At this distance I'm sure some of them will miss. If they try to close the distance we start shooting," said Wyatt. "They're outlaws wanted for murder. We are outnumbered. We don't wait for them to draw first. Why should we donate our lives? Are you with me?"

"I'm with you Wyatt, just waiting for you."

"Now."

Wyatt and Cory drew and were shooting before any outlaws had their guns out of their holsters. Only one outlaw was able to draw. He only got one shot off, and it went harmlessly into the ground at his feet. Celia was the only person left standing. She looked around her, then started running towards Wyatt with her hands in the air. Crying with tears flowing down her checks, she fell into Wyatt's arms.

While Wyatt was holding her, Cory pulled the gun from her holster. She checked it and found it empty.

"Wyatt, her gun is empty."

"Doesn't surprise me. Go check the outlaws."

Wyatt pulled Celia from his arms, "I have to check the outlaws. I'll be right back."

Wyatt caught up with Cory who was kicking guns away and taking off gunbelts. All four were dead. After they had the four bodies tied over their saddles, Wyatt asked Celia, "How did you get mixed up with this bunch?"

"I was so hungry. As I got close to their camp, I could smell bacon. I didn't know they were outlaws. I just wanted something to eat."

"Did they feed you?"

"They did. They said I would be paying them back tonight. I'm so glad you and the woman rescued me."

"I'm Marshal Peterson, and my partner is Deputy Jackson. The first thing we must do is take these outlaws back to Harper and let the sheriff know Celia was a prisoner or they'll be sending out posters for her arrest," said Wyatt.

The Harper sheriff saw Wyatt and Cory leading the outlaws into town. "That didn't take long," he said. "I'm sure glad you two marshals came along. I see you caught the girl."

Cory spoke up quickly, "Marshal, this girl is innocent. Her gun was empty. She was their prisoner."

The town marshal looked at Celia. He saw the dirty tearstains on her face. "I'm glad to hear that. I've never seen a woman hung and don't want to."

"We'll be on our way; sorry about your deputy." Wyatt gave the marshal the bag of the bank's money.

"The bank is going to be mighty glad to get their money back," said the town ~~marshal~~ sheriff while taking the bag from Wyatt.

As the three rode northeast towards Viola and Wichita, Cory asked, "Celia, is Baxter your husband?"

"No! Though lately he thinks so. I was eight years old living in an orphan home in Chicago. There were more of us than they could feed so they put twenty of us on what was called an 'Orphan Train.' When it stopped in Wichita Tom Baxter gave the orphanage two hundred dollars for me. I was sold like a slave. Which is what I became. Right from the beginning I was made to clean the house and do dishes. When I was ten gardening was added to my chores. I was told I had to earn my keep, which I agreed with. When I was twelve, I was taught how to cook, and I did the cooking. I worked hard, and I was okay with it. But then he started hitting me. He always found an excuse. The food was cold or something was wrong with it. Then when I was fifteen, he thought I should take on wifely duties. That's when it became too much. I always watched for a chance to run away. Finally, the other day that chance came while Tom Baxter was in town with most of the ranch hands. I only had time to saddle a horse and ride away; there wasn't time to grab any food."

"Don't worry, we won't take you back to Baxter. We'll take you to Wichita with us," said Cory.

"Thank you," said a relieved Celia.

When the trio entered Sedgewick County and Wyatt wasn't looking, Cory switched badges. She was hoping Wyatt would then forget about the Deputy Marshal badge. She would add it to her collection.

The three stopped in Viola and told the sheriff what had happened. The next time Baxter was in town the sheriff would tell him not to expect Celia back.

Celia was taken to the Wichita Children's Home. The home did not want to take anyone in as old as Celia, but when Wyatt made a sizable donation to cover Celia's expenses and more, she was accepted. She would also help with the younger children. Cory promised to find her a job in town when she was ready to leave the home.

Wichita Children's Home
100 North Fountain

That evening Wyatt and Cory were having a few drinks at Paul's Pub. They had been there maybe a half hour when Tuck entered. Cory thought this would be a good time to tease Wyatt.

"Wyatt, how come I shot three outlaws to your one?"

"One! I got two!"

"You got that second one the same time I did, so it doesn't count."

"If he doesn't count for me, he doesn't count for you either. So that leaves you with just two."

Cory grinned, "That's twice as many as you. Shows what a woman can do compared to a man."

"Now I'm going to show you what a man can do to a mouthy woman," said Wyatt while he stood up. He moved quickly to Cory and grabbed her. "I heard you like to be held upside down." Wyatt spun Cory upside down and started shaking her. Her screaming attracted the attention of everyone in the saloon.

Wyatt was grinning, "Tuck give me a hand here."

Tuck grabbed one leg while Wyatt had the other. They were shaking little Cory when a badge fell out of her shirt pocket, dinging on the floor.

"We can put her down now. I would have forgotten all about that badge if you hadn't started on me Cory." The two men put Cory on the floor gently. She came up like a hissing wildcat and punched Wyatt in his stomach. He'd seen the punch coming and tightened his muscles. Cory felt she'd hit a wall and hurt her wrist. "Ouch." She then stomped her right foot. Wyatt and Tuck laughed. When Cory gave Wyatt a fake sad look while holding her right one, Wyatt melted and pulled her close in a hug. Cory winked at Tuck, making him laugh.

"Wyatt, she bites your nose, punches you in the belly and yet you hold her like a daughter."

"One morning she threatened me with a knife too!" exclaimed Wyatt. "But that's okay because we're pards aren't we Cory? I just wish I could talk her into joining us."

"Won't happen pard, I like it here."

"Tuck, I'm glad you're back. We leave in the morning for Las Vegas, New Mexico," said Wyatt.

Cory looked up at Wyatt, "You're leaving so soon?"

"Morgan needs our help."

Morgan waited until the other passengers were asleep, then she would go to the rear of the car where she practiced drawing her revolver and aiming with a two-handed grip. She had blank cartridge cases in the chambers to protect the hammer when it fell. She practiced cocking with her left thumb as Cory had shown her. She also practiced using her short rifle as a club.

The entire time riding on the train Morgan kept her badge in a pocket and when arriving in Las Vegas she left it there. She wanted to reconnoiter without anyone knowing she was a law officer. It was a three block walk to Hotel Vegas, where she rented a room for four days. Thinking she would not need a horse she had left hers in Wichita. If she needed one, she would rent it.

To get a feel for the town, Morgan went for a long walk through the business area and part of the residential area, learning the streets. One saloon named Sidewinder was exceptionally noisy and it was ten in the morning. Morgan was curious who was making all the noise, but she went on past it. Wearing pants with a pistol strapped to her waist and carrying a rifle, she made quite a spectacle and garnered a few looks.

On her way back Morgan stopped outside the noisy Sidewinder Saloon and thought for a moment about going inside. If whoever was this noisy now, come tonight they will surely be causing trouble. Wanting to see who they were, she went inside.

As soon as Morgan entered, the place became quiet. Men were not used to a woman inside a saloon, and this woman wore a gun and carried a rifle.

A man sitting at a crowded table with four friends yelled, "Bartender, give this woman a drink on me." The man and his friends looked like hard case troublemakers.

"I buy my own drinks," said Morgan in a calm voice that surprised herself.

The man stood, "So you're too good to let someone buy you a drink. I think you need to be taken down a notch," the man grinned, "and I'm just the man to do it."

"Teach her a thing or two Marty," said one of his friends at the table.

Marty moved towards Morgan. When he got close Morgan shoved her rifle's stock into the man's belly, knocking him over and taking his breath away. Morgan held her rifle in her left hand, leaving her right hand free. While lying on the floor Marty's hand went for the gun on his hip. Morgan drew hers. Marty's gun hadn't cleared leather when he found himself staring down the bore of a forty-four. Her speed surprised the man on the floor and his friends. "Pull that hog leg and you're dead," said Morgan in an icy voice.

As Marty stood his eyes had a look of death when he said, "This isn't over."

"Give me your gunbelt and gun," Morgan told Marty.

"Never."

"You have five seconds before I shoot you in the leg and take it from you."

Everyone inside was convinced the woman meant what she said, including Marty. He unbuckled his gunbelt and handed it to Morgan.

"It will be at the sheriff's office."

Morgan backed out through the door and walked

down the street. Her heart was pounding. She couldn't believe what she had just done. "What's become of me?" she wondered.

At noon she stopped in a café for lunch. As she ate the town marshal entered and took a seat. Having finished her lunch, Morgan stayed and drank coffee, waiting for the marshal to finish eating. Seeing Morgan looking at him, the marshal smiled and nodded his head. Morgan returned his smile and nodded her head. The marshal looked to be about thirty with a full beard and mustache. "Won't he be disappointed when he finds out I'm a deputy marshal and not a flirty woman," thought Morgan.

The marshal finished eating and was sitting back enjoying his coffee. Morgan put her badge on and approached the marshal's table. He looked up with a big smile until he saw the badge, then smile turned into a nasty frown.

"What! A woman US Marshal! They sent me a woman! I never heard of such a thing! What can a woman do?" To say he was upset was putting it mildly.

"I'm US Deputy Marshal Morgan Foster. May I sit down?"

The town marshal pointed at a chair, never rising while a woman was being seated as manners dictate. "When they told me a Morgan Foster would be coming to help I thought it was a man. What can a woman do?"

Morgan was expecting this and was ready with an answer, "If Marshal Peterson didn't think I could do the job I wouldn't be here." This is what Morgan had been telling herself the last few days also, while trying to build her self-confidence. "We will talk later when you're in a better mood." Morgan stood. "By the way this belongs to a man named Marty. I think you should hold onto it for a few days." Morgan gave the gunbelt with the gun in it to the surprised sheriff.

"You took this from Marty Healy? He is the man who killed one of my deputies."

"All I know is his friends call him Marty and I didn't like his manners. You wondered what a woman could do, now you know. Why haven't you arrested Marty if he killed your deputy?"

"There's five of them, I'm only one man."

"Now is a good time, he's unarmed. Otherwise, next time I see him I'll arrest him for you."

As the marshal watched Morgan leave, he thought, "That's one hell of a woman!"

Morgan had walked two blocks when she saw a bench outside a store called "Outfitters" and she sat down. She had been doing a lot of walking and needed a rest. Las Vegas was a large bustling town. The street was crowded with wagons and men on horseback. Dust and the smell of horse dung wafted in the air. Being a female wearing a badge, Morgan drew a lot of stares. Most of the men smiled and tipped their hat to her. It was a relaxed Morgan that smiled back and nodded her head. She might be relaxed for now, but she missed Wyatt and Tuck immensely. She was by herself and lonely.

Morgan was watching as a nice-looking man with beard stubble on his face tied his horse to the rail. He smiled at Morgan and tipped his hat. He was about to go inside when he instead asked, "May I sit down?"

Morgan looked up at him and smiled, "Join me. Do I look lonely?"

The man sat next to Morgan on the bench. "I don't know, are you?"

"I am. This is my first time on a mission alone and I miss my friends."

"First time, huh. I never would have guessed that after what you did at the Sidewinder. I was there meeting a friend. You were remarkably calm. But you made that snake look bad in front of his friends. You should have killed him because now he's going to be coming for you."

"I have never fired a shot in anger."

"That will change in this town. I'm Clive Owens. I have a small ranch outside of town."

"Morgan Foster, you're my first friend here."

"I'm proud to be your friend. If you should ever need anything, my ranch is the CO. It's straight west of town as you get to the foothills. I've got to go, nice talking with you."

Owens stood and went inside.

Morgan had been sitting on the bench for a couple of hours. Not knowing what to do, she thought she would go see the sheriff. She didn't even know his name. The sheriff's office and jail were two blocks outside of the business district.

The door to the office was open so Morgan went in. The sheriff was sitting at his desk reading a newspaper.

"Good afternoon sheriff," said Morgan in a pleasant voice. "Let's start over. I'm Morgan Foster."

The sheriff looked up from his paper and stared for a moment. "I'm Sheriff Underhill. Nice to meet you Deputy Foster. I apologize for my remarks earlier. Women seem to be taking over. Next thing you know they'll be allowed to vote."

"Having a say in who is making laws governing me would be nice," grinned Morgan. "Do you have any posters on Marty and his friends?"

Sheriff Underhill pointed to a small stack on his desk. "Help yourself."

Morgan picked up the five posters and looked at them. "I see you have separated these from the rest, so you have been looking at them."

"You said it, I've been looking at them, nothing more."

"Let's take the two shotguns you have on the wall and go arrest them."

"You are joking, aren't you? That would be two against five."

"No, I'm not. We catch them off-guard and arrest them. Then I can go home and maybe with the threat gone you will be able to find another deputy. Do you still have Marty's gun?"

"Hanging there on the wall."

"That makes it two against four. We can handle that."

"This woman is either awful good or awful crazy," thought Sheriff Underhill.

Morgan had never held a shotgun much less fired one, but she'd watched others, and Sheriff Underhill didn't need to know that. Acting like she knew what she was doing, Morgan took a shotgun off the wall, flipped the lever and broke it open. Seeing it was empty she asked, "Where's your shells?"

Sheriff Underhill pulled open a desk drawer and grabbed a box.

Morgan opened the paper box, pulled two shells from it and dropped both at the same time into the two chambers and snapped the shotgun closed.

"You loaded two at a time. You know what you're doing."

Morgan emptied the box into her hand and put them into a left pocket.

Sheriff Underhill rose and took down the other shotgun. He exhaled and said, "If we come out of this alive, I will surely be surprised."

He loaded his shotgun and put shells in a pocket. "I imagine they're still at the Sidewinder."

When people saw their sheriff and a deputy marshal walking down the middle of the street with shotguns, they knew something was about to happen. Being curious, they followed.

Being a deputy marshal, Morgan thought she should be in charge, so she told Sheriff Underhill, "I'll take the front door, you take the back. The doors don't line up with the table where they are sitting, so we won't be shooting at each other. When you hear me scream, that's when we both enter."

Sheriff Underhill couldn't help chuckling, "A woman's scream should cause them to be off-guard."

"Off-guard and looking my way, which will make it easy for you to get behind them. I think we can do this without a shot being fired."

When the two got to the Sidewinder, Sheriff Underhill went around back. Morgan gave him a couple of minutes, then she screamed.

They both entered with shotguns pointed at the table where Marty sat with his friends. They were taken completely by surprise. Seeing two double-barreled shotguns pointed at them, they quickly raised their hands.

"Slowly set your guns on the table and move away from it," yelled Morgan authoritatively. "One false move and your bodies will develop a lot of leaks."

Marty was the first to move away while the other four put their guns on the table, then joined him.

"Sheriff, check them for guns and knives," ordered Morgan.

Sheriff Underhill found three boot knives and one pocket pistol. "Pete, we'll be back for these guns in a bit," said Sheriff Underhill to the bartender.

After the five were placed inside two different cells, Morgan said, "That went well."

Sheriff Underhill had a funny look on his face, then he burst out laughing, "It sure did. I still don't believe it."

Coming off their adrenaline high, they both laughed in relief.

"You're quite a woman, deputy."

"Thank you, sheriff. I'll see you later, I must send

a telegram to my boss."

Morgan sent a telegram to J.T. Rothschild telling him her mission was complete. Suddenly feeling tired she went to her hotel room for a nap. When she awoke the sun was low on the horizon. She found a telegram that had been slid under her door. It was from Rothschild. He was surprised and pleased she had accomplished her mission for Attorney General Whitaker so quickly. He told her not to go anywhere, as Wyatt and Tuck would be there in the morning. After reading the last part her emotions got away from her and she yelled, "Yea!"

Hungry, she went to the café where she had had lunch earlier. She had just sat down when Sheriff Underhill came in the door and walked to her table.

"May I?"

"Sure, Sheriff, take a seat."

After they had both ordered Morgan couldn't hold it back any longer, "My friends will be here in the morning."

"A bit late for the party, aren't they? Besides, you didn't need them anyway."

Not wanting to ruin her reputation with the sheriff it was all Morgan could do not to tell him it was her first mission alone and she couldn't wait to see Wyatt and Tuck.

After they finished eating Sheriff Underhill said he was going home. Morgan told him she had napped all afternoon and would keep an eye on the two until around midnight.

As Morgan walked the streets of Las Vegas she thought of the day's events. She realized she could do the job she was hired for and her much needed self-confidence and self-image rose. For the most part, it was a quiet night. At eleven-thirty she went to her room and bed.

It was ten the next morning when Morgan and Sheriff Underhill met the train at the depot. When Wyatt and Tuck stepped off the train Morgan had the strongest urge to run up and hug both of them, but she restrained herself. She knew she would look like a weak woman in front of Sheriff Underwood. Instead, she introduced everyone.

With introductions done, Morgan thought she would do some teasing, some might call it bragging though. "What brings you two to Las Vegas?" Morgan asked.

Wyatt looked a bit puzzled, "We were told Sheriff Underhill and you needed help."

Morgan looked at Sheriff Underhill, "What could we need help with?"

The sheriff decided to play along with Morgan, "I don't know. Things are quiet…I know, I'm short deputies for guarding the prisoners. They could help with that."

"That's right, Sheriff. Someone should stay with the prisoners at night. Follow us and we'll show you your job for tonight while the sheriff and I are out having fun."

"Morgan you are trying my patience! Before we left Wichita, Cory was doing that, so Tuck and I held her upside down and shook her."

Morgan grinned, "You best not try that with me. Follow us to the jail."

"Morgan you won't believe what Cory did to Wyatt for holding her upside down! Tell her Wyatt!" said a chuckling Tuck.

"Don't give her any ideas, Tuck," growled Wyatt.

"Then I'll tell her. She bit Wyatt on his nose!"

"Really? You have to be kidding." Morgan was laughing.

"She really did! Wyatt thought part of his nose was missing so I looked at it. There wasn't even a bite mark."

"Sounds like a love bite Wyatt," said a laughing Morgan. "Maybe she's after you," Morgan teased.

"That little imp. I'd sooner be with a bucking mule."

"What a close-knit group," thought Sheriff Underhill.

As the four walked, Sheriff Underhill started

talking to Wyatt. "Morgan is quite the deputy, Marshal. First, she outdrew the leader Marty and took his gun away from him. Later, when she found out they were all wanted she took charge and arrested them all without much help from me."

Walking in front with Tuck, Morgan had been listening. She turned her head and grinned at Wyatt. Tuck reached over and patted Morgan on her back and said, "Good job. I knew you had it in you."

Wyatt looked at the five prisoners, then returned to the office section of the jail. "Those are some tough-looking characters."

"Wyatt, let's get something to eat," said Tuck.

"I'll join you," said Morgan.

"Nice meeting you Sheriff, we'll see you later," said Wyatt.

As the three were eating Tuck asked, "Seeing as how Morgan took care of things, what do we do now?"

"Now we do what Rothschild hired us for, we help those in need," said Wyatt.

"There is a poor section of town I can take you to when we're done eating," said Morgan.

As they walked through the poor section of town, Wyatt wondered how they could help without being mobbed. Wyatt decided the local churches were best suited for helping the poor. Wyatt gave the pastors of each church five hundred dollars. He made sure they understood the money wasn't his but was being donated by an undisclosed benefactor.

That afternoon the three were in one of Las Vegas's many saloons. They'd been drinking and talking for a couple of hours. Morgan was feeling the liquor's effects. "You both have no idea how much I have missed you two. I didn't know what to do when I got here."

"That reminds me," said Tuck, "thank you for all you did getting Lomasi out of Colorado."

"It was my pleasure to help her. You two are perfect for each other. And this reminds me, Wyatt I owe you an apology for what I said about Tricia when we were in Walsenburg." Morgan looked Wyatt in the eyes. Her speech was slurred as she said, "I might have been a bit jealous."

"At the time it hurt. Apology accepted. Tuck we better get her back to her room before she gets any more emotional."

"I think you're right."

As the trio walked to the hotel Morgan tripped. Tuck caught her then walked with an arm around her.

"Tuck my hero. How come Wyatt isn't more like you?"

"I heard that," said Wyatt.

"You were supposed to hear that," slurred Morgan.

KILLER MCBRIDE

Wichita, Kansas late September 1888.

The Marshals had some time off. Morgan was getting her father's bookkeeping caught up. Tuck was spending every available minute with Lomasi. Wyatt was either at Pete's Pub or his hotel room.

It was early afternoon when Cory saw Wyatt sitting outside of Pete's Pub by himself. Cory was on duty, walking along the boardwalk on the other side of the street from Pete's Pub. She crossed the street to the saloon.

"Mind if I join you?" asked Cory.

Wyatt looked at Cory for a moment. "A little company would be nice."

Cory went inside and was back out a moment later with a glass and a chair. She helped herself to Wyatt's bottle, then sat down. For five minutes neither said anything; they both watched the activity on the street.

"Do you know Thomasina in Trinidad?" asked Cory. "People call her Tommy."

"Never heard of her."

"She's a gunsmith. Yesterday I got a letter from her. When Morgan was in Colorado, she visited Tommy. While they were in a saloon Morgan got into a fight with a man. Before they fought bets were placed. Of course, most bet on the man to win. It sounds exciting; wish I'd been there. Anyway, Morgan knocked the man out. The surprising thing, says Tommy, is Morgan then used a wet towel and took care of the man like a mother would her child. After she helped him back to his seat, she felt so bad for him she gave him her winnings."

"Morgan is a fool."

"No, she isn't! She's tough yet compassionate. She has the traits you were looking for in a woman. Tuck told me how she singlehandedly took care of a gang in Walsenburg. She's everything you wanted in a woman, yet you are mean to her."

"What would you know? You're just a little busybody!" yelled Wyatt harshly.

Cory was hurt. She looked at Wyatt for a moment. "How do I know? It's obvious to me! Besides, Tuck tells me things. I was only trying to help you see past your blind self-pity. There's no excuse for the way you treat Morgan."

Cory poured the whiskey from her glass into Wyatt's glass. "Just sit here by yourself and pine away!" It was a hurt Cory that hurried off.

"Cory, I'm sorry. Come back," yelled Wyatt. Cory kept walking. "I just hurt the person I most like," thought Wyatt.

A couple of days later Wyatt sent word to Tuck and Morgan to be at the train depot tomorrow at two in the afternoon with their horses. The train would depart at two-thirty. He would tell them the mission while on the train.

The next day, after getting settled down on the train, Wyatt told Tuck and Morgan they were going to Springfield, in Dakota Territory. The town has a population of about two hundred fifty people. The mayor and several town council members had been killed by Jason McBride, according to Sheriff Carlson. Sheriff Carlson was having trouble finding McBride and the town is worried there will be more killing.

After arriving in Springfield, the three marshals tied their horses outside the Bon Homme Hotel, where they got separate rooms. It was named after Bon Homme County, where Springfield was located.

The three met in Wyatt's room.

"Let's split up and see what we can learn. I'll talk to Sheriff Carlson," said Wyatt.

"I'll check the saloons," grinned Tuck.

"Is that Indian blood of yours looking for some firewater?" grinned Wyatt.

"Saloons are the best places to get information," said Tuck, defending himself.

Not saying anything, Morgan went downstairs and mounted her horse. Tuck watched her ride out of town and wondered where she was going.

After getting a mile out of town, Morgan took off her badge and began riding in a circle around the town. She watched for tracks and places a wanted person might hide out. She had almost completed her circle when she saw a lone rider riding away from Springfield. She gigged her horse and rode after the rider. The rider saw someone riding fast towards him. Noticing it was a woman, the rider relaxed. He stopped and waited for her. Then as she got closer, he noticed her good looks, then the gun on her hip and rifle in a scabbard, mildly surprising him.

As Morgan got closer, she realized the rider and horse met the description for Jason McBride. The horse was a brown bay with black stockings, the same as McBride rode, only this rider was young. He looked to be only seventeen or eighteen. She decided to play a lost woman running from someone. With a big smile she rode close to the young man and held out her hand, "Hi, I'm Morgan Foster."

The young man took her hand, "Nice meeting

you, I'm Jason McBride."

Morgan was so stunned she could have fallen off her horse. This young, honest, easygoing man is a killer? She wanted to get to know him better so she lies, "I'm running from someone and need a place to hide. Would you be able to help me?"

"I know a place. I'm headed there now. You're welcome to stay with me."

Morgan smiled again, "That's very kind of you."

As the two rode side by side, they talked.

"Who is chasing you?"

"A man that is determined to marry me has sent men to take me to him."

"Some men are that way; they have power or money, and they think they can take whatever they want."

"Where did you learn such wisdom?" Morgan was beginning to like this kid.

"I'm dealing with the same kind of person as you are."

Hearing a number of gunshots from in front of him, Jason said, "Someone may need help. You stay here." Without waiting for a reply, Jason galloped off. Of course, Morgan followed.

As the two came out from a stand of trees to a road, they saw a wagon with an older couple being chased by two men shooting at them.

Jason pulled his pistol. Morgan rode up alongside. Surprise was on Jason's face when he looked at Morgan. Morgan smiled, pulled her pistol and said, "Let's get 'em." Morgan and Jason galloped towards the bandits from their left side. As they got close, they started shooting. One fell from Morgan's shot, the other fell from one of Jason's many shots.

The old couple on the wagon stopped. With her gun in her hand, Morgan dismounted and checked the two bandits. They were both dead, one from a wound to his head, and the other from where a bullet had entered his side, penetrating to his heart.

Morgan mounted her horse and rode to the wagon. "Are you two alright?"

"We're fine. We wouldn't be if not for you two though," replied the man. "I'm Morrice and this is my wife, Gertrude."

"I'm Morgan Foster." Morgan didn't want to give out Jason's name and was surprised when he boldly told the couple he was Jason McBride.

"Why were those two trying to kill you?" asked Morgan.

"I guess because we're old they thought we had saved lots of money," chuckled the old man.

"They might be worth some money. Why don't you take them on into town and see if there isn't a reward you can collect," suggested Morgan.

"I couldn't do that. Any reward should be yours."

"I'm not interested in it," said Morgan, "Are you, Jason?"

"Not me. That town doesn't much like me."

"Gertie and I could sure use the money. I'll turn this wagon around and we'll load 'em up."

Before loading the outlaws onto their horses, Morgan took the gunbelt and gun from one and handed it to Jason, "An extra gun might come in handy."

"Good idea," replied Jason as he hung the gunbelt from his saddle horn.

After loading the bodies onto their horses and tying them to the back of the wagon, Morgan told them they should keep the horses after delivering the bodies to the town's undertaker.

Morrice shook hands with Morgan and Jason. "You two are good folk. Thank you for all your help." He climbed up onto the wagon, released the brake, snapped the reins and drove off.

"It doesn't look like you have any food with you. Follow me and I'll fix us some coffee and something to eat," said Jason.

As the two rode, Jason said, "We make a good team."

"We do. You're going to be a good catch for some

woman."

"I've already been caught."

"You have. You mean I'm too late?" laughed Morgan.

"Not too late to catch my eye, just too late to catch my heart."

Wyatt found Sheriff Carlson in his office.

"Good afternoon, Sheriff. I'm Marshal Peterson. I was sent here to help find McBride."

"I never asked for help and I don't need your help. I suggest you go back where you came from."

Wyatt was surprised by the grouchy response. "I'm not going anywhere. I was sent here to find McBride and I will do my job. You can help by telling me all you know. Let's start with the witnesses. How many are there and what are their names?" Wyatt pulled a piece of paper from a pocket along with a pencil.

Sheriff Carlson mumbled for a moment, then said, "One of the witnesses is Mack Bernhardt. He's usually at the Golden Egg Saloon. The other is Mike Hartford. I don't know where he lives."

"You only have two witnesses for four shootings? How do you know McBride did all four?"

Sheriff Carlson shrugged, "He's the only one killing people."

"You put a dead or alive wanted poster out on the word of what sounds like a worthless drunk and another man that doesn't have a home? I want that poster pulled immediately."

"You can't come into my town and start telling me what to do!" said the belligerent sheriff loudly.

"As a U.S. Marshal I sure can. I can also remove you from office if you don't cooperate."

"I have a strong backing. You're one lonely marshal. You don't stand a chance."

"Are you threatening me?"

"Take it however you want. Just get out of my office!"

As Wyatt stepped out of the sheriff's office a wagon stopped in front. Wyatt saw the two bodies lying over the two horses. An old man climbed down from the wagon and went inside. Being curious, Wyatt hung around as Sheriff Carlson and the old man came outside.

"These two men tried robbing me but were thwarted by a young man and woman. They said there might be a reward for these two and I could have it."

Sheriff Carlson looked at the two men. "Yep, there is. One hundred dollars apiece. They're two-bit outlaws from Nebraska. I'll have you sign some papers then take you to the bank for your reward. Did you get the names of the two that helped you?"

"Yeah, the woman said she was Morgan Foster. The young man was Jason McBride."

Wyatt almost fell over when he heard those two names. What could that crazy woman be up to now?

"McBride you say. Can't be, he's a killer himself."

"That's what he said his name was."

"He must've been lying. Come on inside for the paperwork."

Wyatt noticed the worried look on the sheriff's face. He then went looking for Tuck. The town was only big enough for three saloons. Wyatt found Tuck in the second one he entered. Tuck was sitting at a table with three others. When he saw Wyatt come in, he met him at the bar.

Wyatt ordered a whiskey. "How'd you do Tuck?"

"Jason McBride is only a kid and he's well-liked. He doesn't sound like a killer."

"I just left Sheriff Carlson; I have no use for that man. I have the distinct impression he's into this mess up to his gunbelt. He sure doesn't want us looking into the killings. He thinks I'm here by myself and he actually threatened me."

"Isn't he in for a surprise. Say, where's Morgan? I haven't seen her all afternoon. I'm worried about her."

"You should be worried. She's with McBride. Her and McBride got into a shootout with a couple of outlaws. Killed them both."

A big grin took over Tuck's face. "She's one heck of a woman. You need to ease up on her. She's perfect for the job."

"Cory told me the same thing. I then got upset and told her off. She went away with tears in her eyes."

"How could you do that to little Cory? She's only trying to help you."

"I don't know. I need to get my head together."

"The best way to do that is to let Morgan in. You need to accept her and who she is. Once you've done that, you need to live for the future. Then, I think you will be fine."

Wyatt thought for a long while. "I think you're right. Thanks for being honest with me."

Two men entering the saloon caught Wyatt's eye. It was Sheriff Carlson and another man. When the sheriff saw Wyatt, he started to turn back, but then changed his mind. Seeing an empty table in a corner the two men went to it.

Both Wyatt and Tuck noticed the sheriff's hesitation. Tuck chuckled, "I don't think the sheriff was too thrilled to see two marshals."

Wyatt grinned, "I think you're right. We need to find out who that is with him."

"This is where I live; it's not much but it keeps me dry when it rains," said Jason.

Morgan looked at the shack. "Are you sure? It looks ready to collapse at any moment."

Jason grinned, "It has a few leaks. You just have to avoid those places. If you start a fire, I'll take care of the horses."

"You have a deal."

Morgan went inside. She was surprised how nice the one room shack was inside. The dirt floor was swept. A bunk against the wall had a bedroll on it. There was a table with two chairs in the kitchen area. The table showed a woman's touch with a tablecloth on it.

Ten minutes later, Morgan had a fire going in the cookstove when Jason entered the doorway, which was missing the door. Jason pulled a pot from a cupboard and pumped water in it from the well at the sink. As he put the pot on the stove to heat, Morgan was bent over adding wood to the stove when her badge fell out of her shirt pocket. Morgan grabbed it and quickly put it back in her pocket. She looked up to see Jason staring at her with a sad, disappointed look on his face.

"I never heard of a woman sheriff. Are you going to arrest me? I thought we were friends."

"We are friends. I'm a Deputy U.S. Marshal, and no, I'm not going to arrest you. I don't believe you've done the things they say. I like you and want to help you. Let's get some food cooking and we'll talk about it while we eat."

A look of relief engulfed Jason's face, followed by a grin. "I'm so glad I won't have to shoot you."

"You wouldn't shoot me anyway," smiled Morgan.

While the two ate Jason told Morgan how his father, in a fit of rage, had ran him off from the family ranch in Montana. He somehow found himself in Springfield and went to work as a cowboy on Adam Carlson's ranch, the largest ranch in the county. While working there he fell in love with Adam Carlson's daughter, Jennifer. When Adam found out about his daughter seeing a poor, worthless cowboy he had a fit and ran him off. It wasn't long after that he was blamed for a number of murders.

"Do you think Adam Carlson had anything to do with you being blamed?"

"I have no idea. When he ran me off, I found this place and have been living here since. I'm trying to get Jennifer to run away with me, but she doesn't want to leave her mother. How can you, a woman, help me?"

"I should punch you. What a terrible thing to say to your partner after our run-in with those two outlaws. I'm as tough as any man. Besides, I'm not alone; I have two other marshals here with me. Do you know you are wanted dead or alive?"

"No, I didn't. Now you are scaring me. Are you going to stay the night here?"

"No, she isn't!"

A startled Morgan had her gun drawn and pointed at the doorway where a girl stood.

"Don't shoot her! That's Jennifer!" yelled Jason.

Morgan holstered her gun.

"Who's she?" asked Jennifer loudly.

"She's U.S. Deputy Marshal Morgan Foster," answered Jason.

"A woman marshal? I bring you food and find you with another woman and you tell me she's a marshal."

"Morgan, show her your badge."

Morgan pinned her badge to her shirt.

Jennifer looked hesitant but seemed to accept it and came the rest of the way inside. She was carrying a large sack. She set it on the counter by the kitchen sink. "Here's the food I said I'd bring you."

The rider that followed Jennifer Carlson had

seen enough. He wheeled his horse around and headed back to the Carlson ranch where he reported to Adam Carlson.

"She's at the Crouther's old shack with McBride."

Adam thought for a moment. "Jake, I want you and Bart to be at that shack when the sun comes up. When McBride steps outside in the morning to relieve himself, I want you to kill him. Then take his body to my brother."

Jennifer returned to the ranch an hour after Jake and was busy stabling her horse when her father, Adam Carlson, entered the barn.

"Where you been young lady?" he asked angrily.

"Just out riding, Father."

"Were you visiting that killer McBride?"

"He's not a killer! Someone made all this up!" Jennifer ran to the house and upstairs to her room.

"Are you going to stay here tonight?" Jason asked Morgan.

Morgan thought for a minute, "I don't have my bedroll with."

"I have some extra blankets and there is a second bunk."

Morgan thought some more. Her friends probably heard from the couple they saved that she was with Jason, so they shouldn't be worried.

"Yes, I think I'll stay and look after you."

Jason smiled, "I like the idea of being looked after by you. Just don't tell Jennifer I said that."

Morgan chuckled, "You're just like all men."

It was three in the morning when Morgan woke. The wood in the bunk was half-rotten and something was sticking in her back. Thinking the dirt floor would be more comfortable, she grabbed her two blankets. It was too dark to see where she was going, so she felt her way to a clear place on the floor and went back to sleep.

It was false down, just a faint light on the horizon, when Jason woke. He was half-asleep as he rose to go outside. Knowing the way to the open doorway he wasn't concerned about being able to see inside the cabin. Moving groggily, he tripped over something on the floor and fell on top of it.

"Ugh! You're on my stomach! Get off me before I wet myself!"

Jason got off Morgan, "I was trying to go outside. I didn't see you."

"I got firsts. You're going to have to wait for me now."

"But I got to go!"

"You fell on me. Now I can't hold it any longer. If you step outside before I'm back, I will beat you to a pulp!"

Morgan hurried outside. Seeing the outhouse was partially collapsed, she dropped her pants in the overgrown yard. While she was going, she heard whispering. Knowing someone was watching her she didn't move her head, only her eyes. To get a better look at Morgan, someone had stuck their head out too far from a tree and Morgan saw him. She stood and pulled up her pants. "I hope he enjoyed the view because It's going to cost him his life," she thought to herself.

As she entered the doorway Jason tried to push his way past her. She shoved him back.

"I got to go, get out of my way!"

"Someone is outside and it's not me they want, at least not right away. I think they're here to kill you. Just go over in the corner. I won't look," stated Morgan. "I'm going to saddle my horse and pretend I'm leaving, then I'll slip up behind him."

"Aren't you afraid they'll shoot you?" questioned Jake.

"No, if they wanted to, they would have done it already. Just wait inside."

Morgan saddled her horse, mounted and yelled so everyone could hear, "I'll be back in a couple of hours," and rode off.

"She's getting away," said Bart to Jake.

"We'll wait for her inside, and when she comes

back, we'll have our fun."

"Good idea, Jake, she's a real looker."

When Morgan was out of sight of the two men, she dismounted and tied her horse, Raven, to a tree. She pulled her rifle from its scabbard and walked back towards the men. As she got close, she started moving from tree to tree. She was careful not to step on a branch and snap it, alerting the two men. Now she could see them, but she needed to get closer. She was almost where she felt she needed to be when one of the men heard her coming. He was fast getting his rifle pointed at her and started shooting. The bullet hit the tree next to her, spattering pieces of wood into her eyes. A couple of splinters stuck in her cheeks. She yelled, "Ouch," and moved behind the tree. Now both men were pelting the tree she was behind with bullets.

Hearing the gunshots, Jason rushed from the cabin towards the gun smoke. His only thought was helping Morgan and not his safety. Seeing one of the men, he took two quick shots with his pistol, hitting him. The man dropped his rifle and fell. When the other man saw his partner fall, he turned towards Jason and fired. His bullet nicked Jason's left arm. Seeing her chance, Morgan shot the other man in the back, killing him.

They found both men were dead.

"I know these two. I used to work with them at Adam Carlson's ranch," said Jason.

"Let's load these two on their horses and I'll take them to the sheriff. You need to find a new place to hide out." Morgan thought for a moment. "Maybe I can put you under protective custody. Let's get them loaded on their horses while I think about it."

The two bodies were loaded onto horses and everything was ready.

"This land is so flat there really isn't any place to hide, is there?" questioned Morgan.

"There are some low hills about three miles west of town. Why?"

"Good. Here's what we'll do. I want you to find a place to hide in those hills while I take these bodies to the sheriff and report what happened. Try to hide your trail. When Adam's men don't return, he'll be sending more here. They will probably try tracking you. I'll come get you at dusk. No, I'll come sooner in case you need help. We'll wait until dark, then I'm taking you into town. You'll be in my custody."

"Where are you going to take me?"

Morgan grinned, "To my hotel room."

Jason's mouth fell open.

Morgan laughed, "Don't get excited. You will be sleeping on the floor."

"But your reputation will be soiled."

"I don't know the people of this town, so I don't care. As to my two friends," Morgan shrugged her shoulders, "if they want to think bad of me, that's their problem. Your life is worth more than my reputation and this is the only way I know I can keep you safe."

Jason looked at Morgan with an appreciative look. "You are a special person. I hope the man that captures your heart fully appreciates you."

"Jason, that was sweet. You're pretty special yourself. Twice now you have saved someone without thinking of your own safety by entering a hail of bullets. You are a brave man."

Morgan mounted her horse and was leading the other two horses with the dead cowboys when she yelled, "Get going and watch your back trail. I'll see you soon."

Jason waved at her and thought, "I wish she wasn't so much older than me; maybe I'd have a chance."

Seeing a woman in town leading two horses with dead men over the saddles caught a lot of interest. At least two dozen people followed Morgan. Sheriff Carlson was sitting in a ladderback chair on the wooden porch in front of his office. Seeing a woman wearing a badge, leading two horses with dead men slung over them surprised him and piqued his curiosity to say the least. As the woman got down, he was looking at the dead men.

"These are my brother's men. Did you kill them?" asked Sheriff Carlson in an angry voice as he walked towards Morgan.

"I did. They were shooting at me, so I shot them."

Sheriff Carlson was angry, "I don't believe you! These were good men. You're under arrest. Give me your gun."

"You want my gun, you will have to take it."

When Sheriff Carlson reached for Morgan's gun, she punched him in the solar plexus. When he doubled over in pain and out of breath, using the heel of her right hand, she hit him with an uppercut to his chin. The sheriff fell to the ground. The bystanders clapped and cheered. As he lay on the ground his hand went to his gun. Morgan yelled, "You pull that gun, you are a dead man."

Sheriff Carlson didn't like backing down to a woman, but somehow he knew she would kill him. He moved his hand away from his gun and stood up. To save face he said, "This isn't over."

More clapping and derogative comments aimed at the sheriff angered him even more.

"It seems you are not a very popular sheriff." Morgan turned towards the crowd, "Will someone please get the undertaker?" She saw a man hurry off.

Sheriff Carlson headed to Jeremiah's Stables where he kept his horse. He saddled up and rode to his brother Adam's ranch.

Morgan led her horse two blocks to a clothing store where she bought a black hat and long black duster. She had the owner put everything in a large gunny sack so people wouldn't see the clothing.

While she was shopping, Wyatt and Tuck entered a restaurant called Jimbo's Joint. It was packed. There was one empty table. They hurried to it and took seats. While waiting for the waitress, they realized everyone was talking about a woman marshal that brought in two dead men and beat up the sheriff.

"Now what has she done?" questioned an upset Wyatt.

Wyatt might have been upset, but Tuck sure wasn't. He was laughing his head off. "That's our girl. I told you she was perfect for this job. Morgan has found McBride, rescued an old couple, and killed four men. What have we accomplished? Nothing!" Tuck laughed some more while shaking his head.

"I have to admit, she has surprised me."

"She's one tough woman," grinned Tuck, "we're lucky to have her. Hah, here she comes now!"

Wyatt turned towards the door to see Morgan

entering carrying a sack and her carbine. She leaned the short rifle against the wall and took a seat at their table.

"Did you buy me something?" asked Tuck laughingly.

Morgan ignored Tuck, "I'm starving. I've worked up an appetite this morning."

"We've heard you have been busy," laughed Tuck.

Wyatt got right down to business. "So, who were the dead men you brought in? And more importantly, where is McBride?"

"I have him hiding out. I'm planning on moving him tonight."

"Wait a minute. There's something wrong here. You have taken over. I'm the one in charge; you can't just do things on your own without my approval."

Morgan stared at Wyatt. "I've accomplished a lot; what have you got done?"

Tuck started laughing which angered Wyatt.

The waitress interrupted things.

While the three were eating, Tuck looked into the bag without Morgan noticing, "Nice. Is there a new man in your life?"

"Tuck, leave that alone!" Morgan pushed away from the table and her unfinished breakfast, grabbed the sack and her carbine and hurried out the door, letting Wyatt pay for her food. She slipped the rifle into its scabbard, tied the bag to her saddle horn and was about to mount her horse, Raven, when she saw a bakery across the street. She led Raven over to it and tied him to the rail. Inside she purchased a loaf of bread and some biscuits. Seeing some jerky and hardtack, she bought a dozen of each.

Once outside she put the new items into the large gunny sack and tied the strings. She mounted and rode west.

Back inside the restaurant Wyatt asked Tuck, "Did she say where she was moving McBride to?"

"Nope."

"We need to find someone trustworthy and have them tell us what has been happening in town," said Wyatt.

"That older fellow that runs the stable seemed to be level-headed. I'll talk to him," responded Tuck.

"I think his name was Rick. Let's meet here at noon," said Wyatt.

The Carlson Connected Ranch owner, Adam Carlson, was talking to his foreman, Nick Angle. "It's been six hours. Bart and Jake aren't back so something must have happened to them. I want McBride dead. Do we have anyone that's good at tracking?"

Nick thought for a moment, "John is fair to middling."

"Do we have anyone left that will follow orders and is willing to kill McBride?"

"I don't think so, but I know of a couple men that don't like to work and will do anything for a dollar."

"All right, take John with you and hire those two. Give them fifty dollars each with another fifty after the job is done. Have them start at that shack where McBride was staying. I can't imagine McBride took out Bart and Jake by himself."

Nick found John getting ready to ride fence. "John, I have something else for you to do. Wait for me while I saddle up. We're riding to town."

Morgan had been riding west for forty-five minutes when she saw the grassy low hills. Not knowing where to find Jason, she rode into the hills hoping he would see her. Jason suddenly appeared from around the base of a hill and startled her.

Jason grinned and said, "Follow me."

They rode over a hill and down into a low valley where there was a good size stream. Jason rode into it and followed it downstream in a southerly direction. They stayed in the stream for three miles. They exited the stream on the west side and rode up and over a hill where they stopped.

Jason picked up a leafy branch and said, "I'm going to brush out our tracks."

Morgan watched as Jason went back to the stream and brushed out all their tracks going up the hill.

"Good job Jason. Using the stream and brushing out our tracks it should be hard to find us."

Jason liked getting a compliment from Morgan and grinned like he had won a prize. Jason led Morgan another two miles where he had a camp with some hard-to-find firewood. A small fire was burning with a pot of coffee being kept warm. Jason had found a couple of rocks somewhere and they were placed around the fire for sitting on this cool late September day.

"Have you eaten?" Morgan asked Jason.

"Yeah, I brought some food with from the shack."

"I didn't think of that. I brought some bread and biscuits."

"Bread sounds good. Could I cut off a piece?"

"Sure, help yourself." Morgan handed Jason the gunny sack.

Morgan watched anxiously as Jason opened it.

Jason had a bigtime smile as he asked, "Whoa, what's this? For me?" He tossed his old hat and put on the new black one, then slipped into the duster.

Morgan was smiling, "It's to hide your identity when we walk from the livery to the hotel."

"Do I get to keep 'em?"

"They are all yours."

"You sure are good to me, thank you."

Jimbo's Joint was packed again. All the tables were taken. Tuck hadn't ordered; he was sitting at a table for two waiting for Wyatt. Two rugged-looking men approached. They had scraggly oily hair and filthy clothes that hadn't seen soap and water for a month or more. When they arrived at Tuck's table, he noticed their bad smell. One of the men sat down in the empty chair.

The other said, "I want that chair," to Tuck.

"If you want it, you will have to take it," said Tuck while standing.

The man took a swing at Tuck. Tuck stepped sideways and the punch missed. Tuck kicked the man in the groin. He fell to the floor. He was laying on the floor in a fetal position moaning as his partner rose from the chair he had taken and charged Tuck. Tuck was still off-balance from his kick when the man collided with him, knocking him onto a table with four people. One person at the table was knocked to the floor and the table full of food broke from Tuck's weight. While

Tuck was laying on top of the broken table on the floor, the man started kicking him in the ribs. The slippery food and plates were making it hard for Tuck to get up and he was taking a beating. The man who had been kicked was now up and about to join the fight when Wyatt hit him from behind with the handle of his gun. The man collapsed on the floor unconscious. Wyatt did the same thing to the man that had been kicking Tuck.

Wyatt helped Tuck up. "Thanks Wyatt, but if you had been on time this wouldn't have happened."

"Grab a leg, Tuck and let's drag these two outside." They each grabbed a leg and dragged one outside then came back in for the other. They didn't show any pity for their heads as they banged along. Both were left lying in the street. Jimbo and the waitress were busy cleaning up the mess.

They both sat down at Tuck's table and waited for Jimbo and the waitress to finish cleaning.

"Keep an eye on the door; they might be back," warned Wyatt.

"They will probably backshoot us when we don't expect it," said Tuck.

"You are probably right. What did you find out today?"

"Jim Baxter is the stable owner. He has lived here

for twenty years. What's happening scares him. He said Adam Carlson, who owns Carlson Connected, is trying to take over the town. He's a big rancher with a lot of sway with people. If people don't owe him money, they owe him a favor. Having people indebted to him gives him power and control over others. And when he can't get his way, according to Baxter, he has them killed, such as the previous sheriff. Sheriff Brent Carlson and Adam are brothers. When someone killed the previous sheriff, Adam managed to get Brent appointed sheriff with promises of an election in three months. The three months came and went without any election," said Tuck.

"That about sums up what I found out also," said Wyatt. "I spoke with the owner of a feed store and a clothing store. I never spoke with the mayor because both store owners said he was in cahoots with Adam Carlson. They also told me Jason McBride is only eighteen and was working for the Carlson Connected. McBride and Carlson's sixteen-year-old daughter started sparking, which angered Carlson. He didn't want his daughter to have anything to do with a lowly cowboy. It seems Jason McBride is well-liked and no one thinks he killed anyone. The two business owners suspect Adam Carlson had someone do the killings and made sure McBride was blamed for them," said Wyatt.

"So, what do we do?"

Wyatt pondered for a moment, "Let's wait and see what Morgan does. In the meantime, we keep looking for information."

"And watching our backs."

"That's a good point, Tuck. Besides those two saddle tramps we threw out, both Carlsons would probably like to see us dead."

"Wake up Jason, it's time to go. By the time we get to town it will be close to midnight. Toss your old hat and get your new stuff on."

As the two rode through the large barn door of the livery, Rick the owner saw them. Recognizing Jason, he said, "Hi Jason. Aren't you taking a risk coming to town?"

"Naw, the woman I'm riding with is a federal marshal."

"A woman marshal, interesting. There are two other marshals in town. Maybe with three of 'em here things will get straightened out. I've got your horses. Take care of yourself, Jason."

"You too Rick."

"Jason, pull your hat down and put an arm around me so we look like a couple."

Jason slipped an arm around Morgan and said, "I like this."

"Don't let it go to your head."

"Do you take that rifle with you everywhere?"

"I do."

Seeing the desk clerk in the Bon Homme Hotel with his head on his desk sound asleep, Morgan and Jason walked quietly through the lobby and up the stairs.

As the two walked down the hallway Morgan whispered in Jason's ear, "No talking."

Inside Morgan's room Jason looked around and whispered, "It's going to get cold tonight; I need a blanket."

Morgan glanced around the room. "Just keep your duster on."

Jason grimaced. Morgan pulled off her duster and boots. Jason had laid down on the wooden floor. Morgan looked at him and felt bad. She whispered, "Jason, this is a double-size bed; if you stay on your own side, you can join me."

Jason stood quickly and with a big grin took off his duster and boots and was under the covers quicker than a rattlesnake. Both were wearing their clothes in bed.

Wyatt and Tuck were up at six the next morning and having breakfast at Jimbo's.

"I wonder if Morgan is in her room," commented Tuck.

"No way to tell without knocking on her door

and waking her. If she's there, she got in late and will probably sleep late this morning."

Wyatt and Tuck had been drinking coffee and talking for a couple of hours when Morgan and a stranger entered and came to their table.

"Wyatt, Tuck, this is Jason McBride." Wyatt and Tuck stood and shook hands with Jason.

"You're younger than we had expected," commented Tuck while sitting down.

Morgan noticed the way Wyatt was looking at her. Her Irish temper was about to explode, but before she could say anything Tuck asked, "What are your plans, Morgan? Why did you bring Jason to town?"

"He has nowhere to go. Carlson found out where he was staying and tried to kill him yesterday morning. If I hadn't been there, he'd be dead. I think we need to take him to the county sheriff and put him under the sheriff's protection."

Wyatt and Tuck were thoughtful.

"That's a good idea," said Wyatt, "Sheriff Carlson doesn't have a case against Jason. I think we should talk to the judge and press for a trial to clear his name."

Morgan waved the waitress over. Morgan and Jason gave their order.

With a stern look on his face, Wyatt asked, "Jason, did you stay with Morgan in her room last night?"

Before Jason could answer, Morgan's Irish temper took control of her. She stood and gave Wyatt a look that could kill. She said loudly, "If I want to take a man to my room I will. It's none of your business. I'm sure you have taken women to your rooms many times!"

Everyone in the restaurant heard her. A couple of women looked aghast. Some of the men laughed. Tuck's eyes rolled.

Trying to defend Morgan, Jason said, "I slept on the floor," but no one paid him any attention.

In a huff Morgan stormed out of the restaurant. Not knowing what to do, Jason looked at Wyatt and Tuck, then followed Morgan.

"I hope you didn't get them both killed," said Tuck angrily to Wyatt. "I'll follow them at a distance," said Tuck while rising. He left Wyatt with a sad, confused look on his face.

Tuck hurried to catch up to Morgan and Jason. He followed them into a small café. They were taking seats at a table when Tuck joined them.

"What do you want?" asked Morgan angrily.

"Hey, don't take it out on me. I didn't say anything."

"You were thinking it. How come women are held to a different standard than men?"

Tuck shrugged his shoulders. "For both your protection, let me join you. If Sheriff Carlson sees Jason, there will be trouble."

Morgan nodded her head yes.

Tuck laughed, "I wonder what Wyatt's going to do with all that food!"

Tuck's laugh affected Morgan, so she relaxed and laughed also.

"Jason, where's the county seat?" asked Tuck.

"It's Tyndall, and it's only fifteen miles north of here."

"About a four hour ride then," said Tuck. "Morgan, if I can calm your boyfriend, I'll bring him back and when you two are finished eating we'll ride to Tyndall."

"He's not my boyfriend!"

Tuck grinned, "He worries over you like he is." Tuck stood and was moving towards the door.

"Stay here," Morgan told Jason as she hurried to catch Tuck. She caught his arm and stopped him.

"Tuck, nothing happened last night."

Tuck looked into Morgan's pleading eyes, "It's not like you to make someone sleep on a hard floor. He slept in your bed, didn't he?"

Morgan put both her hands on Tuck's waist and pulled him close to her. "He did, but nothing happened."

Tuck looked into Morgan's wet eyes, "I believe you, and as far as Wyatt is concerned, Jason slept on the floor."

"Thank you, Tuck. It's important to me that you believe me."

"I know. See you in a bit."

After Morgan sat back down, Jason said, "You two are close."

"We're real close. He's my best friend. Tuck has the perfect woman waiting for him in Wichita."

"That doesn't disappoint you, does it?"

"Not at all. I'm incredibly happy for him."

Their food arrived and the talking ended. The two had just started eating when Sheriff Carlson stepped in for a coffee break. Doing as Wyatt always did, Morgan had sat facing the door. The sheriff's eyes and Morgan's met at the same time. Then he saw Jason McBride and his hand went for the gun on his hip. But Morgan was quicker. She had hers out and pointed at the sheriff.

"Sheriff, Jason is in my protective custody. I'm taking him to the county sheriff in Tyndall today."

"And who are you?"

"I'm Deputy U.S. Marshal Morgan Foster."

"I've never heard of a woman marshal! And where's your badge?"

Morgan pulled the badge from her pocket and held it up. "As I just showed you, a woman can pull a gun as fast or faster than any man." She put the badge back into her pocket.

Being shown up by a woman in front of others irritated the sheriff and he stormed outside, slamming the door behind him. As he left, Wyatt and Tuck entered.

They saw Morgan holstering her gun and knew there had been trouble.

"What happened?" asked Wyatt.

"Carlson was going to shoot Jason. I outdrew him and he left."

"She's fast!" exclaimed Jason with a big smile.

"Let's get our horses and get out of town before Carlson tries something else," said Wyatt.

While Wyatt and Tuck were going out the door, Morgan and Jason were wolfing down the rest of their breakfast. Morgan laid a five-dollar bill on the table and hurried to the door followed by Jason.

As they stepped outside and turned in the direction of the livery, Morgan saw two men behind Wyatt and Tuck lifting their rifles into a firing position. Morgan yelled, "Wyatt!" causing one of the riflemen to turn around. The other was about to shoot Tuck when Morgan's bullet hit him in the back. Jason now had his gun out and he shot the other rifleman before he could shoot Morgan. The man Jason shot was still alive and drawing his revolver when Morgan put another bullet in him.

Wyatt and Tuck approached the downed men while Morgan and Jason approached them from the other direction. They were both dead.

"These are the same two fellows we dragged out of the restaurant yesterday," said Tuck.

A crowd was gathering. "Morgan, put your badge on," ordered Wyatt. To the crowd Wyatt yelled, "The three of us are United States Marshals. Everything is fine. I'll give a dollar to someone that will get the undertaker."

A man rushed up with a big smile and held out his hand. Wyatt put a silver dollar in it. "Tell the undertaker he can keep whatever he finds on these saddle tramps."

"Got it," said the man, then hurried to the undertaker.

"Let's go," said Wyatt.

As they walked the rest of the way to the livery stable, Wyatt said, "You both realize if you would have missed you might have hit Tuck and me."

Morgan had a smart retort but decided not to say anything.

"Thanks, you two," said Tuck appreciatively.

As the marshals and Jason were saddling their horses, the stable owner, Rick, mentioned Sheriff Carlson had gotten his horse fifteen minutes earlier and seemed to be in a big hurry.

When Sheriff Carlson arrived at his brother's CC ranch, he tied his horse to a hitching rail outside the large ranch house. Without knocking, he hurried through the front door, slamming it behind him and startling everyone inside.

Adam Carlson left his office with gun in hand running to the front door. "Brent, you just scared the crap out of me and the housekeeper! What's up?"

"Three marshals have McBride and they're taking him to Tyndall. I don't know what they're up to, but they have something going on. If you hurry you can dry gulch them at Indian Hills Gap."

Adam Carlson thought for a moment and said, "Good idea." He went outside and yelled at three cowboys by the corral, "Saddle up and have your rifles." Adam saddled a horse for himself. In five minutes they were galloping north towards Tyndall.

The marshals and Jason were about three miles south of Tyndall when Wyatt stopped. As the other three stopped alongside, Morgan asked,

"What's up?"

Without answering, Wyatt reached back into a saddlebag and pulled out a pair of binoculars. He studied the road in front for a moment. "Jason, tell me about those small hills ahead."

"They are called Indian Hills. Where the road goes through them, they call it Indian Hills Gap."

"How much will it add to our trip if we go around them?"

"I don't know, maybe five miles. I've always stayed on the road."

"We'll go around the east side."

"Five miles. That will add over an hour to our trip," complained Morgan, "and we'll be riding through brush."

"Let's go. We're turning off here," said Wyatt.

"Wyatt is worried about an ambush," Tuck told Morgan.

"Who would ambush us? No one knows we're going to Tyndall."

"Wyatt is a careful man. That's why he lasted more years than most with the Texas Rangers."

While they rode, they munched on the jerky and hardtack that was still in Morgan's saddlebags. Jason even ate the stale biscuits.

It was evening when they arrived in Tyndall, tired and hungry. Seeing a small café, they stopped to eat. They were about finished eating when a man wearing a badge entered. Seeing the badges of the marshals, he went to their table.

"Good evening. I'm Sheriff Green, may I join you?" he asked. As Wyatt started to rise Sheriff Green quickly told everyone to remain seated.

"Sure thing, Sheriff. Grab a chair from another table and we'll make room," said Wyatt.

Jason made room for Sheriff Green by scooting his chair close to Morgan. He gave her a big smile.

"I was told some lawmen were eating here..." Sheriff Green looked at Morgan and frowned. "I never heard of a female lawman...er lawwoman. That doesn't even sound right."

"Lawwoman works for me," smiled Morgan. "I'm Deputy Morgan Foster."

"I'm glad to meet you, Deputy Foster."

"I'm U.S. Marshal Peterson," spoke up Wyatt. "Next to me is Deputy Tucker, he's Tuck to us. The young man next to you is Jason McBride. He's in our custody."

Sheriff Green looked at Jason, "McBride, yes there's a warrant out for him. Why is he eating with you and not in jail or irons?"

"We feel he is innocent and the charges against him are trumped up. Someone did this so no one looks for the real killer," answered Wyatt. "We're here to talk to a judge about having a trial so his name is cleared. We feel the real killers want to kill Jason so there isn't a trial. They know with a trial he will be declared innocent, which will shift the hunt to the real killers."

"Besides that," spoke up Morgan as she put a hand on Jason's shoulder, "he has saved my life and the lives of an elderly couple. He thinks of others before himself."

"Then for his own safety and adherence to the law, he should be in my jail until trial. Judge Walker will be busy in the morning with another trial. He should be free in the afternoon."

Wyatt looked at Jason. "You are right Sheriff. When we finish here, we'll follow you."

Morgan looked at Jason and squeezed his shoulder, "I'll be there with you."

With a sad face, Jason said, "Okay."

After Jason was locked up, Morgan brought her saddlebags and bedroll into the jail and took over an empty cell. After rolling out her bedroll on the cell bed, she said to Tuck, "I'm not leaving here so please bring me some food once in a while."

Tuck smiled, "I'll see to it. Jason is lucky you are so loyal to your friends. I'll take care of Raven for you."

"Thanks Tuck."

"This isn't a hotel!" complained Sheriff Green to Morgan. "By staying here, you are insulting me and my deputies. You're insinuating we can't do our job."

"I don't mean to insult anyone. Just think of me as an extra deputy. I just want to keep my friend company. If I have to leave, then he goes with me."

Sheriff Green gave Wyatt a stern look.

"She's stubborn. It would be a whole lot easier to just let her stay," said Wyatt.

"I want a key to his cell also," said Morgan.

"Why would you want that? To let him out during the night?" questioned Sheriff Green.

"If I was going to help him escape, I wouldn't allow him to be locked up in the first place. It's in case of fire or some emergency."

Sheriff Green reluctantly gave Morgan a cell key.

After everyone had left the cell area of the jail, Jason was standing at the bars between the cells looking at Morgan. "You are a special woman and a great friend. I feel a lot better with you here."

Morgan smiled, "You are special yourself; that's why I'm staying."

As Wyatt and Tuck rode their horses and led Raven to the livery, Tuck said, "Morgan has to be the most compassionate, caring, and loyal person I've ever met."

"I have to agree," said Wyatt quietly.

Adam Carlson decided they had waited long enough at Indian Gap. "McBride must have gone around. Let's head on to Tyndall."

As Adam Carlson and his men road into Tyndall they spotted a saloon. They tied the horses at the rail and went inside. Carlson bought a bottle to share with his hands. After they were feeling their drinks he said, "Jeb, I want you to go to the sheriff's office. Tell whoever is there you're a bounty hunter looking for McBride and ask him if he knows where McBride might be. Then come back here."

Jeb left and was back five minutes later. "McBride is in the jail."

"Good. Mike, ride around behind the jail and see how many windows there are and report back."

Five minutes later Mike was back. "One window in the middle of the building."

Carlson nodded, got up, went to the bar and brought back another bottle.

Carlson checked his watch. It said midnight. It was time. His hands had been sleeping with their heads on the table for the last two hours. He woke them. "Here's what we're going to do. Jeb, I want you and Hal to find a spot across from the jail where you can shoot through the window at the deputy. Don't kill him. Just try to put a bullet in his shoulder. Hal, if Jeb misses, take the shot.

Mike, I want you to ride around back and shoot McBride through the window. When you three are done, meet me outside of town on the road to Springfield."

"I don't much cotton to shooting a lawman," said Jeb.

"Here's a hundred-dollar bonus for tonight." Carlson gave each man a hundred-dollar bill. "When we leave here, we'll ride all the back to the CC. If anyone should ever ask, we never left."

"Sounds good," said Jeb.

"All right, everyone has five minutes to get in place. Mike, you wait until you hear Jeb shoot, then take out McBride."

"Got it boss."

When Mike got behind the jail this time, he realized the window was so high he would have to shoot from his horse. Working his horse close to the wall, he scraped a stirrup against it, making a noise. Then his horse spooked as a cat ran past, causing him to bang his knee into the wall, eliciting a swear word. This was enough to awaken Morgan.

Morgan reached through the bars and grabbed Jason's leg. She squeezed it. As Jason raised his head Morgan whispered, "Someone is outside the window. Get under your bed."

Morgan moved over to the window. It was too

high for her to see out, so she waited. When she saw a gun poke through the bars, she grabbed it and twisted it, breaking someone's trigger finger. The would-be assassin let loose of the gun and galloped away. Then Morgan heard a gunshot and breaking glass. She grabbed her rifle and ran into the office area. A deputy was laying on the floor, holding his bloody shoulder. Morgan ran outside. Seeing two men with rifles getting on horses, she shot at one of them. Missed. She levered in another round and fired again, and again. One of the men fell off his horse. The horse continued alongside the other horse and rider.

Morgan moved quickly to the cells and let Jason out. Back in the office area she asked the deputy, "Is there any clean rags or towels?"

"There's a few towels in that cabinet against the wall."

Morgan grabbed a towel and placed it against the deputy's shoulder. "Hold this tightly."

The gunshots had woken half the town. The first few people to arrive were drunk cowboys from the nearby all-night saloons. Wyatt and Tuck soon arrived.

"What happened?" Wyatt asked Morgan.

"Some men tried to kill Jason. They all got away but one. Come on Jason, let's see if you recognize him."

The man Morgan had shot had a broken neck from falling off his horse.

"That's Jeb Hawthorne. He rides for Adam Carlson," said Jason.

Morgan, Jason, Wyatt, and Tuck returned to the sheriff's office to find Sheriff Green and another deputy there. Wyatt wanted so badly to say something about Morgan staying at the jail. Sheriff Green was quiet about Morgan being there, but Wyatt could tell he was glad she had been there.

"So now what do we do with Jason?" asked Sheriff Green.

"He's still safer in the jail than wandering the streets with us," said Wyatt. "How do you feel about it, Morgan?"

"I agree with you, Wyatt. I'll continue to stay with him, except from now on his cell door won't be kept locked."

"Fair enough," said Sheriff Green.

"Let's go back to bed and see if we can't get back to sleep," said Tuck.

"Sounds good to me," said Morgan.

"I'll take my injured deputy's shift," said Sheriff Green.

Wyatt and Tuck were late getting up the next morning.

"Tuck, let's see if Morgan and Jason have eaten yet. If they haven't, let's take them to breakfast."

"I'm sure they would appreciate that."

When they arrived at the jail Morgan and Jason were still asleep.

"Let's go you two sleepyheads. This is your breakfast posse," yelled Wyatt with a grin.

Morgan woke with a big yawn. "That's nice of you Wyatt. Get up Jason."

When they finished breakfast Morgan and Wyatt took them back to the jail.

"There's nothing for us to do this morning. How about a game of cards?" suggested Tuck.

Everyone liked the idea, so they played until noon, then everyone went for lunch. It was close to one o'clock when they finished eating. All four went to the county courthouse to meet with the judge and the prosecuting attorney.

The marshals told the judge and attorney they suspected a warrant for Jason was a scam with no intentions of taking him in for a trial. It was just an excuse to kill him and end any investigation into the killings.

The judge said he would have the sheriff go to Springfield, investigate the killings and report to the prosecuting attorney. After the sheriff's report, a decision of the matter would be made in a couple of days.

The four talked as they walked back to the jail.

"Sounds like we have a few days off," said Tuck.

"No, we don't. We now have time to do Rothschild's work," said Wyatt.

"I'd forgotten all about that," claimed Morgan.

"What kind of work?" asked Jason.

"Social welfare," answered Wyatt. "A rich man we know wants us to help him give away his money."

"I'll take it," grinned Jason.

"Jason, you live in the area. Who do you know that needs help the most?" asked Morgan.

Jason thought for a while. "Hmm...on the east side of Springfield there is a small group of Dakota Indians. They're dirt poor."

"Why aren't they on the Yankton Reservation?" asked Wyatt.

"I'm not real sure. I've been told they feel the reservation will trap them into the old ways. To succeed they feel they need to learn the white man's ways. Trouble is no one wants to hire an Indian."

"I know that story keenly," lamented Tuck.

When Jason frowned, Morgan told him Tuck was half-Indian. Jason was surprised.

"The trouble with us Indians," said Tuck, "our

pride gets in the way. We want to continue in the old way of dressing and personal hygiene, such as long hair. Too be assimilated into the white man's world we need to look like them. Wyatt convinced me to lose my long hair, headband, feather and buckskins. It worked too. Actually, it wasn't him that convinced me, it was money I could make if I did."

After arriving at the sheriff's office, the four took seats in the jail section and continued their discussion.

"As far as helping the Indians on the reservation, there are too many of them. It would quickly bankrupt Rothschild. We'll let the government continue to care for them."

"It seems to me these Indians in Springfield are going to need more than one handout. Once the money we give them is gone, they'll be right back the way they were," suggested Morgan.

"I agree with you Morgan. I will set up a monthly stipend," said Wyatt. "Maybe Tuck can talk to them about changing their ways. Tuck, how about we leave now? There's enough time yet today to ride to Springfield."

"Sounds good to me."

It was evening when Wyatt and Tuck got to Springfield. They would visit with the Dakota Indians in the morning. They got rooms and stabled their horses.

After eating at Jimbo's Joint they went to the nearest saloon. As they entered, Wyatt noticed the sign next to the door simply read 'Saloon.' They took a table by the rear wall. Wyatt sat so he could see the doorway. A saloon gal in a low-cut dress came and took their order.

Wyatt and Tuck had been drinking and talking for about thirty minutes when Wyatt saw Sheriff Carlson enter. The sheriff's eyes, not being accustomed to the dimly lit saloon, never noticed the two marshals sitting at the rear wall. He went straight to the bar. When Wyatt saw the sheriff stumble, he suspected the sheriff had been drinking for a while.

Sheriff Carlson had only taken a couple of swallows from his glass when he looked at the man next to him and started rambling in a loud voice about the three marshals being in cahoots with the killer McBride. He was pretending to be talking to the man to his right when in actuality he was talking to everyone in the saloon.

"Those phony marshals said they were taking McBride to the county jail in Tyndall, but they never showed. Instead, the gang escaped to rob and kill elsewhere."

"I've heard enough," Tuck said to Wyatt as he was starting to stand.

"Wait, let's hear what else he has to say. Let him dig his hole deeper," Wyatt whispered as he grabbed Tuck's arm and pulled him back into his seat.

"I know this for a fact because I was on the road to Tyndall and they never passed me," said the sheriff even louder.

"Now I've heard enough," said Wyatt as he stood.

Wyatt moved quietly towards the bar. When he was behind the sheriff, he pulled the sheriff's gun from its holster and tucked it into his waistband.

"Wha…" said the sheriff as he turned to face Wyatt.

"So, my gut instinct was right, you were waiting to ambush us at the Indian Hills Gap. When we didn't show, you came back here. We took the long way around. What you don't know is your brother rode to Tyndall and tried to kill McBride while he sat in the jail."

Wyatt grabbed Carlson's badge and yanked it, ripping a hole in his shirt. "You are no longer sheriff and I'm arresting you for conspiracy to commit murder, unlawful activities and anything else I can think of."

"You can't arrest me! I'm the sheriff!"

"Not anymore and I just did. Now let's go."

As they exited the saloon a couple of men clapped. Someone said, "Good riddance."

When they got to the sheriff's office the door was

locked. Wyatt held out his hand. Carlson ignored him. "We can do this the easy way or the hard way, you decide. There's nothing I'd like more than to punch you in the gut."

Carlson then dug in a pocket and produced the key.

After he was locked up Tuck asked, "Should someone stay with him tonight?"

"I don't think it's necessary."

The next morning after breakfast Tuck asked Wyatt, "Shall we take the horses?"

"Tough question. It's a long walk but saddling and unsaddling horses can be a pain. Let's walk; the exercise will do us good."

After walking ten blocks they arrived at the edge of town. Across a large grassy and weedy area were four crude houses. Wyatt and Tuck walked towards the houses. Young, barefoot dirty kids were playing in the dust. Older children were sitting in an outdoor classroom. Wyatt realized they were being taught English. As they moved past the outdoor classroom an elderly Indian approached them.

"Hello, I'm Jeffrey Mathew. What can I do for you?"

Expecting an Indian name, Wyatt was caught off-guard and stuttered for a moment. "I'm United States Marshal Peterson and this is U.S.

Deputy Marshal Tucker, we call him Tuck. We heard there were a few Dakota living in Springfield trying to adopt the white man's ways and wanted to see how you were doing."

The old Indian stared silently at Wyatt for almost a minute before saying, "Look around, does it look like we are doing well? I could tell my name confused you. My Indian name is Red Hawk. We have taken white man's names to help us blend in, but as you can see, we are having much difficulty. No one wants an Indian working for him."

"We might be able to help you," said Wyatt. "Tuck and I will return tomorrow. Until then here is three hundred dollars for food and clothing. Winter is coming."

As Wyatt held out the money the Indian pushed Wyatt's hand away.

Wyatt thought a moment then said, "Don't let your pride make your children suffer. Everyone at some time needs the help of others. This money comes from a rich man that wants to give his money away helping people. Please take this money and get what is needed most."

Slowly a smile appeared on the Indian's face. He reached out and took the money from Wyatt. "May the great spirit smile on you."

"I plan to be back in the morning. We'll talk some more then."

"I will look for you then."

As Wyatt and Tuck walked back to the center of town, they made plans on how to help the Indians.

"Tuck, this afternoon I'd like for you to talk to business owners. Offer them free help for six months. At the end of six months, they must pay the regular rate to keep the worker. During the first six months Red Hawk will pay the Indian worker with money he gets from a monthly stipend."

"That's a good idea. I can't imagine anyone not wanting free labor."

"Hopefully it will be a start for the Indians, but they must wear clean clothes and be neat. While you are doing that, I'll be looking into building four or five new houses for them."

"Lucky Indians," said Tuck.

"They deserve it. We'll meet at Jimbo's at five," said Wyatt.

At five they met again to eat and compare notes.

"Tuck, how'd you do?"

Tuck grinned, "Good. I have a promise from a grain store that is looking for a strong back. A dress shop wants a dress-making apprentice…"

Wyatt interrupts, "A dressmaker apprentice. I never heard of such a thing, but it sounds good."

"And the local bank would like a free teller," the owner's words made Tuck laugh.

"It's a good start. I'll help look tomorrow after our meeting with Red Hawk." Wyatt chuckled, "I guess we shouldn't be calling him Red Hawk. And I almost forgot, we need to feed our prisoner."

"Why don't we let him out? Maybe he'll get himself into more trouble," suggested Tuck.

"You're right. We took his badge away, that's good enough. We do need to find a temporary sheriff before we can leave though."

"Rick the stable owner knows everyone. I bet he'd have a good idea who would make a good sheriff," said Tuck.

"Good idea. Let's go see him right now."

"Hello Rick, we'd like our horses ready at seven tomorrow morning. Yesterday I took Carlson's badge from him and locked him up. Do you have any thoughts on who'd make a good new sheriff?" asked Wyatt.

"That's easy, James Boden. You'd probably find him working at the sawmill tomorrow."

"Thanks Rick. Now let's go let the ex-sheriff out of jail," said Wyatt.

As Carlson was being let out of the jail, he said loudly, "You haven't heard the last of this!"

"Yes, we have because we will be leaving in the morning. County Sheriff Green is taking over this investigation," said Wyatt.

Carlson stormed out the door.

After breakfast the next morning Wyatt and Tuck got their horses from the stable then went back to their hotel rooms and got all their stuff and checked out. After meeting with Jeffrey Mathew, also known as Red Hawk, they would ride back to Tyndall.

As Wyatt and Tuck were riding to the sawmill, Tuck said, "I bet the sawmill could use some free help."

"That's another good idea, Tuck."

The two marshals found James Boden stacking planks. They noted how muscular he was. "He looks like he could handle himself in a saloon fight," quipped Tuck.

"I think you're right. Mister Boden, may my partner talk to you for a minute?" asked Wyatt.

Boden stopped stacking planks and walked over to the two marshals. "What can I do for you?"

"I'm U.S. Marshal Peterson and my partner is U.S. Deputy Marshal Tucker. Rick at the livery said you would make a good town sheriff. Would you be interested in the job? It would be temporary until an election is held."

Boden glanced at the badges Wyatt and Tuck wore. "Pleasure meeting you both. Yeah, I'd like the job. It pays better than this and isn't so physical."

"If I have someone here tomorrow to replace you, would you be able to start right away?"

"Sure. Sounds good," smiled Boden.

"Also, I have started a program to help the town's Indians find work. I'll explain it to you tomorrow. I'd like you to run it."

"The Indians need help. I'm looking forward to hearing about this program."

"The program would also work with an Indian as a deputy," said Wyatt.

"I'm sure that won't work," said Boden.

"Why's that?"

"Because people won't accept taking orders from an Indian."

"Tuck here is Indian and he doesn't have any trouble."

Boden looked at Tuck. "You don't look like an Indian."

"That's right, and that's what you need to accomplish. Making the working Indians not look like they are Indians," said Tuck. "At least where it's not real noticeable."

Tyndall, Dakota Territory:

After a boring day of card playing with Jason in the jail, Morgan decided she would go to a saloon for a few drinks. Jason begged to go along, but Morgan refused. Before entering the Badlands Saloon, Morgan put her badge in a pocket. They had a keg of beer, so Morgan bought a beer and took a seat in a dark corner. She leaned her carbine against the rear wall next to her chair. Every eye in the place had followed her to that corner. Morgan had been sipping her beer and listening to other's conversations when a handsome cowboy of about thirty years of age came to her table.

"Evening ma'am. Would you like some company?"

Morgan looked at the man for a moment. He was nice-looking, clean-shaven, and wearing clean clothes. "Sure, why not? Have a seat."

The cowboy grinned and sat down across from Morgan, "I'm Frank Jessup. Foreman for the Ben Wainwright ranch."

"I'm Morgan Foster of Wichita, Kansas."

"Nice meeting you Morgan. You're a long way from home. What brings you to this cold godforsaken place?"

"Just had to take care of some business up here."

Jessup looked at Morgan's carbine against the

wall. "The way you are armed and dressed it appears to be quite serious business."

Morgan took a swallow of beer, "Nothing special."

"You're an interesting woman. I've never met anyone like you."

A small smile crossed Morgan's face. "I find wearing men's clothing is much more comfortable and easier to get work done."

"Ah, now we're back to your work. What is it you do?"

Morgan's smile got larger, and her eyes sparkled, "Would you believe me if I said I was a Deputy U.S. Marshal?"

Jessup stared at Morgan for a moment, "I don't know. It sounds crazy, but when I look at you, I think it might be possible."

With a sly smile on her face, Morgan asked Jessup, "May I buy you a drink?"

"You are full of surprises. Yes, you may. Kentucky Whiskey."

Morgan glanced at her carbine. She wanted to take it with her but knew she couldn't carry it and drinks, so she left it.

Jessup noticed Morgan's quandary.

As she was standing at the bar waiting for the drinks she had ordered, she felt someone put their hand on her butt. Her first thought was Jessup had followed her to the bar. When she realized it was the fat smelly man standing next to her, she angrily elbowed him in his ribs, eliciting a groan. As she backed away from the bar, she slapped him across the side of his face. When the man laughed it off it angered her even more.

As Morgan was returning to her table with the drinks, she saw Jessup returning to his chair. "If you were going to help me out you were a bit slow," said Morgan with a smile.

"I might have been slow, but you were slow at removing his hand."

"At first I thought you had come up behind me."

"So, what you're saying is, my hand on your fanny is okay."

Morgan only grinned as she took a swallow of the Kentucky Whiskey she had switched to.

An hour later Morgan was feeling the effects of the whiskey when Jessup said it was late and he had to be getting back to the ranch. Morgan said she should be leaving also. Jessup walked Morgan outside and asked, "Do you have a room at the hotel?"

"No."

"I can get us one."

"Okay."

Jessup put an arm around Morgan and walked her to the hotel. When they got to the door Morgan said, "I changed my mind," as she pulled away.

"What'd ya mean ya changed your mind? Ya can't just change ya mind!" Jessup's anger and whiskey were affecting his speech.

"I'm sorry but…"

In a fit of rage Jessup reached out with both hands and grabbed Morgan by her shoulders and pulled her to him. "Then I'll just have you in the alley!"

Whiskey had slowed Morgan's reflexes, allowing Jessup to grab her, but her anger put her mind and body into a fierce response. She swung the barrel of her carbine upward between Jessup's legs with all her might. He fell to the ground laying in a fetal position and groaning in unbearable pain.

Morgan straightened her clothes then walked quickly to the sheriff's office. The deputy sheriff on duty looked at her and asked, "Are you alright?"

She ignored him and went into the jail section. Jason noticed how upset Morgan was and came to her asking, "Morgan, what happened? Are you okay?"

"I'm fine. Leave me alone." She was madder at

herself than at Jessup. She pulled off her boots, rolled out her blankets on the bunk and got under them, facing the wall. Eventually she fell asleep.

Morning, Springfield, Dakota Territory:

After breakfast the next morning, Wyatt and Tuck got their horses from the stable then went back to their hotel rooms and got all their stuff and checked out. After meeting with Jeffrey Mathew, also known as Red Hawk, they would ride back to Tyndall.

When Wyatt told Mathew that construction on five new homes would begin in two weeks and four jobs were available for Indians, he was a smiling happy man. Wyatt told him he needed to find a young woman to learn dressmaking, a strong man to work at the sawmill, a boy or man to work at a grain store and someone good with arithmetic to work at a bank. They all should be wearing nice, clean clothes, especially the person for the bank and the dressmaker.

Jeffrey Mathew asked the marshals to wait while he spoke to different people. It took him over an hour. When he returned Wyatt and Tuck were sitting in the grass while their horses grazed. He introduced the workers one at a time. The first was Betty Thornburg. She was a pretty woman of about twenty. Her dark hair was in two braids down each side of her head. She wore a nice green dress. She was to be the teller. Next, he introduced the dressmaker. Her dark hair was also in two braids. She wore a new blue dress. The two young men looked strong and capable of handling heavy bags of grain or lumber. Their hair was cut short, unlike most Indians. Everyone had smiles and looked happy.

Wyatt said he would take everyone to their new jobs. He also told Jeffrey Mathew to come along to open a bank account while they were at the bank. Mathew asked Wyatt to wait a minute while he went and changed into nicer clothes.

Wyatt and Tuck were leading their horses as they walked with the Indians. As they entered townspeople watched. A couple of cowboys yelled hello and tipped their hats to the two pretty Indian girls. Embarrassed, but smiling, they dropped their eyes to the ground.

The first stop was the sawmill. Next, the grain store. The owner looked at the strong arms on the Indian and looked pleased. He knew with the big Indians around he would get no trouble from the usual troublemakers.

The owner of the dress shop was an older woman who lived by herself upstairs. She took one look at the nicely dressed Indian girl and gave a big smile. "I know we are going to get along just fine," she said with that big smile. "It will be so nice to have someone to talk to while I work. I will be buying us lunch at the café across the street. Thank you, gentlemen."

"You are welcome," grinned Wyatt.

The last stop was the Bank of Bon Homme County. The first thing Wyatt did was open an account for Jeffrey Mathew. Wyatt deposited five hundred dollars into his account. He told Mathew this was not his money, but his people's and he should use it wisely. He could take forty dollars a month out for his own use though. Also, he must pay the workers thirty dollars a month for the first six months until they receive pay from their bosses.

"Money will be put into your account every month; I don't know how much though. The new sheriff will oversee everything and help others to find work," said Wyatt to Mathew. Wyatt then asked to see the bank president. The teller went to an office in the rear of the bank and returned a few minutes later with a pasty-faced, bald-headed man wearing glasses.

"I'm George Mays, president of the bank. What can I do for you?"

"I'm Marshal Wyatt Peterson, my deputy Tuck and this is Jeffrey Mathew. He just opened an account. You will be seeing him regularly. The young woman is Amy Watts. She will be taking the teller position."

The bank president studied Amy for a moment. He then wrote some figures on a piece of paper. "Miss Watts, I want you to tell me the answer to add these two figures." He handed her a pencil.

Amy glanced at the figures and without writing told Mays the answer. Mays was impressed. He wrote down larger numbers. Again, Amy gave the answer without using the pencil. Next, he gave her a long division test. This time Amy used the pencil, and again her answer was correct. Mays had a quizzical look on his face when he looked at Wyatt. Without saying anything he wrote down a difficult multiplication problem. Using the pencil, Amy had the correct answer in half a minute. Mays couldn't contain his smile, "You have the position of teller. I'm sure you will go a long way at this bank."

Amy smiled coyly, "Thank you Mister Mays."

"Tuck, Jeffrey, wait for me outside," said Wyatt. After they had left, he asked Mays, "Do you give all your applicants mathematics tests?"

"Yes, but none as difficult as I gave Ms. Watts. Her intelligence impressed me, and I was trying to stump her. I can see her becoming the head teller quickly. Thank you for bringing her in."

"I'm glad to hear it. Nice meeting you, Mister Mays."

Outside, Wyatt handed Mathew a piece of paper, "Here's my address in case you need any help.

~~Nick~~ James Boden is taking over as sheriff. He will work with you. If you need any help, see him. Tuck, ~~do~~ you have anything to add?"

"Nope."

"Then let's ride to Tyndall and see how much trouble Morgan has gotten into."

Tuck laughed, "Knowing Morgan, I'm sure something happened!"

The two marshals arrived in Tyndall in time for supper but first stopped at the jail to find Morgan and Jason playing cards. As Morgan looked at her two friends a big smile crossed her face. She rose and went to Tuck, giving him a tight hug. "I'm so glad you two are back."

Wyatt looked at Morgan and thought to himself, "I knew it. Something has happened." He then said, "Let's get something to eat."

All four left the jail and walked a block to a café where they found Sheriff Green eating and sat with him.

"I've put the fear of God into Adam Carlson. He knows I'm looking for evidence against him. He won't be any more trouble. I almost forgot; Judge Walker will see Jason in the morning. There's nothing to worry about; all charges will be dropped."

Jason smiled, "Sheriff Green, thanks for all your help. The same to you marshals." Jason was looking directly at Morgan.

When supper was done all four got rooms at the hotel where they had stayed a few days ago. Morgan and Jason had baths in their rooms while Wyatt and Tuck stabled their horses.

The next morning after breakfast, Wyatt sent a telegram to Rothschild and Attorney General Whitaker letting them know their mission had been completed. Wyatt also alerted Rothschild to the arrangement with some Dakota Indians.

An hour later Wyatt and Morgan were being sent to Wyoming about horse rustling. Tuck was sent to Arizona to hunt for a missing boy.

WYOMING

Tuck would be riding the train with Wyatt and Morgan to Cheyenne, where he would take a train south through Denver to Las Cruces, New Mexico, then west to Phoenix.

As usual, Morgan sat next to Tuck behind Wyatt.

"More wooden benches. Why don't they pad these seats?" complained Tuck.

"That man at the front of the car looks comfortable," whispered Morgan with a smile.

Tuck looked towards the front, "I'm sure you're right; he's got more padding than a bear before hibernation."

At a one hour stop for water, coal and passengers, Tuck and Morgan were walking together, and Morgan said to Tuck, "When we get back on, I'm going to sit next to Wyatt."

"Why? I like you sitting next to me."

"Because I don't want Wyatt to think the only reason I'm sitting next to him after Cheyenne is because you have departed for Arizona."

"What difference does it make? He's not nice to you anyway."

"I want to change that."

"Are you still after him?"

"He's just going through a rough time; maybe I can help him through it. Besides, what would Lomasi think if she knew we always sat together?"

"We're just good friends; she wouldn't think anything of it."

"We are that, but Tuck, you don't understand women. You don't ever want to take a chance on losing her. Let's get back on before the train leaves without us."

Wyatt was sitting in the center of the bench seat. Morgan stood looking down at him with a smile, "Well, are you going to move over or make me ride standing in the aisle?"

Wyatt had a surprised look on his face as he slid over next to the window without saying a word. Morgan sat down and said, "Thank you."

It wasn't long before the gentle rocking of the car made Morgan sleepy. When her eyes closed her head fell onto Wyatt's shoulder. He was caught by surprise, but when he realized she was sound asleep he put his left arm around her, drawing her in closer. In her sleep she snuggled up to him.

Tuck saw everything and smiled to himself. Tuck felt the two were meant for each other even if they didn't know it.

An hour and a half later Morgan opened her eyes. When she realized she was curled up on the bench seat with her head in Wyatt's lap and he had an arm laying on her she smiled and closed her eyes and went back to sleep.

While Morgan was sleeping Wyatt had to go to the car's toilet in the worst way, but he didn't want to wake her, so he suffered. When Morgan finally woke, Wyatt said, "Excuse me," and hurried to the toilet at the rear of the car. After seeing where Wyatt went in such a hurry, both Tuck and Morgan laughed.

When Wyatt returned Morgan teased, "Wyatt, that was the best I've slept on a train yet."

At Cheyenne Wyatt and Morgan got off the train to stretch and say goodbye to Tuck. They followed Tuck to the rail corral where he showed the ticket stub for his horse. The saddle was on loosely. Tuck cinched up the latigo. He was getting ready to mount when Morgan grabbed him. "Tuck, you aren't going anywhere until you say a proper goodbye!" Morgan gave Tuck a tight hug and said, "You take care of yourself."

Tuck pushed Morgan away so he could look into her eyes, "I will miss you."

"I'm going to miss you too," said Morgan.

Tuck shook hands with Wyatt, "Wyatt, take care

of her."

"I think it's more likely she'll take care of me," grinned Wyatt. "Watch your back."

Tuck's train wouldn't leave until eight the next morning, so he rode off feeling lonely, looking for a hotel.

Wyatt and Morgan got back on the train and sat in the same seat. The train would take them another hundred miles west to Medicine Bow. From Medicine Bow it would be two hundred miles by horseback to Buffalo.

It was late afternoon when Wyatt and Morgan arrived in Medicine Bow. The town was named after the Medicine Bow River. If not for the transcontinental railroad the small town of less than one hundred people would never been built. The land was flat and mostly treeless. Mountains were way off to the north. A cold wind was blowing, making the thirty-degree temperature feel even colder.

The horses had been unloaded from the stock car and were waiting for them in the railroad's corral. Wyatt and Morgan showed their tickets and collected their horses.

"First thing let's buy some warm clothes, then we'll get rooms," said Wyatt.

"Sounds good, it's freezing. Lucky Tuck got to go to Arizona."

Being only one trading store in town, the prices were high. They bought Sherpa lined coats, beanies with flaps over their ears, extra socks, warmer boots and wool union suits.

"We'll get our supplies in the morning. Let's get rooms and find a place to eat," said Wyatt.

After putting her things in her room Morgan crossed the hall to Wyatt's room. "It's as cold in my room as outside. There's no fire in the stove. I'm going downstairs to see about this."

"Wait up and I'll go with you."

When asked why their rooms were so cold, the clerk simply pointed to the bundles of firewood against a wall. The sign on them said fifty cents apiece.

Morgan looked at Wyatt and said, "You might have company in your bed tonight."

Wyatt was caught off-guard by the comment. Not having any idea what to say he only stuttered.

Morgan grinned, "What's the matter Wyatt, don't know what to say?"

"Let's get something to eat."

Morgan laughed, "That's the best you can do?"

After eating, the two entered the only saloon in town. Besides having a few drinks Wyatt wanted information about the road to Buffalo. Two men were standing at the short bar talking. Two more were at a table. Everyone looked to the doorway as Wyatt and Morgan entered. Wyatt looked around, "Let's go to the bar." Wyatt asked the bartender if he had any beer. The bartender said yes and opened a door to a cold room and drew two beers from a keg. Wyatt and Morgan were pleased to have cold beer.

After buying the two men at the bar drinks, the men became friendly. Wyatt found out it would be a four or five-day ride of two hundred miles to Buffalo. There were two trading posts that had become tiny towns along the way. One was Casper, the other KC. Some were now calling KC, Kaycee.

Wyatt and Morgan learned their biggest danger along the way would be outlaws.

"Why are there so many outlaw gangs in this area?" asked Wyatt.

"Just west of Kaycee is the Hole-in-the-Wall. It's in the end of a box canyon. There's only one way in or out and it would take an army to get past the shooters above the canyon. Kid Curry, Black Jack Ketchum, Butch Cassidy and the Sundance Kid use the Hole-in-the-Wall to hide out. They have cabins, livestock and enough food for the winter."

"I'd heard of Hole-in-the-Wall but never knew where it was," said Wyatt, "For some reason I always thought it was in Missouri."

"Same goes for me," chimed in Morgan.

"Outlaws are always comin' and goin' on the road to Buffalo, so be careful," warned one of the two men.

Hole in the Wall

Hole-In-The-Wall Ranch house Spring of 1898 E. Bezona

Author's note: Notice the similarities of the background between the modern-day picture and the one from 1898. It appears to me the cabin is a bit further in, and the picture is taken from a different angle.

"And Buffalo is no place for a woman," said the other man.

"Why do you say that?" asked Wyatt.

"Even if your woman is wearing pants and a gun, she's a nice-looking woman. Buffalo is a lawless small town; half of the men are probably outlaws. If ya aren't killed on the road and yore woman taken, they'll git her in Buffalo."

Morgan was about to let the men know she wasn't Wyatt's woman, but then she realized she liked being called his woman. Wyatt seemed to ignore the remark.

It was getting late when Wyatt thanked the two men. As he and Morgan walked the block to the hotel, Wyatt said, "Glad we're not wearing our badges. This is no place for a lawman."

"Or a lawwoman."

"Lawwoman, that's not a word. It doesn't even sound right."

"Best get used to it," grinned Morgan in the dark.

Both bought two bundles of firewood. It took each of them two trips up the stairs with their bundles.

Wyatt had a fire going in his stove and was brushing his teeth over the basin when he heard a crash coming from Morgan's room. He grabbed his gun from where he had laid it on the bed and rushed to Morgan's door and tried it. It was locked, so he banged on it.

When Morgan opened the door, Wyatt pushed his way past her looking for someone to shoot.

"Wyatt, what's the matter? You barge into my room with a gun in your hand!"

With a confused look on his face, Wyatt looked around, "I heard a crash. I thought…someone had you. What happened?"

Morgan looked embarrassed as she said, "I stumbled into the chair and fell against the wall."

Wyatt looked at the broken chair laying on the floor by the wall. "How could that happen?"

Not wanting to answer, Morgan stood quietly.

"Well…?"

"I was practicing."

Wyatt gave an exasperated sigh, "I've gotten answers from outlaws easier than this."

Morgan looked at the floor. Without looking up she said, "At night I always practice drawing my gun and swinging my rifle."

"What do you mean swinging your rifle?"

"I pretend I'm in a saloon fight and using my rifle as a club, like Cindy."

"Like Cindy! You'll never be like Cindy!" As soon as the words were out of his mouth, Wyatt regretted saying it.

Tears were flowing as Morgan yelled, "Get out! Get out of my room!" as she pointed towards the door.

Wyatt started to leave, stopped and turned around, "Morgan I…"

"Get out! Now!"

Back in his room Wyatt sat on his bed. Talking out loud he said, "First I hurt Cory, now Morgan. Two people I deeply care for. What's wrong with me?" Wyatt pulled off his boots, crawled under the three blankets and fell into a fitful sleep.

After knocking on Morgan's door the next morning and not getting an answer, Wyatt went downstairs and across the street to the only place in the tiny town to eat. Morgan was sitting at a table drinking coffee with a rough-looking cowboy. Wyatt sat at a different table and gave a waitress his order.

Wyatt was still eating when Morgan and the cowboy got up and left. Wyatt was surprised at himself when he realized he was jealous. He finished his food and left for the livery, thinking he would now be alone on this mission. Seeing another man with Morgan made Wyatt realize how much he cared for her.

When Wyatt got to the livery, he was surprised to find both his horse and Morgan's saddled and ready to go. He looked at Morgan and asked, "Has the liveryman been paid?"

Morgan only nodded.

"Let's get our supplies."

They led their horses the one block to the general store, picked up the supplies and rode north.

Wyatt and Morgan had been riding north towards Buffalo for an hour when they saw two men riding south. Wyatt didn't like the looks of the two and said, "Once we're past them, draw your gun and turn around. If they turn around with guns in their hands start shooting. The one on the west side of the road is mine, the other is yours."

Wyatt saw the lecherous looks and heard the comments the men gave Morgan and he knew they were determined to have her. Knowing he would be their target, as soon as Wyatt had passed the two men, he was drawing his gun and twisting around in the saddle to face them. Sure enough, they also had guns in their hands. As Wyatt was about to shoot, he heard two gunshots and both men fell from their saddles. Wyatt looked at Morgan and saw the smoking gun in her hand.

Morgan looked at Wyatt, "I'm better than Cindy."

Wyatt knew Cindy couldn't have done as well. Leaving the two men lie where they fell, Wyatt and Morgan continued their ride north.

Coming to a creek they stopped and watered their horses and took a break. Morgan pulled a sack of biscuits from her pack. "Wyatt, would you like a biscuit?"

Wyatt was surprised and pleased that Morgan thought to bring biscuits from the café. "Thanks Morgan."

After the thirty-minute break while they were riding, Wyatt said, "You make me a target."

"How's that?"

"It's like Joe said last night, every man that wants you, knows he has to kill me first."

Morgan stared at Wyatt for a minute then said sarcastically, "I apologize for being a woman. If I were born a man, I'm sure we would get along much better."

"That's what you need to do. You need to become a man. We'll both live longer."

Morgan reigned her horse. "And how do you want me to do that?"

"Cutting your hair and losing your...ah figure."

"You want me to cut my hair and tie something around my chest," said Morgan angrily. "Well, it's not going to happen! I'm a woman and proud of it." Morgan gigged her horse and galloped away.

"Stubborn woman will get us both killed." Wyatt let Morgan ride up ahead by herself for half an hour before relenting and catching up to her.

Morgan kept her eyes and face straight ahead, ignoring Wyatt. The never-ending Wyoming wind was blowing hard, making the thirty-five-degree day feel even colder. Morgan was looking forward to crawling in her bed roll with extra blankets.

The next morning Wyatt found Morgan with her head hidden, buried in blankets. He left her alone as he built a fire and started breakfast and coffee. The smell of coffee and bacon frying got Morgan up. She was pleased to find Wyatt had biscuits baking in the small Dutch oven. As they were eating Wyatt baked more biscuits to save for lunch.

As the two rode, the cold wind stopped, and the day warmed. Coats came off and were hung over saddlebags. The warm weather put Morgan in a fine mood, "Wyatt, thanks for the good breakfast."

"My pleasure."

At noon they stopped to rest the horses near a creek. After watering the horses, they loosened cinches and hobbled them in a grassy patch close to the creek. They were eating the leftover biscuits and jerky when three grizzled rough-looking bearded older men, also riding north, stopped. For a whole minute they only stared at Wyatt and Morgan.

Wyatt knew they were trying to decide it they could kill him and take the woman and their supplies. He said forcefully, "You are outmatched, now get on your way."

Without a word one rider turned his horse and continued north; the other two followed.

"With them ahead of us, we will need to be more alert," said Wyatt.

"It would have been better if they'd tried something," said Morgan, "then we'd be done with them."

Surprised at her confidence, Wyatt looked at Morgan. She had done well alongside of him against the two men, but it wasn't a true test of her capabilities. The city marshal in Las Vegas had high praise for her. Wyatt hoped she was as good as portrayed by the marshal and Morgan's confidence.

Ten minutes later they were again riding north. Both studied every potential ambush site. Wyatt knew he'd be the one to be shot. Three rifles would blast their deadly missiles at him. The stress was wearing on Wyatt. Seeing a good place to spend the night off the road a ways to the east, Wyatt called a halt. It would be a cold camp, only eating jerky and hardtack. Wyatt didn't think they needed to take turns on watch.

It was morning of the last day of their trip. The two stopped on a high point of the road. Wyatt studied the terrain. To avoid an ambush, he decided they would ride parallel to the road, on its west side. Riding through the brush would be slower, but the terrain looked suitable.

They had been riding for two hours when Morgan spotted three horses tied to a tree. Wyatt reached back and took his spyglass from a saddlebag. After studying the area, he said, "Those three men are hidden from the road with their rifles pointed at it, waiting for us."

"They were going to shoot us down in cold blood," exclaimed Morgan.

"You mean shoot me then take you."

"As long as I have a gun, they wouldn't have taken me alive."

"They would wait until your gun was empty."

Morgan knew Wyatt was right. They would have gotten her. She dismounted, tied her horse to a scraggly tree and pulled her rifle from its scabbard. "Are you coming?"

"I'm not one to shoot men in the back."

"You know they have killed in the past to get what they have wanted and will continue to prey on innocent people. How many other women have they taken this way? They need to die. If it makes you feel better, you can warn them first, and hope they miss when they shoot at you."

Wyatt was surprised at Morgan's cold thinking, but he knew she was right. He tied his horse to the same tree. The two snuck from tree to tree and rock to rock until they were in rifle range. They stopped about fifty feet apart from each other.

"I have the one on the right," said Morgan as she rested her rifle on top of a large round rock. Wyatt aimed his rifle at the one on the far left. He waited for Morgan to shoot, then fired just after her. After shooting the first two, they both swung their rifles to the man in the middle and fired.

Morgan was starting to walk towards the downed men when Wyatt said, "Wait. Get back behind the rock. Let any wounded bleed out."

They waited fifteen minutes then moved forward.

"This one was waiting for us to come close. See how he's holding a pistol after dropping his rifle? It's a good thing we waited."

"Are we going to bury them?" asked Morgan.

"Even if I had a shovel, which I don't, I wouldn't bother. The buzzards and animals can have these vermin. Let's take their guns and horses." Morgan hung the three gunbelts from her saddle horn. Wyatt tied the three rifles inside their scabbards alongside his bedroll. Extra ammunition was put in their saddlebags.

The town of Casper was the halfway point. They got rooms, much needed baths and a good night's sleep. The next morning, they restocked and were on their way.

Two days later they were entering Buffalo. Seeing a livery stable on the edge of town, the two stopped.

The liveryman met them just outside the large door. "I'm Wallace. What can I do for you?"

"These three horses and tack are for sale," replied Wyatt.

"You have three saddled horses for sale. That tells me they're stolen."

"Not stolen. Just taken from three ambushers that have no need of them anymore."

A small smirk showed on Wallace's face, "I'll take 'em. What are ya going to do with those extra guns?"

"Sell them to a gunsmith," answered Wyatt.

"No gunsmith in town. I know someone that will want them. I'll take the lot for eighty dollars."

"They're yours for a hundred."

"Wyatt, I want to keep one of these pistols and belt," spoke up Morgan.

"One less handgun, but I still want a hundred," declared Wyatt.

Wallace grimaced, "I need to be able to make a profit. Take it or leave it, there's nowhere else you can sell them."

"Okay, you have a deal."

"Does the town have a hotel?" asked Morgan.

"No, but Nancy Boarding House is on the north edge of town."

"How far is it?" asked Wyatt.

Wallace grinned, "Within walking distance. Just two blocks."

"In that case, how much per day for our horses?"

"Dollar a day per horse."

As Wyatt and Morgan walked, they noticed gaps between some buildings and a couple of empty ones. When they came to the 'Pig Pen Saloon,' Wyatt stopped, opened the door and looked inside. The bartender and two patrons looked at him. Wyatt backed out, closed the door and said, "It's not much."

Seeing a sign reading, 'Nancy's Boarding House,' they went to the door and knocked. An elderly woman answered, "I'm Nancy. Are you interested in a room?"

"Hi, I'm Wyatt. Yes, two rooms please."

"I only have one room available."

"We'll take it."

"No, you won't. I'll not have a man and woman living in sin in my house."

Nancy was closing the door when Wyatt put his foot in front of it. "We're married. This is my wife, Morgan."

"If you are married, why did you ask for two rooms?"

"We've been fighting so I thought two rooms would be better."

"I think you are lying. Now take your foot from the door."

"Ma'am, we've been five days on the road from Medicine Bow. We're tired and dirty and badly need a place to stay. We should be staying for a week. I will pay you double."

The woman thought for a moment. "I charge two dollars a day per person. That includes breakfast and supper. Breakfast is served at seven. Supper at six. If you are late, you miss out. I won't hold a meal. Baths cost twenty-five cents. I want two days paid in advance. That would be eight dollars, but for you it will be sixteen."

Wyatt paid her. "I would like a bath as soon as possible for my wife. I will use her water when she has finished."

As Nancy took the quarter, she studied Wyatt a moment. "I don't want any foolishness taking place in my bathtub."

Morgan chuckled, "Believe me ma'am, there won't be!"

"The bath will be ready in twenty minutes. I almost forgot; I do laundry. I charge by the amount. Come and I'll show you to your room. Boots and shoes stay here at the door."

Wyatt and Morgan took off their boots. Nancy looked at their dirty socks and made a face.

The room was nicely furnished with furniture and carpeting, giving it a comfortable look. It was a corner room with a window on both outside walls. Wyatt and Morgan both looked at the large bed then gave each other a stony look. If Nancy noticed, she didn't say anything.

After Nancy had left, Morgan said sternly, "You're sleeping on the floor."

"You didn't make Jason sleep on the floor."

"I liked Jason. He was a sweet boy. Besides this floor has a carpet."

Wyatt looked at the floor, then looked longingly at the bed. "I wish we got along better."

"So do I." Morgan got busy pulling her dirty clothes and last change of clean clothes out of her saddlebags. She then sat in a chair and pulled off her dirty socks. Seeing Wyatt looking at her dirty feet she said, "Don't you have anything to do?" embarrassing Wyatt. He quickly got busy taking things from his saddlebags.

After a knock on the door someone announced the bath was ready.

Morgan grabbed her things and said, "I'll hurry so you have warm water." Inside the bathroom Morgan saw a clean towel and a place for dirty clothes. She got undressed and into the bathtub. After washing herself she leaned back, enjoying the hot water. She knew she should get out right away, but the hot water felt so relaxing. Twenty minutes later she was dressed in clean clothes and feeling good. She found Nancy in the kitchen preparing supper. "I spent too much time in the bath. Could you please get another bath ready?"

Nancy yelled, "Hattie, we need another bath."

A girl of about fourteen appeared. "Yes Mrs. Berkshire."

"Please get another bath ready."

Back at their shared room Morgan told Wyatt, "I spent too long in the tub. It'll be another twenty minutes before your bath is ready."

Wyatt also enjoyed a long bath. When he got back to the room he found Morgan gone. Thinking the only place she could be was the Pig Pen Saloon, he went there. As he was about to enter, a man with a smashed bloody nose came out asking where a doctor was. Wyatt told him he didn't know. Inside, Wyatt saw a man lying on the floor unconscious. Someone was bending over him. Seeing the saloon was full, Wyatt realized it was Saturday night. He saw Morgan sitting at a table playing cards with two men.

With a bad feeling, Wyatt went to the bar and ordered a beer and asked what happened.

"See that woman over there playing poker? She gave those two over there," the bartender pointed at the unconscious man and the one next to him, "and the one that just left, a lesson on manners."

"How did she do that against three men?"

"She was a whirlwind with that short carbine next to her. She used it as a club and a spear as she spun, punched and jabbed. That's quite a woman."

The bartender left to take care of someone else. Wyatt watched Morgan play as he sipped his beer. She was smiling and winning. When it was five-forty-five Wyatt went to Morgan's table.

"Nancy will have supper ready in fifteen minutes. We should leave."

Morgan looked up, smiled and nodded. "I'll be back in an hour boys."

"In case you don't make it back I just wanted you to know I had fun losing to you," said a man across the table from Morgan.

"Thank you, Mike," said Morgan with a nice smile

as she rose.

Wyatt and Morgan stepped down the steps from the saloon into the street. Wyatt's peripheral vision caught movement to his right. The man with the smashed nose was drawing his gun, so Wyatt went for his. But before his gun cleared leather there were two rapid shots and the man fell. Wyatt looked to his left to see Morgan's pistol pointed at the downed gunman as she walked towards him. She kicked the gun from his hand. He wasn't breathing so she assumed he was dead. In the meantime, a crowd was gathering.

"Is there an undertaker in town?" asked Wyatt.

"I'm an undertaker," said a man out of breath from running to the shooting. "I heard the gunfire and figured there would be work for me."

"Whatever you find on him is your payment," said Wyatt.

Knowing the gun and holster alone would be worth ten times what he usually charged, he had a huge smile.

As the two continued to Nancy's, Wyatt said, "I'm impressed with your alertness and shooting."

"Thank you. Men aren't the only ones that can have fast reflexes."

"You are right. We men sometimes are blind and stupid."

Morgan slipped her arm around Wyatt's, surprising him. Seeing his surprised look, she said, "We need Nancy to think we're married."

Thinking he would be allowed to sleep in the bed tonight, Wyatt smiled to himself.

At Nancy's they washed up and joined four other people at the large table. A respectable looking man of about forty was sitting across from Wyatt. Curious about Wyatt, he introduced himself as James Beeker, a horse purchaser for a horse racing association back east and asked Wyatt what brought him to Buffalo.

"I'm Wyatt. My wife, Morgan, and I are also here to look at horses, so I guess we're in competition with each other."

After supper Morgan wanted to continue playing poker so Wyatt accompanied her back to the saloon. After watching her from the bar Wyatt realized Morgan was an expert poker player. Her style of play and her sex made it difficult for men to realize her winning was more than a simple lucky streak. Wyatt realized Morgan was good at reading faces, a skill that was greatly needed in law enforcement. When the pile of cash in front of Morgan started to disappear, Wyatt was surprised.

After losing all her winnings Morgan stood, "Gentlemen I've enjoyed tonight, but now it's time for my beauty sleep. Maybe I'll see you again tomorrow night."

"Beauty sleep? You certainly don't need that," said one of the players.

Morgan smiled at the man, "That's sweet of you Jim, but I'm tired."

As she walked past Wyatt she said, "Let's go."

Their first stop was the outhouse behind Nancy's boarding house where they took turns. When they entered the house, they pulled off their boots at the entrance and walked in their stockings to their room. The kerosene lamp in the hallway let enough light into their room to see where they were going. Wyatt lit the lamp on the nightstand. Morgan grabbed her cup and toothpowder and went to the bathroom. Filling her cup from the large jug of water, she brushed her teeth and spit into the basin.

When she returned to the room Wyatt left to brush his teeth. While Wyatt was gone Morgan took off everything but her drawers and got into bed.

Wyatt returned to find the lamp turned down low and Morgan in bed. He didn't know what to do. He knew he had to undress first so he did that. After looking at his bedroll for a second, he blew out the lamp then pulled the blankets back on the bed and was about to get in when he heard the loud click of a gun hammer being cocked. The fear in his voice was very evident as he said, "Wait! Morgan, don't shoot!" He jumped back from the bed. "Careful, that gun has a hair trigger!"

"Yes, it does! The nerve of you! You thought you could share my bed without being asked. And you, the one that insinuating I was a wanton whore to let Jason share my bed when I felt sorry for him sleeping on the floor. You didn't believe me when I told you nothing happened. I do my best to be thoughtful of others. Like tonight, I could have taken those men for every dollar they had, but I didn't. They were family men and shouldn't have been gambling. I was only playing because I enjoy the game. I let them win their money back. The next time you try to crawl into bed with me I won't be playing games like little Cory."

"I didn't get into her bedroll, she got into mine!"

"You expect me to believe that after what you just tried to do!" Morgan knew Cory had crawled into Wyatt's bed and had fun threatening him with her knife, but she wasn't going to give any quarter to Wyatt. When she heard Wyatt expel the breath he had been holding, she smiled to herself. She knew she had taught him a lesson.

The next morning Morgan scooted over in the bed to look down at Wyatt's bedroll. It was empty. Morgan grinned, "I bet he didn't sleep a bit."

Expecting it to be a cold day, she put on her men's union suit then her pants and shirt. She found Wyatt in the dining room drinking coffee. She smiled at him and said, "I slept great last night, how about you?"

Wyatt turned away and looked out the window.

When they finished eating, they got their guns and collected their horses from the livery. They told Wallace they would be back in a few hours.

"What's the first place we're going to?" asked Wyatt.

"It's the Triple T. It's owned by Tom Tillerman. Supposed to be two miles north."

"Where did you get this information?" asked Wyatt.

"Mike. One of the guys I was playing poker with. He has a cattle ranch."

The house Wyatt and Morgan rode up to was small and plain. The barn was also small compared to most barns. A man of about twenty-five came out of the front door holding a shotgun. He quietly looked Wyatt and Morgan over. "What can I help you with?"

"I'm U.S. Marshal Wyatt Peterson, my partner is Deputy U.S. Marshal Morgan Foster. We're investigating a complaint of stolen horses." Both Wyatt and Morgan showed their badges, then put them back into their pockets.

"I had two of my best horses stolen last night. One was a stallion, the other a breed mare. By the way, I'm Tom Tillerman."

"Did you follow the tracks?"

"Yep, followed them out to the road where they mixed in with all the other tracks. They could be anywhere."

"It sounds like the thieves were after your most valuable horses," surmised Wyatt.

"Yep, that's what they got. I can't afford to lose those two."

"Show me their tracks."

"Last night I had them in the dirt lot just behind the barn."

Wyatt got down low and studied the tracks, looking for any identifying characteristic. Not finding anything he followed them through the gate where they met up with another set of tracks. Wyatt studied these and saw a nick on the left rear shoe. He stood, "We'll let you know what we find out. By the way don't let anyone know we're U.S. Marshals. We don't want anyone to know an investigation is going on."

"You got it."

"One more thing," mentioned Wyatt, "if you were the thief where would you hide horses until you could move them?"

"Hole-in-the-Wall."

"That's too far. There must be a place around here they would keep them before moving them to Hole-in-the-Wall."

Tom shrugged, "I dunno, but without those two horses I'll lose my ranch."

"Have there been any strangers around lately?" asked Morgan.

Tom thought for a moment, "No…wait. Yes, someone was here last week wanting to buy top of the line horses."

"Was his name James Beeker?" asked Morgan.

"Yeah, that was him."

As Wyatt and Morgan returned to their horses, they saw a young mother with two little children standing on the porch.

"Where's the next place?" Wyatt asked Morgan as they were riding down the lane to the road.

"Another mile further north. A single woman named Darcy owns it."

As they approached Darcy's place, they saw a woman digging up potatoes and putting them in a burlap bag. When she saw them, she dropped a potato and pulled the pistol on her hip and walked towards the two riders, her gun pointed at the ground.

Wyatt showed his badge, "Hello ma'am, I'm U.S.

Marshal Wyatt Peterson. With me is Deputy Marshal Morgan Foster. We're investigating horse thefts in the area."

Morgan noticed the way Darcy stared at Wyatt. "I'm Darcy Higgins. I breed horses but none of mine have been taken."

"Has anyone been around looking to buy horses?" questioned Morgan.

Darcy never took her eyes off Wyatt as she answered, "No."

"Any strangers?" asked Wyatt.

"None."

"Thanks, we'll be letting you get back to your work," said Wyatt.

"Wait," said Darcy, "I was about to fix something to eat, would you like to join me?"

"Yes, that would be nice," replied Wyatt.

After they had entered the well-kept house, Darcy said, "Make yourselves comfortable while I get out of these dirty coveralls."

Wyatt and Morgan took seats at the dining room table. They both noticed how clean and well-appointed the house was.

"It was nice of Darcy to invite us, don't you think?" asked Wyatt.

Being suspicious of Darcy's motives, Morgan did not reply.

Darcy chatted happily through the entire lunch about her ranch and horse breeding. She spoke of everything but why she was running a horse ranch alone. Morgan did not think Darcy looked her way once the entire time, instead focusing on Wyatt, who seemed to enjoy the attention.

With the meal over, the three were sitting in the main room having coffee. When Wyatt went outside to use the outhouse, Darcy asked Morgan, "Is there anything between you and Wyatt? What I mean to ask, are you two a couple?"

Morgan shot daggers at Darcy. After flirting with Wyatt all through the meal she now asks if there is anything between Wyatt and her. After what seemed like minutes to Darcy, Morgan answered, "No, there is nothing between us." It was at this time that Wyatt closed the door behind him. Morgan wondered if Wyatt had heard her.

"Wyatt, we need to be going. There are more people we need to talk to."

"But we have lots of time." Noticing Morgan's icy stare, he capitulated, "I guess you're right. Darcy, it's been nice meeting you. We're staying at Nancy's Boarding House. If anything comes up be sure to come see me."

Morgan noticed Wyatt had said, "Come see me," instead of "Come see us."

The owners of the next two ranches said they did have breeding stock stolen. Morgan noted both ranches had been visited by James Beeker. She didn't think Wyatt caught the coincidence; his mind was probably on Darcy.

While having supper at Nancy's, Morgan smiled and asked, "Mister Beeker, did you purchase any horses today?" Morgan watched Beeker's face intently.

Beeker didn't answer right away. Morgan didn't understand the look on his face when he returned her smile and said simply, "Not today." Morgan wondered why he didn't ask how their day had gone.

Beeker stood up and said, "Please excuse me, I have a meeting to attend." He grabbed a coat hanging by the front door and left.

Morgan started to get up to follow him when she saw Wyatt shake his head sideways, so she sat back down and finished her meal.

After supper Morgan went to Nancy and said, "I noticed an empty place at the table tonight. Did someone leave?"

"Yes, Mrs. Sims had been visiting relatives here. She went back east."

"I'd like to rent her room."

"It has been cleaned and clean sheets are on the bed, so it's ready for you."

"I'm staying where I'm at. I'll tell Wyatt to move."

Nancy laughed, "I can tell you're the one in charge."

Morgan found Wyatt in their joint room. "Wyatt, why didn't you want me to follow Beeker?"

"Waste of time. He's not a rustler."

"How do you know?"

"After dealing with outlaws for years I just know."

"We'll see. I'm tired. I'm going to take a bath then go to bed. I rented a room for you. See Nancy, she has it ready for you." Morgan noticed Wyatt's surprised look.

Wyatt looked Morgan in her eyes, "Sleeping on a bed tonight will be wonderful." Wyatt shoved all his things into his saddlebags and left without another word.

The next morning after breakfast Morgan asked Wyatt, "What do you have planned for today?"

"First thing we'll talk to Wallace at the livery. He's a horse man, so he might have some ideas as to who is stealing horses and where they may be keeping them."

"After that?"

"I don't know. You have any ideas?"

"No. It seems we have to catch this thief in the act."

"You're right. One of us should be at the Higgins

ranch all the time."

"You'd like that wouldn't you, Wyatt."

"What does that mean?"

Morgan shrugged her shoulders, "A good-looking, single woman with a profitable ranch…"

"I admit I was a bit taken by her in the beginning but not anymore. Besides, she can't hold a candle to you."

Morgan was taken aback, and it showed on her face as she whispered, "That's the last thing I expected you to say."

Wyatt moved close to Morgan, put his arms around her and kissed her. Morgan's heart was pounding as she returned the kiss. When Wyatt pulled away, she almost collapsed. Morgan noticed Nancy standing behind Wyatt with a smile on her face. Embarrassed, Morgan rushed out the front door.

Wyatt followed her out and said, "You might want these."

Morgan turned to see him holding her boots. She looked down at her feet and laughed. "Thank you," she told him as she took the boots from him and pulled them on.

As Wyatt and Morgan approached Wallace's livery, they both noticed a fourteen-year-old boy talking to Wallace. The boy mounted a horse and galloped away.

"I think it's time for us to wear our badges," said Wyatt.

When Wallace saw Wyatt and Morgan coming towards him wearing badges, he became agitated. He tried to hide it with an overdone, "Good morning to you two." Wallace squinted at the badges. "You both are marshals?"

"Good morning Wallace. Yes, we are. We're here to ask you a few questions about the horse rustling that has been going on around here."

"I wouldn't know a thing about that," Wallace answered quickly.

"If you were to steal someone's horses, what would you do with 'em?"

When Wallace tried to answer he stuttered, then finally said, "I'd hide 'em somewhere until I had what I wanted, then sell 'em to the outlaws at Hole-in-the-Wall."

"Outlaws pay good money for the fastest horses they can get, don't they?" asked Wyatt.

"I imagine they need fast horses to make their getaways," replied Wallace.

"Would you have any idea where a person would hide horses before taking them to Hole-in-the-Wall?"

Wallace scratched his head then said, "No idea at all marshals."

"Thanks for your help. We need to talk to someone else and would appreciate your helping us saddle up."

"Sure thing."

Fifty minutes later Wyatt and Morgan were at Darcy Higgin's ranch.

"Good morning Ms. Higgins," said Wyatt.

"Good morning…Marshal." She looked quickly at Morgan. "You are both U.S. Marshals? A woman?"

"Yes, we are both U.S. Marshals. We were sent here to investigate the horse rustling. Is everything still okay here at your place?"

"It's great. Yesterday I sold four of my best horses. I only kept a breed mare so I'm not much worried about rustlers. Wanting to improve my breeding stock, I ordered an Arabian stallion. He should be here in a couple of weeks."

"Who did you sell your horses to?" asked Morgan.

"That same fellow you mentioned to me, James Beeker."

"I wonder why he didn't say anything last night when I asked him," questioned Morgan.

"We need to go and talk with Wallace some more," said Wyatt.

"Wallace? I think Beeker is the man we need to ask the hard questions."

"Beeker is not the man we want; he paid for

horses yesterday when he could have stolen them. I have a gut feeling about Wallace."

"I am confused about Beeker, but Wallace seemed like a nice man to me."

As the two marshals approached the livery, Wyatt said, "I'm going to go hard on Wallace. I think he will break easily. Please stay out of it."

"Back already?" asked Wallace.

"Yep. We found out all we needed to," replied Wyatt. "Let's take care of these horses then I'll take you to dinner."

Wallace had a suspicious look on his face. "Why do you want to do that?"

"Just to have a talk with you. How's the food at Alice's Café?"

"Good. Alice is a great cook."

With three doing the work it didn't take long to put the tack away and brush the horses.

Through the whole meal Wallace kept waiting for Wyatt to say something but he never did. When they finished eating Wyatt said, "Let's go to the Pig Pen and have a drink."

Wallace had a worried look on his face as he said, "Sounds good."

Being early afternoon in the tiny town only a couple of saddle tramps were in the saloon.

"Morgan, take a table while I get a bottle."

Wyatt paid for a bottle. He brought it and three glasses to the table and poured two fingers in the three glasses. For the first thirty minutes it was small talk until the bottle ran out. Wyatt got another. Wallace was loosening up and telling jokes and laughing. Wallace was quite inebriated; Wyatt knew it was time.

In a friendly manner Wyatt asked Wallace, "Where did ya hide the horses?"

Without thinking Wallace said, "North Ridge."

As soon as he said it, Wallace's head dropped to the table in despair. Morgan gave a surprised look to Wyatt.

"Where's North Ridge?" asked Wyatt.

When Wallace raised his head, Morgan noticed his wet eyes and scooted her chair next to him. "Just five miles west of here. The horses are in a nice grassy canyon."

"I know you had a good reason for taking them; what was it?"

"I did it for my wife Beth. She has consumption and paying Doctor Barkley to come all the way from Medicine Bow is expensive. Now he says she needs to go to a warmer, drier area. He told me I need to take her to Arizona, but we don't have any money." By now tears were rolling down his cheeks.

Morgan put a reassuring hand on his shoulder and said, "We can help you," which exasperated Wyatt as he sighed loudly.

"Morgan, you are talking out of turn."

"He hasn't hurt anyone! We can fix this!"

"Morgan, your concern and thoughtfulness for others is affecting your judgment and legal responsibilities."

Seeing Morgan's pleading facial expression melted Wyatt. "With that being said, yes, I think we can help him."

Morgan grinned, "Hah, I've got you Wyatt!"

"Don't push it," said Wyatt with a grin. "Wallace, tell us how you took the horses. Did anyone see you? Did anyone get hurt?"

"My boy Jessup did all the rustling. He knows horses as well as me and knew which ones to steal. He claims no one ever saw him."

"Was that your boy we saw you with this morning?" asked Morgan.

"Yes."

"I noticed he wasn't armed. Does he have a gun?" asked Wyatt.

"No, he doesn't have a gun. He thought he needed one to steal horses, but I told him a gun would just get him or someone else killed."

Wyatt took a swig of whiskey and was quiet for

a few minutes while he thought. "Here's what I want you to do. Have Jessup quietly return all the horses to their owners at night. If no one is missing property, they can't claim theft. When he has all returned, come find me. If it works out, no one needs to know you were involved."

A large smile took the place of the tears on Wallace's face as he thanked Wyatt and Morgan.

"Wallace, there's something else Wyatt will do for you, isn't that right, Wyatt?"

"Morgan, you're out of turn again, but yes there is. If you get everything accomplished without anyone the wiser there is something I can do to help your wife." Wyatt looked at Morgan, "Now are you happy Morgan?"

Morgan winked at Wyatt, "Yes, I knew you would do what's right. Thank you, Wyatt."

Wyatt let a big breath exhale, "Morgan, you're just too much for me."

Morgan had a seductive smile as she said, "We're only just starting to get to know each other."

"That's what scares me."

Two days later Wyatt and Morgan were riding south to Medicine Bow. Riding with them for security rode James Beeker, leading the four horses he had bought from Darcy Higgins. He had explained he thought it best to be quiet about the purchase because they were looking for horses also and he didn't want to make them feel badly. Also in the group was Wallace, driving a carriage with his thin wife. He had given his business away to a young, industrious cowboy. Jessup was on his horse riding alongside the carriage.

ARIZONA

From Cheyenne Tuck took a train south through Colorado to New Mexico. From New Mexico he took a train to Phoenix. From Phoenix he would ride horseback the twenty-three miles to Fort McDowell.

After tiring of looking at the scenery going by, Tuck had nothing to do but think about how his life had changed. He'd come a long way from being a drunken half-breed. He now had good friends, nice clothes and money. He was curious why a Deputy United States Marshal was needed to hunt for a missing boy.

Tuck arrived in Phoenix early in the afternoon. The telegraph office was in the train depot, so he telegraphed Attorney General Whitaker as he had been instructed. He left word he would be at the Phoenix Hotel.

When Tuck returned to his room after his bath down the hall, he noticed a telegram had been slid under the door. He picked it up and opened it and laid on his bed to read it. As he was previously told, he was ordered to Fort McDowell where he was to meet with Captain Mathew. It would be a twenty-three-mile ride taking almost a full day, so he would wait until morning to leave. Apaches were still waring, so he knew he would have to worry about Indians. He was tired and fell asleep.

When Tuck awoke, he realized his horse was still hitched to the rail in front of the hotel. He felt bad. He hadn't intended on taking a nap. He had planned on riding and exploring the city. It was November and not real hot. The first thing he did was to take his horse to a water trough, where he drank greedily. Then he rode it to a stable on the outskirts of the small city.

Tuck was walking along a side street when he heard a scream. He hurried around a corner to find a girl crying over a man lying on his back with a bloody face. He appeared to be her father. Two men were standing behind her. One reached down and pulled her up. "Ya are comin' with us," said the man to the girl, his slurred speech an indication of having had too much to drink.

"Let go of the girl!" yelled Tuck.

The drunk pulled the girl in tightly to him and said, "I'm takin' her to Mason."

His partner turned, and seeing only one man, started to move towards Tuck with ill intent. Tuck sprung towards the man while drawing his gun. He hit the man over the head with its barrel.

Now looking towards the man with the girl he saw the man bringing his gun level to shoot him. For fear of hitting the girl, Tuck didn't fire. The drunken man's shot missed Tuck. He was about to shoot again when the girl's father struck the drunk holding his daughter on the head with a board, breaking it. The blow wasn't hard enough to subdue the man, but it was enough of a distraction for Tuck to move forward and grab the gun away.

"Mister," said Tuck to the man that had used the board, "get the other one's gun." The man did what he was told. "Now you," said Tuck to the drunk, "get over next to your pard. Any wrong moves and I will shoot you. Now what's going on here?"

The girl started talking first, "These men were beating my father!"

"What's your name?"

"Eva Barlow, and that's my father Jim."

"You two skunks, what are your names?"

"Go to hell," said the drunk.

"I might, but in another minute, you'll be there way ahead of me," said Tuck, while cocking the hammer of his gun which emitted a loud click. It was enough to scare the drunk.

"Don't shoot. I'm Jake and my pard on the ground is Crow."

"Is Crow his real name or nickname?"

"No one knows. Everyone just calls him Crow."

"Now that you're talking so well, is there a reason other than she's a girl, that you grabbed her?"

"I was following orders from my boss."

"Who's your boss?"

"Plimpton, ah, Greg Plimpton. Barlow owes him money, so I was told to grab the girl."

"I've heard enough for now. Barlow, lead the way to the sheriff's office. These two are going to jail."

"You can't arrest us!" said Crow while holding his head.

While still holding his gun in his right hand, Tuck used his left to pull the badge out of his shirt pocket. "I'm a Deputy U.S. Marshal. You two are under arrest for attempted kidnapping and attempted murder of a federal officer."

"Plimpton will have us out in no time, then we'll be comin' for ya Marshal," said Crow while holding his head.

"I hope you do because then I'll have an excuse to rid the world of two scumbags. Let's go Barlow."

Barlow looked at his horse-drawn empty wagon; thinking it would be okay to leave it, he led the group three blocks to the sheriff's office. The girl, who Tuck figured was about fourteen, walked beside Tuck. Tuck noticed she kept looking up at him and smiling. Tuck thought, "That's all I need, a love-struck little girl."

When they got to the sheriff's office, Tuck announced, "Sheriff, I'm Deputy U.S. Marshal Jed Tucker, though most call me Tuck. I'm arresting these two scumbags for attempted kidnapping of Eva Barlow and attempted murder of a federal officer."

"That federal officer is you I suppose, and the girl is Eva Barlow," said the sheriff.

"That's right."

After the two were locked up Tuck asked, "What can you tell me about Plimpton?"

"He's the owner of a saloon he calls Plimpton's Place, and he's also a loan shark."

"Where is his saloon?"

"Six blocks west of here towards the edge of town."

"I'll be headed there next. What's he look like?"

"Short, bald and fat. About fifty years old. And just so you know, he always has two bodyguards around. Keep an eye out for 'em," replied the sheriff.

"Sheriff, how do you feel about Plimpton? Is he an asset to this town?"

The sheriff chuckled, "It would be great if he disappeared."

"Thanks. If you hear any gunfire, ignore it. Nice meeting you, Sheriff. Barlow, let's step outside and talk."

Once Tuck and the Barlows were outside Tuck said, "I'm about starved to death. If you two would lead me to a place to eat I'd like to buy supper. We can palaver a bit while we eat."

"That'd be very kind of ya Marshal."

"I've never eaten anything but Ma's cookin'," said the girl with a bit of excitement.

Tuck looked at Eva and grinned, "I guess there's a first time for everything."

Taking a seat in the restaurant at a table for four, Jake Barlow sat across from Tuck while Eva sat to his right.

"Mister Barlow, I know it's a personal question, but how much do you owe Plimpton?"

When Jake looked nervously at Eva, Tuck knew Jake didn't want his daughter to know about the family's finances. "Eva is almost a woman; sharing your financial situation might be educational for her."

"We're farmers, Marshal. I have an orchard that does well but the leafy greens I grow need irrigating if it doesn't rain. Last year was so dry I couldn't even irrigate. I needed money. The bank wouldn't loan me any. Said farming was a bad risk so I went to Plimpton. This year things look good, but Plimpton won't wait until harvest for his money, he wants it now."

"How much?"

"Five hundred plus interest."

Tuck whistled. "Where is your farm?"

"On the northeast edge of town."

"Good, that's on my way to Fort McDowell." Tuck took a hundred-dollar bill from the money belt under his shirt. "It's early yet so when we finish here, I want you to take your daughter shopping for a new dress and anything else she might need. Buy yourself and your missus anything you need also. Use what's left over for food. I'll be stopping by your place in the morning." Tuck looked at Eva, "A pretty girl like you should be wearing a pretty dress."

Eva blushed and said, "Thank you Marshal Tuck."

"Eva, we can't take his money!"

"Mister Barlow, it's not my money. It was given to me for purposes like this. Please accept the help without any shame or embarrassment. I must go now. I'll see you in the morning. Eva, I'll be expecting to see you wearing a pretty dress."

As Tuck stood, Barlow said to him, "You are a very kind man. Thank you for your help."

"As I mentioned, it's someone else's money. I'm just delivering it. Have fun shopping."

Riding boots were made for riding, not walking. Tuck wished he had his horse as he walked west through the city. By the time he got to Plimpton's Place, Tuck's feet were sore and he was in a foul mood. He stepped through the batwings, then moved to the side while his eyes adjusted to the dim light. Once his eyes became accustomed to the dim saloon, he spotted Plimpton behind the bar. At the far left end of the bar sat a giant of a man, and he was not drinking. Tuck pegged him for a bouncer or bodyguard.

Tuck moved slowly towards the bar, his eyes lingering on all around him. The clientele of Plimpton's Saloon appeared to be the dregs of Phoenix. It looked like a place a man wearing a badge could have his hands full. Tuck never saw who he thought might be the other bodyguard.

"What can I get for you Marshal?" asked Plimpton.

"A shot with a beer chaser. You must be Plimpton." After paying for the drinks, Tuck downed the shot in one gulp.

"I am. I suspect you didn't come here to drink. What's on your mind, Marshal?"

"I'm here to pay Jim Barlow's debt. How much does he owe?"

"Six hundred dollars."

Hearing that, Tuck almost came unglued. He was giving Plimpton a steely-eyed glare. The bodyguard at the end of the bar knew his boss was in trouble, so he got up from his seat. A fast spin to the left and lightning draw had Tuck's gun pointed at the huge bodyguard. "Get back where you were with your hands on the bar. If I see them anywhere else, I will shoot you!" said Tuck sternly. Tuck was wishing he knew where the other bodyguard was when he saw someone come in the rear door. When he saw Tuck with his gun pointed at the big man, he drew his gun. Tuck saw him draw and shot him. When Tuck saw the big man's right hand drop below the bar, Tuck shot him also. Tuck knew both men were dead because he had shot them both in the heart.

Keeping one eye on Plimpton, Tuck glanced around the saloon and said, "Anymore takers?" No one answered. Tuck pulled a wad of bills from a pocket, counted out six hundred dollars and laid it on the bar. "I want a receipt."

Plimpton quickly wrote a receipt.

"Plimpton, if I hear the Barlows have trouble of any kind, I will come looking for you. Understand?"

Plimpton was too scared to talk so he shook his head yes, causing the fear-driven sweat to fling from his face.

"And, if I ever hear you treated some other poor

family like you have the Barlows, I will come looking for you."

Tuck was leaving when the sheriff and a deputy entered. "We were headed this way when we heard shots," said the sheriff.

"Plimpton needs two new bodyguards," said Tuck as he walked calmly out through the batwings.

It was about eight the next morning when Tuck arrived at the Barlow's place. Jim met him in front of his house. "Good morning Marshal. Would you like to step down for coffee or breakfast?"

"Good morning Jed. I would appreciate that. I left without eating this morning. I'm on my way to Fort McDowell."

"Come on inside and meet my wife, Francis. She has breakfast just about ready."

Tuck stepped inside, took his hat off and said, "It shore smells good."

"Her cookin' is the best," said Jed proudly.

"Would you like coffee?" asked Eva with a large smile.

"Yes, thank you Eva. By the way, you sure are pretty in that new dress. Thanks for wearing it for me, but don't wear it for work; that's what your old one is for."

Eva placed a cup and plate on the empty side of the square table. Tuck was waiting for Francis to sit before he did. Jed noticed Tuck waiting, and as he sat, he said, "Take a seat Marshal."

Tuck sat and started sipping his coffee. "Good coffee."

"Thank you Marshal," said Francis with a nice smile as she placed a plate full of scrambled eggs and biscuits on the table. "Help yourself."

Eva had been watching Tuck's coffee cup, waiting for it to be empty. As soon as she saw it was empty, she was up and grabbing the coffee pot, "More coffee, Marshal?"

Tuck looked up at her standing next to him and smiled, "Yes, thank you Eva."

Francis noticed how her daughter had been acting around Tuck and smiled to herself. Just a young girl's crush on her handsome knight in shining armor.

The food was so good there was very little talking. When everyone was finished eating Tuck said, "Jed, could you step outside with me please?"

"Sure thing Marshal."

When they were alone on the porch Tuck handed the receipt to Jed. Jed looked at it. His eyes got wet and he didn't know what to say. Seeing Francis step out on the porch, he handed the receipt to her. She read it and her tears flowed. She moved quickly to Tuck and threw her arms around him in a tight hug.

With the hug over, Francis took off her aprons and said, "Thank you for everything, Marshal, this is the dress Jed bought me. He has such good taste."

Tuck was embarrassed, "Please, everyone, call me Tuck, and remember it wasn't my money. I've got to go now. I'll stop by and see how things are going on my way back. Don't know how long I might be in Fort McDowell."

Tuck shook hands with Jed and was starting to turn towards his horse when Francis said, "You are going to hurt her feelings if you don't allow her to give you a hug."

Tuck looked at an embarrassed Eva and said, "Come here."

Eva gave Tuck a quick hug then ran into the house. Jed and Francis laughed.

Tuck mounted and waved as he rode off.

Fort McDowell 1870s

It was about four in the afternoon when Tuck rode into Fort McDowell. As with most forts, a small town grew up next to the fort and its protection. The fort itself was made of adobe with a wood roof and wood shingles. A tall fence surrounded the fort's perimeter. Apparently, the area was secure enough from attack that guards at the gate were not needed. Riding inside, Tuck saw a building with a sign reading 'Colonel Fredrick.' Tuck rode to the building and tied his horse to a post and went inside. Seeing a sergeant at a desk, Tuck went straight to him.

"I'm looking for Captain Mathew."

"Next building to the right as you exit."

Tuck turned around and left. Entering the next building to the right, a corporal was seated at a desk.

"I have orders from the US Attorney General to

see Captain Mathew," said Tuck to the corporal.

"Your name sir?"

"Deputy U.S. Marshal Jed Tucker."

The corporal stood and knocked on an open door behind him.

"I heard Corporal, send him in."

The corporal motioned to Tuck to enter.

"Mister Tucker, close the door and take a seat and tell me what you know."

Tuck shut the door and sat down at a chair in front of the captain's desk. "All I know is I was sent here to investigate a child's kidnapping, which makes little sense to me."

The captain studied Tuck for a moment. "It's not just any kidnapping. It was Colonel Fredrick's grandson that was kidnapped. I have been put in charge of recovering the boy."

"If the army can't find the boy, how is one man supposed to do it?"

"It's not a matter of finding him. We know where he is."

Tuck was getting frustrated and it showed on his face. If they knew where the boy was, why didn't they just go and get him?

Captain Mathew noted the frustration on Tuck's face and chuckled. "I know you're thinking, why don't we just go and get him? It's not that easy because he is being held by his father, who is a Yavapai Apache." The captain stopped talking when he saw Tuck shake his head and look at the floor.

"So, you want me to go into their camp and grab this boy and bring him back! That's the craziest thing I ever heard!" Tuck wanted to get up and leave but he knew that would cost him his badge.

"No, I don't expect you to ride into their camp and take the boy. You have friends in high places. One of those people highly recommended you, though I cannot fathom how they figure you can get this done. As far as the army going and getting the boy, if we attacked with a large force there would be untold deaths on both sides and probably the killing of the boy by his father. So, that leaves you. Anything you want is at your disposal."

There was silence for several minutes while the captain let Tuck think. Finally Tuck said, "It will probably be the death of me, but I will try. What is the father's and mother's name, and is the mother married to him?"

"The mother's name is Faith Fredrick. The Indian is Nantan Lupan or Grey Wolf. No, they are not married. When Faith was fifteen, she was being escorted by twelve cavalry soldiers to Phoenix when they were attacked. The twelve soldiers died trying to protect her. An Indian named

Nantan Lupan took her to be his wife. A year later they had a son. Grey Wolf named him Tarak, meaning Star. When Faith was twenty-four, she was able to escape with Tarak. Tarak was eight years old at the time. He is now twelve."

"I need to learn more about the boy. Where can I see his mother?"

"I don't think you will find Ms. Fredrick of any assistance. She has been completely uncooperative with us. She hates Grey Wolf with a passion of hate unlike anything you have ever experienced."

"How does she feel about Tarak?"

"I am not sure, but from what I have heard she treats him poorly." Captain Mathew thought for a moment, then looked Tuck in the eye, "I shouldn't tell you this, because if word gets out it will end my career. Colonel Fredrick is an avowed Indian hater. He never visited his grandson, and I am sure he doesn't want him returned. Trying to recover his grandson is just a big charade to make him look like a good grandfather… Corporal Smith."

The corporal entered the office quickly, "Yes sir?"

"Escort Marshal Tucker to Faith Fredrick's house."

"Yes sir."

Faith Fredrick's house was well maintained but small. Having brought Tuck to Faith's house, the corporal turned his horse and rode back to the fort.

Tuck knocked on the front door. A pasty-faced woman answered. "Yes?"

"Hello, I'm Deputy U.S. Marshal Tucker. I'm conducting the rescue of your son Tarak."

As quickly as Tuck got the words out of his mouth, Faith tried to slam the door. Tuck had been expecting this type of reception, so he was ready. His foot was quick to block the door. "Please help me Ms. Fredrick."

"Why? Grey Wolf can keep Tarak. I don't want him. The four years he was here with me were hell! He looks just like his father. My life is ruined, I just want to live by myself!"

"Ma'am, it sounds like you don't even want him back."

Faith's anger exploded, "Of course I don't! I don't ever want to see him again! That's why I took him to Grey Wolf!" As soon as the words were out of her mouth Faith knew she said too much and regretted it. She had said Tarak had been kidnapped.

"So, he wasn't kidnapped, he was abandoned. After I've rescued him, I'll bring him here and see how you feel."

"You, rescue someone from an Indian tribe! Hah! You don't know a thing about Indians and how they live and think! Now leave and don't bother me again!" screamed Faith.

Looking for a general store and finding one, Tuck bought a pair of used Mexican white cotton pants and a used buckskin shirt. From the store he went to a boarding house and got a room. He rented it for a month. After supper in the boarding house, he went to a small saloon where he had a few drinks and thought about what he was about to do. He knew his chances of surviving were slim. Back in his room that evening Tuck wrote a note to the landlady telling her what to do with his things if he was not back in thirty days. He also left a letter that was addressed to both Lomasi and Morgan. These he would leave on the bed in the morning with the note to the landlady.

The next day after breakfast at the boarding house, he put on the used clothes he had purchased. He then pulled on his knee-high moccasins. He used a leather strap for a belt from which he hung his eight-inch knife. Finding his old headband and feather in one of his saddlebags, he put that on.

Tuck hadn't cut his hair since joining Wyatt so it was long enough that he could pass for an

Indian. He knew after a few days riding in the desert he would be dirty enough to look more authentic. Leaving his guns and all his possessions in his room, he went downstairs and walked to the livery for his horse. Only putting reins on his horse, he left all other tack behind. When he road into the desert bareback, he only had his fire starter, a bag of jerky, two blankets, and two canteens.

Tuck rode east into the mountains. He wasn't worried about finding the Apaches; they would find him. As he entered the mountains, he knew he was being watched. The young deer he saw ahead would make the perfect opportunity to impress his audience. Tuck dismounted and left his horse ground hitched. He moved quietly towards the deer, using every bit of cover. Finally, he was at the distance many Indians would use a bow and arrow to take an animal. Tuck pulled the knife from the sheath on his right hip, held it behind his head for a moment, then with tremendous strength and speed sent the knife sailing towards the deer. The knife penetrated the deer to its hilt, reaching the heart. The deer fell dead. The three Apaches that had been watching had never seen anyone take a deer by throwing a knife, especially from that distance, and were impressed.

Tuck went back to his horse and led it to the deer. After throwing the deer over his horse, he tied its feet together underneath the horse. He then called out to the Apaches using the Waco, language which of course the Apaches did not understand. This way they would know for certain Tuck was an Indian.

The Apaches came out from hiding and joined Tuck. Using sign, they told Tuck to follow them, which he did. The Apaches did not have horses, so they did a slow run towards their encampment. Holding the reins to his horse, Tuck ran behind them.

Walking down into a valley, Tuck saw close to a hundred teepees and numerous campfires. People were going about their daily lives. The three Apaches led Tuck to the center of the camp. Tuck noticed people pointing at him and talking. Everyone seemed to know he didn't belong. By the time they got to the center of the encampment several warriors had come together to meet the arrivals.

A muscular older Indian, who must have been the chief, stepped in front of the warriors and spoke directly to Tuck. Of course, Tuck didn't understand the Apache language, so he responded in the Waco language. It seemed the chief didn't know what to make of Tuck or what to do with him. Tuck knew the Apache also spoke Spanish. They'd been fighting Spaniards then the Mexicans for centuries. The name Apache has its roots in Spanish. But Tuck didn't speak Spanish. After a minute of talking back and forth at each other, Tuck decided to try English. The chief recognized English; he even knew a few words. He turned to a warrior and said something. The warrior hurried off. A minute later he was back with a scared and worried young boy.

The chief spoke to the boy. The boy turned towards Tuck, "Chief Dahkeya wants me to translate. What is your name?"

"Red Hawk. I am Waco from Texas."

The boy turned to Chief Dahkeya and spoke in Apache. Turning back to Tuck he said, "Chief Dahkeya wants to know what you are doing in Apache lands."

"White skins have killed my people. I am looking for another place to live."

The boy translated to the chief. Turning back to Tuck, the boy said, "Chief Dahkeya says you are a great hunter and may make a good warrior. You are welcome in our camp until it is decided what to do with you."

The boy was turning to go when Tuck said, "Wait, are you Tarak?"

There was a look of surprise on the boy's face, "Yes, I am Tarak. How did you know?"

"I have spoken with your mother."

"If you wish to live, never mention this again."

"Where do I stay? What do I do with my horse?"

Tarak looked at Chief Dahkey and asked those questions in Apache. Tarak had a small smile when he looked back at Tuck. "I have been put in charge of you. Follow me. We will leave the deer at my father's teepee. His woman will prepare it. Her name is Onawa or Wide Awake. My father's name is Nantan Lupan or Grey Wolf."

After leaving the deer with Onawa, Tarak led Tuck to the edge of the Indian village where a few other horses were. "Leave your horse here. Now we go eat. Because of your deer, we will eat good tonight and in the morning."

Tuck grabbed his canteens and blankets. Tarak led Tuck back to his father Grey Wolf's teepee and took him inside.

Grey Wolf said something angrily to Tarak. Tarak grabbed Tuck's arm and led him back outside. "You must leave your things here. You will eat and sleep alongside the teepee. You are not allowed inside."

Tuck was surprised, "What's his problem?"

"That's the way he is. He is not nice to me either; I don't like him. I'll sit here and wait with you."

A half-hour later Grey Wolf's woman, Onawa, brought a large bowl from the cooking fire and gave it to Grey Wolf inside the teepee. A minute later she returned with three much smaller bowls. She gave one to Tarak and one to Tuck. The last bowl was hers, which she took inside to eat.

The food looked and smelled good to Tuck. Other than the deer meat and some wild onions, Tuck had no idea what else was in the bowl, but it tasted good. Tuck and Tarak ate with their fingers.

Ten minutes later Onawa collected the bowls and took them to the large creek to wash.

Tuck and Tarak didn't know it at the time, but Tarak eating with Tuck angered Grey Wolf. He was further angered when Tarak spent the night outside with Tuck and was in a foul mood the next morning.

It was about a half hour after a breakfast of the same food as the night before, when Tuck heard a large commotion from the center of the village. Tuck and Tarak went to see what it was. Grey Wolf was in a fierce argument with another warrior. As Tuck watched, the two warriors moved towards a grassy area on the perimeter of the village. All the men in the village followed. The women stayed back.

As Tuck followed Tarak he asked, "What's going on?"

"Grey Wolf is angry with another Indian and challenged him. I think his name is Wiyot."

A circle was formed around Grey Wolf and Wiyot. When Grey Wolf saw Tuck at the back of the circle of men, he angrily pushed two men in the front aside and yelled to Tarak.

"Grey Wolf wants us in the front," said Tarak worriedly.

Once Tuck and Tarak were in the front of the circle, Grey Wolf pulled the knife from his waist. Looking at his foe he took a crouched fighting position. Everyone, including Tuck, knew Grey Wolf expected to win. He wanted Tuck close to the fight so he would be intimidated.

Wiyot did his best not to show fear, but his eyes gave him away. Grey Wolf strutted confidently in a circle around Wiyot. Suddenly, springing at Wiyot like a mountain lion, he slashed his knife across Wiyot's chest. Blood flowed from the long horizontal slice. Ten seconds later Grey Wolf tried the same tactic. This time Wiyot was ready for him and slashed Grey Wolf's shoulder that was holding the knife. Grey Wolf smiled and backed off.

Grey Wolf did a fake to his left, then sprung right, slashing Wiyot across his thigh muscle, making the leg almost useless. Grey Wolf was again smiling as he circled the crippled, slow-moving Wiyot. Grey Wolf made a fake jab to his left then sprung straight ahead, plunging his knife into the side of Wiyot. Grey Wolf held the knife inside

Wiyot's chest, keeping Wiyot from falling. He then brought his right foot up and pushed Wiyot off the knife. Wiyot fell to the ground to die a moment later.

Grey Wolf looked right at Tuck while giving an Apache warrior yell. Tuck knew eventually he would be in the ring with Grey Wolf, and he knew he would be in big trouble.

Chief Dahkeya called Tarak aside and said something to him. When he had left Tarak said, "Because you are a hunter, Chief Dahkeya wants you to help supply meat."

Happy with the order to supply meat, Tuck asked Tarak, "Do you know how to make a bow and arrows?"

Tarak grimaced, "No, Grey Wolf treats me bad. Has me learn woman's work."

"Then I will teach you. While you get my horse, I will get the deer guts we will need for string."

Grey Wolf was watching as Tuck and Tarak left the village. Tarak was proudly leading Tuck's horse.

As they walked through the pine forest, Tuck watched for the perfect branch to make a bow out of. He also watched for the perfect smaller branches that would make arrows. When Tuck came across the remains of a mourning dove, he grinned as he squatted and picked up feathers. A little further on he found the perfect branch for a long bow. He and Tarak took a seat on a log. Tuck showed Tarak how to make grooves at the end of the stick for the gut string. Using a strip of leather, he made an arrow rest in the middle of the stick. Next, he fashioned a string out of the deer gut.

Once again, they were walking through the woods. After cutting off three small branches they again took a seat while Tuck made the arrows using the mourning dove's feathers. Tuck tested his bow. He was pleased with it. Now they were ready to hunt.

That evening Tarak proudly led Tuck's horse, which was loaded with a dead deer, a ringtail cat and a jack rabbit. Chief Dahkeya noticed and rewarded Tuck with a small teepee of his own to live in. Tarak immediately told Chief Dahkeya that Tuck was teaching him how to make bow and arrows and hunt and he needed to live with his teacher. The chief agreed. When Grey Wolf found out he swore he would find a way to call Tuck out.

Things had been going well for two weeks. Tuck and Tarak made a good hunting team and were doing more than their share of supplying meat to the village. Tuck and the boy were growing close. Tuck took the place of Tarak's unlikeable father and Tarak was becoming the boy Tuck never had. Tuck had been teaching Tarak how to ride and thought it was time he had his own horse. That night Tuck snuck out of the village. He rode in the dark to a ranch he had passed once. Seeing a fifteen-hand Morgan, Tuck stole it. He didn't like stealing the horse and hoped he would be able to repay the owner.

It had been a long ride and a long night. The sun was up when he rode into the village leading the Morgan. He tied both horses on a post next to his teepee. Tarak had breakfast prepared and had been waiting for Tuck. Tuck sat and began eating. He didn't say anything about the other horse. He saw how Tarak kept looking at the horse. When Tuck had finished eating, he said, "Every hunter needs a horse. This one is yours. Let's go hunting."

Tarak's eyes got as large as his smile. Tuck bent over and locked the fingers of both hands together, making a step for Tarak. In an instant Tarak was on his horse.

The two rode to the edge of the village where horses were kept. Tuck dismounted, saying, "My horse is tuckered out, I'll leave him here and walk." Tuck grinned at his own little joke.

The next morning when they went to hunt, Tarak's horse was missing. They looked around. Off a way they saw Grey Wolf sitting on Tarak's horse. He had a broad grin on his face as he rode close to Tuck. In Apache he said to Tarak, "This horse is meant for a warrior, not a boy."

Tarak looked like he was about to cry. Tuck knew this was his challenge. This would be his most dangerous fight ever and he knew he had to accept. He pointed to the spot of Grey Wolf's last fight. Grey Wolf understood and grinned. He would kill this poor excuse for an Indian and have an impressive horse.

Wichita, Kansas

The train Wyatt and Morgan were on was just rolling into Wichita. They were returning from Arkansas where they had easily captured a small outlaw gang. They found them passed out in an abandoned house. The four dimwits had challenged each other to see who could drink the most bottles of whiskey. After robbing a small bank, they stopped a teamster on the road. To the delight of the young outlaws, he was hauling whiskey from Kentucky for deliveries in Fort Smith.

After finding an abandoned house they commenced to see who could drink the most bottles.

"I don't understand why Rothschild hasn't heard from Tuck," complained a worried Morgan. "It's been what, three months since Tuck arrived in Fort McDowell?"

Wyatt was also worried. Not knowing what else to say he said, "Tuck's fine, he can take care of himself better than anyone I know."

"As soon as we get off this rocking boat of noise and smoke, I'm going straight to Lomasi. Certainly, she's heard something."

"Let me know if you find out anything."

Lomasi was now renting a room at a boarding house. Morgan knocked on the door. The owner, Mister Phillips, answered, "Hello Morgan. I suppose you are here to see Lomasi. Come on in. She's in her room, so go right ahead."

"Thank you, Mister Phillips."

Lomasi could hear Morgan talking, so she opened her door. Seeing the opened door, Morgan walked right in. As soon as Morgan saw Lomasi's face, she knew something was terribly wrong and said, "It's Tuck, isn't it? What's happened?"

Without saying a word, Lomasi handed Morgan the letter from Tuck. As Morgan read it, tears were rolling down her cheeks. When she had finished, she fell on Lomasi's bed crying.

"The letter came seven weeks ago. I cried for three days straight," said Lomasi. "After crying myself out I realized if Tuck were dead, I would feel it in my heart. Our hearts ride the same horse. If he were to fall off, I would know."

Morgan sat up, "You think he's still alive after three months?"

"I'm scared, but yes, I feel he's still alive and will

return to me."

Lomasi's comment eased Morgan's fears a bit. "Let's go find a saloon," said Morgan while wiping her tears.

Arizona

Tuck, knife in hand, was standing in the center of the circle of Indians looking at a grinning Grey Wolf. Grey Wolf was light on his feet as he started circling Tuck. Just as in his last fight, Grey Wolf feinted left then sprang towards Tuck, slashing his blade across his stomach. Tuck was able to move rearward enough that the slash wasn't as bad as the one to Wiyot. Tuck was desperate, then he suddenly realized Grey Wolf always leads every attack with a feint to his left. From watching Wiyot's fight, Tuck knew Grey Wolf liked to go for the body. Tuck knew he only needed to slice Grey Wolf's hand to win. With Grey Wolf's hand the target, Tuck wouldn't have to get as close, which would be far less risky. The next time Grey Wolf feinted to his left, Tuck would be ready. Grey Wolf had become overconfident. His jabs and slashes towards Tuck's body had lost their fancy footwork.

When Grey Wolf did his usual feint to his left, Tuck knew Grey Wolf would come straight at him. Tuck dodged to his left. While Grey Wolf passed him on Tuck's right, Tuck slashed out to

Grey Wolf's knife-holding hand. The razor-sharp knife cut cleanly through all the tendons and muscles, only stopping when it hit bone. Grey Wolf's hand became useless and caused the knife to fall to the ground. Grey Wolf quickly picked it up with his left hand. Grey Wolf had trained with his left hand, but he just wasn't as good with it. He tried his usual attack but this time he feinted to the right, then lunged forward.

Tuck responded the same as earlier, only this time Tuck dodged to his right, slashing Grey Wolf across his shoulder. Blood was pumping from Grey Wolf's shoulder as he tried vainly to attack Tuck. Grey Wolf was becoming weaker by the second. In a last desperate attempt, Grey Wolf reared his left arm and threw the knife at Tuck. Tuck spun away. Weakened, Grey Wolf dropped to his knees. He uttered something in Apache, then fell face-forward. Tarak ran to Tuck and they hugged.

Not many in the tribe had liked Grey Wolf, so Tuck didn't notice any animosity about him winning. Two warriors picked up Grey Wolf's body and took him to their sacred burial grounds.

The two walked together back to Tuck's teepee. The bleeding on Tuck's stomach had mostly stopped. "Now let's go hunting," Tuck said to Tarak. They grabbed Tuck's two canteens and went where the horses were kept. Tarak was pleased to have his horse back and was rubbing its nose.

Tuck enjoyed his weeks hunting with Tarak, but when plans were being made to attack some families that had moved into the area, Tuck knew it was time to go. After they ate that evening, they sat inside their teepee and talked.

"Tarak, you have lived with white men and you have lived with Indians. How do you want to spend the rest of your life?"

The question caught Tarak by surprise. He thought for a moment, "I have enjoyed our time together. I like what we do."

"I feel the same. Do you realize there is a big new changing world away from here? The way of the Indian is gone in most places and is dying here. In the next year or two the Apache will no longer exist the way they are now. We will not be hunting but instead will be dependent on the white man to feed us."

Tarak was stunned by Tuck's words. "How do you know these things?"

"I have seen it. It has happened everywhere but here. The Apache is the last holdout of the Indian ways, but it will be over soon."

Tuck continued, "How do you feel about killing white men? Are you willing to give your life helping the Apache fight until the Apache is no more?" Tuck could see Tarak was deep in thought.

"When I lived with my mother I went to school and learned things. I liked going to school; I had many friends I now miss. I don't know why, but my mother doesn't like me. She brought me here and gave me to Grey Wolf. Grey Wolf never liked me either."

Tuck noticed Tarak's moist eyes. He knew the boy was doing his best to be a man and not cry. Finally, he could not hold back any longer. The tears flowed and he cried. Tuck scooted close to Tarak, put an arm around his shoulder and pulled him close. It was the first time anyone had ever shown any affection for Tarak, and he welcomed it. After a few minutes Tarak pulled away, "What is it you want to do? You are now my true father; I will go with you."

"I have a woman waiting for me. I wish to marry her. She would love you in a way a mother should. I will return to her. You are welcome to come with me. You will see new things and go to school."

"If you leave, I will have no one here. Let us go, tonight."

Tuck smiled, "No, we will leave in the morning. It will look like we are going hunting."

In the morning after breakfast, they made the usual preparations to go hunting. As usual they rode north out of the village, but after riding for two miles they turned west until they were out of the mountains. Then they rode southwest towards Fort McDowell.

As they rode, Tuck thought about what they would do when they arrived in Fort McDowell. He planned to arrive after dark when they would be less likely to be seen. The first place he would go would be to the boarding house, hoping some of his things might still be there. Then he would take Tarak to see his mother, Faith Fredrick.

It was all dark at the boarding house. Tuck repeatedly knocked on the door. When the female owner opened the door, Tuck realized he had forgotten her name. Seeing two Indians at her door she shrieked and backed inside. Tuck pulled off this headband and feather and said, "Ma'am, it's me, Tuck. We are not going to hurt you. Light a lamp so you can see who it is."

The woman nervously lighted a lamp, then held it by Tuck. "Is it really you, Tuck?"

"Yes, I survived after all. Do you still have any of my things?"

"I do. I put them away in a chest, then forgot all about them. They are still in your old room. I haven't been able to rent it."

Tuck looked inside the chest. His guns, clothes, even his money belt was still there. He smiled at the woman. "I will pay you ten dollars to heat up a bath for us and let us spend the night in my old room." Excited about making that much money, she agreed to do it.

Using borrowed scissors, Tuck cut Tarak's hair, then Tarak cut Tuck's hair. After their baths the tired two went to sleep, with Tuck on the bed and Tarak on the floor.

Tuck enjoyed wearing his regular clothes the next morning. Tarak wore some of Tuck's oversized clothes to breakfast.

After breakfast Tuck walked the four blocks to a general store, where he purchased a set of clothes for Tarak. Once Tarak had regular clothes to wear they would come back so he could find shoes that would fit.

After the second trip to the general store the two walked to Tarak's mother's house. When Tuck knocked on the door a young woman answered.

"Miss, we are looking for Faith Fredrick."

"She doesn't live here anymore."

"This is her son. Could you tell us where we can find her?"

Tuck noticed the confused look on the young woman's face. After a moment she said, "Sir, would you step inside please?"

The woman closed the door behind Tuck, leaving Tarak outside. "I'm sorry to tell you this, but she's dead. She shot herself in the head six weeks ago."

Tuck was at a loss. Finally, he thanked the woman and stepped outside.

"Let's get our horses and ride to Phoenix."

Tarak knew something bad had happened. He also knew Tuck would tell him when the time was right.

When they were a mile out of town, Tuck was looking straight ahead when he told Tarak, "Your mother is dead."

Tarak looked at Tuck, "How did she die?"

"She was messed up in the head a bit. She shot herself."

"Grey Wolf did it to her. He was always mean to her. Sometimes he would hit her and make her cry."

Tuck looked at Tarak. He was surprised to see he was straight-faced and not crying.

Tuck hadn't forgotten his promise to see the Barlows on his way back. When they stopped by, Jed said everything was fine. Mrs. Barlow invited the two for supper, but Tuck said he wanted to get to Phoenix before the telegraph office closed. Tuck told Jed about the horse he had stolen for Tarak and gave Jed five hundred dollars. Jed promised he would take the money to the ranch where the horse was stolen from. That would be more than double what the horse was worth. It also left Tuck with barely enough money for the train.

The two rode into Phoenix after six. Tuck wanted to send a telegram to Lomasi, but the telegraph office was closed. Instead, they got something to eat.

When they finished eating, they went to the Phoenix Hotel. When the desk clerk asked how many rooms, Tuck was at a loss. He looked at Tarak, "Do you want your own room or what?"

"I want to be with you. I'll sleep on the floor again."

"Okay, if that's what you want. We'll take one room for just one night. I also want a bath sent to our room."

When they were in their room Tuck told Tarak to take a bath, that he had some business to attend to and would be back in an hour.

First, Tuck took Tarak's horse to a livery, then he rode to the west side of town to Plimpton's Place. Tuck entered and walked boldly to the bar and ordered a whiskey with a beer chaser from a nervous Plimpton. "I see you've replaced your bodyguards. I just wanted you to know I'm still around."

Plimpton only nodded his head then scampered to the far end of the bar to be by one of his bodyguards.

Tuck finished his drinks and rode back to the livery where he left his horse. Back at the hotel he took a much-needed bath.

After breakfast at the hotel's restaurant, they walked to the livery, retrieved their horses and rode to the railroad depot. They bought tickets for themselves and their horses. It would be a boring two hours before the train arrived from Los Angeles. In the meantime, Tuck sent a short telegram to Lomasi at the Occidental Hotel.

Never having seen a train before, Tarak was grinning with excitement as the behemoth entered the depot puffing steam and the bell clanging. It would be an exciting, educational trip for him.

Their train ran day and night. Three days later they were in Wichita. Tuck was greatly disappointed not to find Lomasi waiting for him. They retrieved their horses from the depot's corral and rode to the Occidental Hotel. The desk clerk told Tuck that Lomasi had moved out almost two months ago.

"This telegram came for her three days ago, but we don't know where to forward it to," said the desk clerk.

"The telegram was from me. Does Wyatt Peterson still live here?" asked Tuck.

"Yes, he does, but he's not in right now."

"Thanks." Tuck looked at Tarak, "I told you about Morgan; I know where we can find her. She can help us. But while we are here, I'll get us a room."

Hangover or not, Morgan knew it was time to get up. It was a cold morning. There were just enough coals glowing in her bedroom stove to get a fire going. Then, to get a terrible taste out of her mouth, she brushed her teeth. Finding a dress in her closet she would wear today, she walked over to the window with it. She was looking at the street below when she saw a boy and a man on horseback. The man looked familiar. She dropped the dress and ran downstairs and into her father's blacksmith shop. She was running barefoot through the shop in her nightgown when the door opened.

"Tuck! Tuck! It's you!" Tears of joy were running down Morgan's face as she ran to Tuck. She ran into him so hard he was slammed against the wall. She squeezed Tuck in a tight hug.

Tuck was pleased with the reception Morgan was giving him. "Morgan, settle down. It's only me."

Darby had stopped working and was watching his daughter. He was confused. She always talked about Wyatt, but here she was going crazy over Tuck. "I never understood her mother either," he said out loud to himself.

Morgan pushed away. Seeing Tarak she asked, "Who do you have with you?"

"This is Tarak, my best friend. After you of course," Tuck added quickly with a smile. "Tarak, this is Morgan, my best friend."

Morgan moved over towards Tarak and held out her hand, "Nice to meet you Tarak."

Tarak took Morgan's hand and shook it. "It is good to meet you. Tuck has told me all about you."

"Morgan, go put some clothes on and take me to Lomasi!" said Tuck with exasperation.

Morgan looked down at herself and said, "Oops," and ran back up the stairs to the sound of Tuck's and her father's laughter.

The dress Morgan was originally going to wear she left on the floor and pulled on her more comfortable Levis. Wearing a warm coat for the cold November weather, she hurried downstairs and out the back door to their two horse stalls that had been added to the building. Once her horse was saddled, she rode around front and met Tuck and Tarak.

"Lomasi will be working today," Morgan told Tuck loudly over all the street noise.

The three arrived at the Detroit Dining Parlor and went inside. Lomasi spotted Tuck and let out an Indian warrior yell. When she ran to Tuck and threw her arms around him in a big hug and started kissing him, everyone in the place smiled or laughed. Lomasi was well-liked by the regular customers and it showed in the tips they left her.

The restaurant's owner knew Tuck and was aware of his disappearance. He understandingly served his customers in Lomasi's place during the ten minutes it took for the two lovers to greet each other. Morgan watched them with an adoring smile on her face. When Lomasi finally broke away from Tuck she looked at the boy with him. "Who is your friend?"

"This is my good friend, Tarak. I'll tell you more about him later."

Lomasi curiously studied Tarak. "He resembles you. He is not your son, is he?"

Tuck laughed, "I don't know how we could resemble each other, but he is like a son. He is an Apache Warrior," exaggerated Tuck.

Tarak beamed with pride.

"I am so looking forward to hearing about you, Tarak. I am Pawnee," said a smiling Lomasi in Apache, while shaking his hand.

Lomasi speaking Apache surprised Tuck. So much he didn't know about this woman.

Lomasi continued in Apache, which Tuck had learned enough to only butcher the language. "Jicarilla Apache live where I am from. Sometimes we got along, sometimes we don't."

Lomasi was not able to get off early, but she was given the next day off. The clock on the wall never moved so slowly. She would join the celebration for Tuck's homecoming later at the Wichita Watering Hole. It was a large new saloon catering to the well-to-do.

Tuck and Tarak went to the sheriff's office looking for Cory. When Tuck stepped inside, he saw her on desk duty. She looked up, saw Tuck and screamed, "Tuck!" She shot out from the desk and streaked at Tuck like a mountain lion after its prey. Tuck had heard about Cory's emotionally excited leaps and was prepared. Sure enough, when she was within six feet, she launched herself. She hit Tuck like a cannonball. Tuck caught her but wasn't planted as firmly as he thought. The two ended up in a heap on the floor with Cory on top.

Tarak was laughing his head off.

"For crying out loud Cory, can't you control your emotions! Just because you only weigh ninety pounds doesn't mean people can catch you!"

Hearing the commotion, Sheriff Drake came out of his office, "What's going on out here?"

When he saw Cory on top of the pile on the floor, he knew what had happened and couldn't contain his laughter.

"Sheriff, Tuck's alive! He's home!" yelled Cory.

"Are you sure he's alive? I suspect you just killed him."

When the two were on their feet, Tuck was dusting off the back of his pants and said, "There's a bit of a celebration going on at the Wichita Watering Hole for my homecoming."

Sheriff Drake thought for a moment, "Screw the paperwork. Cory, it's a slow day, let's lock up and go celebrate!"

Thinking Wyatt would be in his usual seat in front of Pete's Pub, Morgan went there first. Sure enough, he was sitting outside on the boardwalk with a bottle. "Wyatt, Tuck's back! We're having a celebration at the new Wichita Watering Hole. Climb up behind me."

Morgan took her left foot from the stirrup. Wyatt put his left foot in and swung his right leg up over the horse's rump. After wrapping his arms tighter around Morgan than was necessary, he took his left foot from the stirrup.

Noticing how tightly Wyatt held her, Morgan couldn't resist teasing, "Don't be afraid Wyatt, I'll ride slowly so you don't fall off."

Wyatt gave a quick, short tighter squeeze. Air left Morgan's lungs with a woof sound. "Don't give me any of your Irish blarney."

After catching her breath Morgan laughed loudly, "Okay, I'll behave if you behave." She was enjoying Wyatt's tight hold on her as much as he was enjoying holding her.

Wyatt and Morgan were last to arrive at the Watering Hole. Seeing their friends at a large table in the corner, they went to them.

Making fun of the late arrival, Lomasi said teasingly, "You two are so late, did you party before coming here?"

"A gentleman would never tell," replied Wyatt with an insinuating grin.

"The type of answer I would expect from a man," laughed Lomasi.

Morgan pulled Lomasi close and whispered in her ear, "I wish. It's been a long time since I've been with a man."

"Lomasi whispered back, "Maybe tonight will be the night."

Morgan blushed and said, "I need a drink."

Wyatt offered to buy it, but seeing Cory at the bar Morgan said, "I'll get my own." Morgan pushed in next to Cory and ordered a beer. Looking at Cory she said, "I hear you bit Wyatt's nose."

Cory grinned, "He needed punishing and his nose was right there…"

"You did right. Don't let him take advantage of you because you're small. Where's Grant? I expected him to be here."

"I'm sure Wyatt learned his lesson. Grant should be back in town in an hour or so. I left a note for him at the jail."

"One of the four men at the table behind us has been talking about you and making obscene gestures."

When Cory turned around one of the four grubby men grinned and said, "Hi sweet cheeks."

Cory turned back around and said to Morgan, "I thought this place was too expensive for that type."

"Probably stolen money. I'll see you later, I'm going back to Wyatt."

It wasn't more than fifteen minutes after Morgan had left Cory, when the Tuck celebraters heard a loud commotion by the bar. Sheriff Drake, who had been in a conversation with Tuck, looked at the bar. Seeing Cory having a facedown with the troublemaker from the table behind her, Sheriff Drake said, "Now what's that girl up to? She's always getting in trouble."

Morgan was moving to back up Cory, when she saw the man hand Cory his bottle. Cory took a long swig from it then broke it over his head. Dazed, he fell to the floor in a sitting position. He wiped the whiskey wet hair from his eyes. His buddies were laughing their heads off.

Everyone in the saloon had seen it and were also laughing. Little Cory knew she would be in big trouble when the man got up, so she quickly scooted over behind Morgan saying, "You can take him."

Sure enough, seeing his friends and the whole saloon laughing at him, he got up. When Morgan blocked his way to Cory he said, "Get out of my way or else!"

Morgan took a bottle from a table next to her and broke it over the man's head. This time he fell to the floor unconscious. "See how bad an influence you are on me!" said a grinning Morgan to Cory.

By this time Sheriff Drake was telling the man's friends to leave and take the troublemaker with them. Two of the men each grabbed an arm and dragged the unconscious man out the door.

"Thanks, Morgan," said Cory.

"Cory, you're too small to be getting into bar fights. What was that all about anyway?"

"He grabbed my butt. I told him that wasn't the way to get a woman's attention. That he should offer her a drink instead."

"So, you drank his drink, then conked him with it! You're too much," said Morgan with a chuckle.

Cory wasn't listening, as Grant had just come in the door and was headed to her. In front of Tuck's friends, Grant said, "Why is it I would bet Cory had something to do with that man being dragged outside?"

"You're on a winning streak Grant, best find a

card game," laughed Sheriff Drake.

Grant was shaking his head, "I knew it! Little girl, someday you're going to get beat to a pulp."

"Not as long as I have my gun or knife," said Cory with a devilish grin.

Tarak was curious about Cory; she didn't look much older than him, yet she wore a badge, a gun and knife. Everyone kept buying him sarsaparilla, and there was a table with tiny sandwiches, peanuts and some hard candy, so Tarak was enjoying himself. But thirty minutes later he was fast asleep with his head on a table.

Tuck noticed, so he said a few things quietly to Lomasi. Then he said "Everyone, may I have your attention please. I have an announcement. Tomorrow afternoon Lomasi and I are getting married. I just have to find a justice of the peace," laughed Tuck, "so a little help there would be nice."

"So soon?" questioned Wyatt. Morgan was standing next to Wyatt; she elbowed him in his ribs.

Tuck ignored Wyatt, "As you can see my partner is sound asleep. I've never had so many friends. Thank you all for your love and concern, but it's time for me and Tarak to hit the hay."

"Wait!" said Morgan loudly. "You can't just say you're getting married, then go to bed. You have to make plans. You didn't even say what time."

"The time depends on when we find someone to marry us," said Tuck with a shrug of his shoulders.

"Jed Tucker you are taking advantage of sweet Lomasi's ignorance of our weddings! I should slap you!" said Morgan loudly.

Tuck had a sheepish look on his face. "But I don't know anything about weddings."

"You have good friends that will help. First thing in the morning you are to get rings and a suit. Cory knows this city better than any of us, so she can help you find the stores and either a preacher or judge," said Morgan forcefully.

"Cory! She's nothing but trouble. This afternoon the little she-devil knocked me down! Why can't you help me?"

"Because I'll be busy helping your future wife. Did you just say little Cory took out the renowned warrior Red Hawk? Hah, you're not so tough after all," teased Morgan. "You better take Tarak along to protect you."

While everyone was laughing Wyatt added, "Careful Tuck, Cory has a bite like a cougar!"

"Tuck, why don't you and Tarak meet Cory at the sheriff's office in the morning?"

"Okay." Tuck made a face at Cory.

Cory was grinning as she made plans on how she would get Tuck tomorrow.

"Tuck, I know a retired judge that would enjoy doing the marriage; that will shorten the time you have to spend with my fearless little deputy," said Sheriff Drake with a grin.

"That would be appreciated, Sheriff," said Tuck while looking at Cory to see her sticking her tongue out at him. Lomasi saw it all and laughed.

Morgan continued, "Wyatt, you are to find a place to have the wedding and the reception afterwards." Morgan thought for a moment, "And Wyatt, you need to find a love nest for them."

The "love nest" comment got everyone but the embarrassed Tuck and Lomasi laughing.

Thinking Morgan was finished giving orders everyone started to get up.

"Wait, I'm not finished," continued Morgan, "Sheriff Drake, will you be able to find a small band and someone to supply food?"

Sheriff Drake thought for a moment, "Sure, I just happen to know a few guys that like to do weddings. As far as the food goes, my wife and her friends can handle that."

"That would be wonderful, Sheriff."

Wyatt was laughing, "Tuck, just be glad you aren't marrying bossy Morgan."

"Hey, someone needed to take charge and see things got done," said Morgan defensively.

"Don't listen to them Morgan, you are doing a great job and are a wonderful friend," said Lomasi with feeling as she moved next to Morgan and put an arm around her.

Tuck clapped, which got everyone else clapping. Morgan blushed and looked down.

THE WEDDING

The next morning everyone was busy doing the jobs Morgan had assigned them.

The first thing Wyatt did when he got up, even before breakfast, was to secure the hotel's meeting room for the day. He also rented the hotel's suite on the third floor for two days. Later, while Wyatt was having breakfast, Tuck joined him. "Tuck, here's the keys to the suite on the third floor. I would suggest you move your things to that room and check out of the one you have."

"Thanks, Wyatt, I will. Wait! I'll keep the old room for Tarak."

"I forgot about him. Be sure to tell anyone you see the wedding will be here in the meeting room."

Tuck nodded.

After he finished eating, Wyatt went to the telegraph office and sent a message to Rothschild notifying him of Tuck's wedding and he would be taking a few weeks off.

While Wyatt and Tuck were eating, Sheriff Drake

was leaving his house to visit the retired judge he knew. His wife Ella left at the same time to go shopping for the needed food for the reception. She had two of her friends lined up to help fix and serve everything. Ella planned to surprise the couple with a wedding cake.

When the judge asked what time the wedding was, Sheriff Drake shrugged his shoulders and told him it would be at two. After he left the judge, Sheriff Drake went to 'The Hideaway,' where the small band he wanted to hire sometimes played. The owner told Sheriff Drake where to find the band members. He found two of them and was told not to worry, all four would be at the wedding and reception. Due to the short notice, the sheriff had to pay them double. He considered it his wedding present.

Tuck and Tarak met Cory at the sheriff's office in the morning. As the trio were about to leave, Cory realized she had forgotten something and ran back inside. A moment later she came out with a paper sack.

As the three walked to the jewelry story, Tuck couldn't restrain his curiosity any longer. "What's in the sack Cory?"

Cory stopped and looked up at Tuck with the sweetest, most contrite look she could fake as she said, "Tuck, I feel bad about yesterday, so I baked cookies for you and Tarak." She opened the sack and took out something wrapped in paper. She handed it to Tuck. As Tuck was looking at the wrapped cookies suspiciously, Cory gave one to Tarak. Tarak quickly unwrapped the oatmeal cookie and took a bite. "This is good Cory."

After seeing Tarak's reaction, Tuck unwrapped his and took a bite. As he chewed, he started frowning. Then he started spitting it out. He looked around. Seeing a horse water trough, he went to it, put his face in the water and started drinking. After a few swallows he looked at Cory and said, "You little witch, what was in that cookie?"

Cory was grinning as she replied, "I put sugar in Tarak's cookie, but yours got salt."

Tuck stuck his face in the watering trough again and drank. When he came up for air he said, "I'll get you!"

Tarak had been laughing, but when Tuck made a move for Cory, he stepped between them.

"Whose side are you on?" complained Tuck.

Tarak grinned, "Cory's. She's prettier than you."

Tuck shook his fist at Cory.

"If you hit me, I'll tell Lomasi!"

Tuck made a face. "Take us to a jeweler so we can get this over with!"

Cory moved alongside Tarak and slipped an arm around his arm, making him smile, "Thank you Tarak." A frustrated Tuck followed.

Inside the jewelry store, Tuck was stewing over two different sets of rings. Not being able to make up his mind, he wanted a woman's opinion. Cory knew he wanted to ask for her help. Every time Tuck would glance at her, she simply smiled. She wanted him to ask her for help. Finally, he gave in, "Cory, could you help me please?"

Cory grinned, "I'd be glad to Tuck, if…"

"If what?"

"If you promise to dance with me tonight."

"You want to dance with me?"

"Of course. Lomasi is a lucky woman."

"I thought you didn't like me."

Cory gave Tuck a flirty smile, winked and said, "The set of rings in your left hand are the ones to get. She'll love them."

"Thanks Cory."

Morgan and Lomasi spent the morning looking at dresses and getting their hair fixed.

When Cory got back to the sheriff's office, she found Wyatt waiting for her.

"Cory, would you find everyone and tell them the wedding will be two o'clock at the Occidental Hotel's meeting room?"

"Be glad to Wyatt. I'll just check in with Sheriff Drake first." Cory walked back to the sheriff's office and stepped inside. "Everything okay today?"

"Yep, thankfully everyone is behaving today."

"You know the wedding is at two?"

"I do. I'm the one that decided the time. I'll see you at two, Cory."

Cory left out the rear door to the stables in the rear of the sheriff's office. She saddled her horse Socks, then galloped around the city, finding everyone and letting them know the time and place of the wedding.

Cory owned two dresses. One was light blue. It was her dream dress she purchased while an outlaw. She called it her dream dress because to her, wearing it someday was just that, a dream. Both dresses had hidden pockets sewn into the folds. Being small, Cory felt she should always have a means to protect herself. Today, she would wear the dream dress. She would have her knife strapped to her lower right leg. She knew how to use a knife and was exceptionally good at throwing it. She had killed two men that way. In the dress's pocket would be the small gun her best friend Jenny had given her.

No one other than Grant had ever seen Cory in a dress, so when Cory arrived most commented on how good she looked. Cory was delighted by the comments. All the men were wearing suits except for Grant, who was on duty and wearing a deputy sheriff's badge.

Wyatt was best man and Morgan was maid of honor. After Tuck placed the ring on Lomasi's finger he motioned for the judge to wait. Tuck then said, "In addition to the ring I put on your finger I give to you this necklace that was given to my mother on her wedding day." Tuck reached into a pocket and pulled out a beaded necklace with a stunningly beautiful labradorite polished rock hanging from it. He placed the necklace around the surprised and grinning Lomasi's neck.

Labradorite Stone

After placing the wedding band on Tuck's finger, Lomasi turned towards Morgan, who handed her a package. "Tuck my love, when I was afraid you might be lost to me forever, I made this buckskin shirt for you." Lomasi handed the package to Tuck. Tuck held up the shirt and smiled. He tucked it under an arm and reached for Lomasi. Pulling her in close they had a long passionate kiss. The guests clapped, hooted and whistled.

They were pronounced husband and wife and the ceremony was finished. Tuck gave all the women in attendance a thrill when he took off his suit coat and white shirt. Flexing his bare muscular chest to laughter and cat calls he donned the time-consuming handmade buckskin shirt. Taking his laughing bride by the hand he led her to the food line.

After the dinner it was time for Lomasi to open the wedding gifts. Due to the short notice, there wasn't time for people to shop, so all the gifts but one were money. Lomasi opened an envelope. Inside was a telegram. With a puzzled look on her face, she started reading it out loud. "To the newlyweds. The three-bedroom house at 79 Church Street is yours. J.T. Rothschild." Lomasi couldn't keep the happy tears from her eyes. "Tuck, we have our own home!"

Wyatt started clapping, then others joined him.

After opening the remaining few envelopes with money, Lomasi picked up the only wrapped gift. Lomasi read the label, "From Cory." She pulled the wrapping off of a shoe box and opened it. Tuck peeked inside. As Lomasi picked up an oatmeal cookie Tuck said, "Don't eat it! They're terrible. She makes them with salt!" Lomasi took a bite out of it and grinned, "This is so good!"

Tuck frowned, then he gingerly grabbed one and hesitatingly took a small bite out of it. He chewed slowly. He smiled, "This is good!"

Cory was smiling as she said, "There's a small amount of money in the bottom of the box."

"Thank you, Cory," said Lomasi. Lomasi gave Tuck a menacing look. "Yeah, thanks Cory," said Tuck.

It was now time for music, dancing, and of course drinking.

While Tuck and Lomasi danced the first dance, the guests watched and got drinks from the small open bar. Morgan commented to Wyatt how Lomasi and Tuck made the perfect couple and how happy she was for them.

After the bride and groom finished the first dance, Wyatt and Morgan danced. Cory danced with her beau Grant. Sheriff Drake's wife Ella found time to dance before the food would be served at five.

Having finished her dance with Grant, Cory saw Tarak sitting by himself, so she went to him and asked, "Do you know how to dance?"

"I know an Indian war dance."

"Come on and I'll teach you."

"I was teasing about the war dance. I do know how to dance. The schoolteacher thought it was important to know."

"Good for her," said Cory as she led Tarak onto the dance floor. As they started to dance, Tarak pulled Cory in tight, surprising her. "Tarak, you seem advanced for your age."

Knowing why Cory said that, Tarak grinned, "Warriors take what they want."

"Well, you can't have me because I belong to Grant."

Wanting to change the subject, Cory said, "You dance well, Tarak."

When they finished dancing, Cory saw Tuck having a drink, "Mister Tucker, you owe me a dance."

"I will be glad to dance with you, Cory."

While dancing, Tuck said, "The first time I saw you I was reminded of someone. The resemblance is so strong you could be her twin sister."

"If there is another short woman like me, I feel sorry for her," said Cory with a chuckle.

"Her name was Cory Callahan. But she died in a

shootout with a sheriff and his deputies."

Hearing her former name shocked Cory so much, she stumbled. Tuck caught her.

"A female outlaw, how unusual," commented Cory while trying to control her emotions.

"It is unusual. And like you, she wore a gun and a knife. It was a couple of years ago. I happened to be in Walsenburg, Colorado. I watched the shootout. There was another woman involved in it. She claimed to be a Texas Ranger and fought on the side of the sheriff. She shot and killed the woman outlaw."

Cory wanted to defend Jenny by telling Tuck Jenny did not shoot her. Instead, she chuckled and commented, "Women are taking over."

"It seems that way, but as long as women can't vote, us men are safe. You know the crazy thing about that shootout was the outlaw woman's gun was empty."

"She must have been unhappy with her life and wanted to commit suicide."

"I suppose you are right."

When the dance finished, Tuck went to Lomasi.

"It seems you two had much to talk about," said Lomasi. "Do I need to worry about my new husband already?"

Tuck laughed, "Never. I didn't think she liked

me because she's always mean. This morning she gave me a salted cookie. It was terrible!"

"She teases you because she does like you. That's her way."

"I wish she'd find a better way."

While Tuck and Cory were dancing, Morgan and Lomasi had been talking.

"Did you get lucky last night?" Lomasi asked Morgan.

Morgan blushed, "No, but tonight I will make him mine. Wyatt doesn't stand a chance."

Lomasi laughed, "When it comes to women, men are so weak."

Morgan joined Lomasi's laughter, "I hope so. Guess I will find out tonight."

Wyatt walked up to the women. "What are you two beautiful women talking about that is so funny?"

Morgan looked directly at Wyatt, "How I'm going to bed you tonight. Let's dance." Lomasi let out a gasp. Morgan grabbed Wyatt's hand and pulled him to the dance floor. When Wyatt tried to dance the traditional way, Morgan pushed his hand away and wrapped both her arms around Wyatt's neck and pulled him tightly to her. When she felt Wyatt's response, she knew she would win.

While the two danced, all their friends were watching and commenting. Tuck laughed and said, "Wyatt doesn't stand a chance."

"No, he doesn't," agreed Lomasi. "I suspect there will be another wedding soon."

Wyatt was so embarrassed, "Morgan, you're making a scene."

"I don't care." She pulled his face to hers and kissed him. When he returned her kiss, Morgan knew Lomasi was right, men are weak.

The romantic mood of the evening was contagious. Sheriff Drake and his wife Ella were dancing cheek to cheek. Tuck and Lomasi were close together and dancing slow. While Cory and Grant danced, Cory asked, "When are we getting married? You keep putting it off."

"Soon."

"Soon. That's what you always say. I bet Wyatt and Morgan get married before us."

With the reception over, people were leaving. Lomasi saw Tarak by himself and looking lost.

"Tarak, what is the matter?"

Tarak looked at Lomasi for a moment, "I don't know where to go?"

"Tuck get over here!" Lomasi yelled. When Tuck was close, she asked, "Did you forget about our son? Where's he supposed to stay?"

Tuck looked at Tarak, "I'm sorry Tarak. For the next two days you will stay in my room. When we move to the house you're coming with. You will have your own room." Tuck reached into a pocket, "Here's the key to room 202."

Tarak felt a big relief as he took the key from Tuck. As he walked up the stairs he smiled as he wondered about Lomasi calling him their son.

Thank you for reading *The Marshals*. A review on Amazon would be greatly appreciated. The reviews will determine whether I write a sequel.

Packy

Learn more about the tough, trying life of Cory Callahan, aka Cory Jackson in *The Regulators*. You will learn how Cory transforms from being an unhappy outlaw to a deputy sheriff. Cory's saga starts in Book 3 of *The Regulators*.

The Regulators series is a story of four people going back in time to help others. Most of the time it is in the western days, but not always. The series is historical fiction. All places, events and people, other than our four heroes, are real.

I am hoping to write a Book 8 of the popular Regulators series, if my busy summer allows.

The pictures on the cover of Book 3 are all my kids. Yes, all six! Those are also my horses. The black and white pictures on the covers represent someone in the past.

The Regulators
A TIME TRAVEL ADVENTURE

Book 3

A continuing series

by Packy Trucker

Available on Amazon

The Crew

Sky Moran comes home to find his pregnant wife laying naked outside their burning house with a bullet hole in her back. Seeking vengeance, Sky goes after the killers. Wanting to rid the west of outlaws, he became a bounty hunter.

Twenty-year-old Thomasina Taylor worked in her father's gun shop as a talented gunsmith. Due to her father's failing health, she was destined to take over the shop. Thomasina loved working with guns and shooting them. But Thomasina was troubled because men would not speak to a woman about guns. Women did not know anything about guns and could not shoot. One day out of frustration she cut off her beautiful chestnut colored hair and came downstairs dressed in her father's clothes, shocking him. Dressed as a man called Tom, she was a success.

The day Thomasina waited on soft-spoken, tall, handsome Sky, she was immediately smitten. She was envious of what she saw as an exciting lifestyle. When she told Sky she was good with a gun and wanted to join him, he laughed and said it wasn't a job for a boy. Knowing where Sky was going, she followed him. After saving him from two road agents and impressing him with her gun skills, she was allowed to join him. He called her "Tommy." She knew if Sky realized she was a woman he would never have allowed it.

On one hunt, Sky and Tommy received much needed help from Sedgewick County Deputy, Cory Jackson.

When Rex Davis joined the bounty hunting duo, Sheriff Rice called them "The Crew". The Crew developed a deadly reputation for bringing outlaws to justice.

Will Thomasina be able to hide her true identity from her two partners? Will she be able to keep her growing feelings for Sky a secret?

What will happen when The Crew and The Regulators meet?

Made in the USA
Monee, IL
05 November 2021